We all need to accept the fact that our [illegible]
need to understand and accept that our [illegible]
we can communicate with those who di[illegible] consciousness. I know this from my personal and professional experience. Carolyn's book can help guide you to understanding, healing and the truth.

—Bernie Siegel, MD
Author, *A Book of Miracles* and *The Art of Healing*

Carolyn Coarsey has written a story that rings with real life when tragedy strikes and a loved one dies. Her insights into the raw emotions, stressed relations and lonely pathways of survivors brought tears to my eyes because while the story is fiction, these responses are not. There is also hope throughout the story and a vision of heaven that erases despair.

—Bob Deits
Author, *Life After Loss*

We live in a culture often derailed by tragedy—yet society implores us to get back to normal as soon as possible. Carolyn Coarsey knows there is no such thing as normal for survivors of catastrophic disasters and has dedicated years of her life to helping others navigate the rough waters of loss. *Beyond Dark Skies* is filled with vulnerable and insightful characters struggling to pick up the pieces of their lives after one such tragic loss.

—Dr. Gloria Horsley
President & Founder, Open to Hope

Beyond Dark Skies

Beyond Dark Skies

• • •

Carolyn V. Coarsey, Ph.D.

ISBN-13: 9781450533942
ISBN-10: 1450533949
Library of Congress Control Number: 2010900798
LCCN Imprint Name Santa Fe, NM

Author's Note

This book is a work of fiction. However, all of the examples of other-worldly experiences where family members lost loved ones suddenly and traumatically are taken straight out of my thirty-plus years of interviews. In his book *The Art of Healing*, Dr. Bernie Siegel's words ring true for me and hundreds of other family members I have interviewed who have experienced losses of loved ones: I used to be a skeptic because I didn't know any better. I wasn't trained to look through any other lens. But over time I learned to open my mind to other kinds of communication and possibilities.

Beyond Dark Skies

Beyond dark skies, I know you wait for me;
Beyond dark skies lies beauty that only the eyes of love can see.

The violent winds and rain from the storm
Forced the aircraft down.
The angry flames from the fire
Burned it to the ground.

Yet the souls onboard knew nothing of the pain.
For moments before the crash began,
All the souls, one by one, had traveled home,
To live in heaven once again.

The souls involved are safe and whole;
It is we on earth
Who are left to ponder
What lies ahead for each of us.
We can only wonder.

And so we walk in faith and trust,
Knowing the journey home
Lies ahead for each of us.

I know that dark skies will come again,
And my eyes will close another time
On one more life I lived back then.

I shall not fear,
Nor feel dread in my heart,
For I have glimpsed the light beyond
That guides my way.
I need only do my part.

Beyond dark skies, I know you wait for me.
Beyond dark skies lies beauty that only the eyes of love can see.

Part 1
The Crash

Death is not extinguishing the light;
it is only putting out the lamp because
the dawn has come.

—Rabindranath Tagore

I

Leonard "Lenny" Crawford Sawyer

Twenty-two-year-old Leonard Crawford Sawyer, Lenny to his family and friends, reached down and tightened his seat belt for takeoff. His six-foot-three-inch height created a challenge for sitting in most aircraft seats, but at least on this flight—a fairly short trip—he had managed to get an aisle seat, which made it a little more comfortable. He had nearly missed his flight. Traffic had started to back up early that Friday afternoon. He'd had to drive faster than normal in order to make the flight to Omaha for his best friend's wedding. Lenny was happy for Jim and Rosanne. He was also happy it was Jim and not he who would be taking the walk down the matrimonial aisle. By fall Lenny would be entering medical school. He was about to see a lifelong dream become a reality.

For Lenny, making the grades and getting accepted into medical school had never been the challenge. The problem involved his father. Convincing him this was the right career for his son had taken some work. His dad—Leonard Jr.—had practiced medicine for thirty years, and before that his own father had devoted his life to the field. But it had changed drastically. So much so that Leonard Jr. had resisted the notion of his oldest son following the family tradition. He'd even given his son a different middle name so he would not be Leonard Jackson Sawyer, III. Leonard Jr. had always wanted his son's life to be different from his own and his father's, and encouraged him to pursue a more involved and normal family life than physicians of former generations had experienced. He could not change the fact that his son looked so much like him, with his tall, lean build, sandy-blond hair, and aquamarine eyes, but if possible he wanted to save his son from the disappointments of a medical career.

Finally, with the help of his mom, Celia, Lenny had won the battle. Just after finishing at the top of his undergraduate class, Lenny received his father's support for entering medical school. And, also of great significance, he had been accepted into Emory Medical school where the other Sawyer men had earned their medical degrees.

Reflecting on his past and dreaming about his future lulled Lenny into a light sleep, and he managed to doze off peacefully. Awakening near what he thought might be the final few minutes of the flight, Lenny glanced at his new TAG Heuer Titanium watch, a graduation gift from his parents. It was only about twenty minutes before the plane should be landing. Within a few moments, the pilot came on and announced that shortly they would begin their descent into Omaha. As Lenny looked out the window, he could see lightning in the distance. He knew that somewhere nearby, a major thunderstorm was taking place.

Drifting off for another few moments, Lenny awoke to the familiar sound of the chime signaling the flight attendants to prepare the passengers and cabin for landing. The announcement about seat belts and seat backs followed. Pulling his seat back forward, he glanced out the window again. Driving rain hit the fuselage with horizontal force. The intensity of the rain gave him an uneasy feeling in the pit of his stomach. The flight had not been full, so there was an empty seat between him and the elderly woman sitting in the window seat. Although they had not spoken before, she now leaned across the seat between them and spoke to him with genuine concern in her voice.

"Think they can land in this?" The anxiety in her voice was unsettling.

"I'm sure the pilots know what they're doing." Lenny smiled as he attempted to calm the small, white-haired lady.

Suddenly he felt the forward part of the jet slam down on the runway. Screams erupted as the fierce impact threw passengers forward in their seats. Lenny's head smashed into the seat back in front of him. As the jet skidded down the runway, screeching and grinding noises filled the night—the unmistakable sounds of a violent crash. The passengers bounced back and forth, arms flailing out of control, for several seconds. Finally the aircraft broke apart at the wing section on the left side. Sparks from the broken metal scraping the cement of the runway ignited the leaking jet fuel and caused giant flames to leap into the black sky.

Lenny sensed he had lost consciousness for a few seconds. The smell of jet fuel and the red-and-orange flames leaping into the air suddenly forced him to act. The light from the fire allowed him to see a few people around him. It seemed he was the only one awake. He looked at the white-haired lady beside him. Her glasses had flown off at first impact, and she now appeared lifeless. The way her head rested against the seat back in front of her was unnatural. Lenny knew at once she had not survived. But sounds from the rear of the aircraft assured him others had. "Fire!" someone shouted. "Fire! We must get out!"

Lenny looked up and saw a giant fireball coming toward him. The flames leaped into his row of seats, and the white-haired lady was suddenly ablaze. Lenny felt himself floating up and over her. He could see his own body in the seat beside her as the fire rapidly engulfed the entire overwing section. Next, he was on the outside of the burning jet. Oddly, he found himself peering down into the devastation of the fire.

The entire scenario was confusing, yet he felt no fear. It was as if he was watching a movie, but at the same time he was *in* the movie! Lenny's attention was suddenly diverted by voices. In the light of the fire, he could see two people approaching the airplane. He knew it could not be rescue personnel; it was too soon for that, as the crash had occurred only moments before.

"Meemee and Papa!" Lenny was overcome with joy and relief at the sight of his paternal grandparents approaching him. He had not seen them since their deaths when he was in high school. Looking stronger and more youthful than Lenny remembered her, Bonnie Sawyer, known as Meemee to her grandchildren, wrapped her arms around her grandson and spoke.

"Lenny, we've come to take you with us. You must come now, quickly. There's no reason for you to experience more of earth's suffering."

With the confidence and strength of a much younger man than he had been the last time Lenny had seen him, Dr. Leonard Jackson Sawyer, Sr. grabbed both their hands and led them away from the fire.

Dazed and unable to absorb the magnitude of what was happening, Lenny walked quickly alongside his grandparents, feeling safe and secure in their presence. As he glanced back over his shoulder, he saw the entire airplane was ablaze. He could not imagine how anyone could have escaped. In the distance, he heard the sirens of emergency and rescue vans rushing to save the lives of anyone who survived the devastating impact and brutal fire that followed. He knew the rescue workers would be emotionally impacted upon arrival, when they learned there were no lives to save.

II

Heaven

Lenny yawned and slowly came to consciousness. He felt more rested than he could remember having ever been. He opened his eyes and looked around. He wasn't sure where he was. He was lying in a very comfortable bed covered by a soft, warm, white down comforter that seemed to float across his body. This may very well have been the most comfortable bed in which he had ever slept. The room was bright. There was sunshine streaming through the large, open window across from the bed where he lay. A gentle breeze lifted the tails of the sheer white curtains, which matched the billowing clouds in bright-blue sky outside.

Opening his eyes wider, he noticed a man standing in front of the window. The tall, well-built, sandy-blond-haired man was dressed in khaki slacks and a light-blue long sleeve shirt. His hands were clasped behind his back, about waist high. He stood with his feet shoulder width apart. He appeared to be gazing out the window at the beauty of the day.

Lenny did not recognize the man; he felt he knew him but did not know how or when they might have met. Almost as though he could read Lenny's thoughts, the man turned and smiled at him. His eyes, which matched the color of the sky outside the window, sparkled with friendliness and familiarity.

"Do I know you?" Lenny asked.

"Yes, we know each other well. In fact, we have known each other for a very long time. We enjoy a unique relationship."

Something about the man's voice sounded as familiar as his face looked, yet Lenny could not place him.

"Where am I? Is this a hotel?" Lenny asked.

"Well, more like a rehab hospital of sorts," the man replied, still smiling and looking directly into Lenny's eyes. "On this side we call this a healing room."

Something about the way the man said *this side* heightened Lenny's curiosity. "What do you mean *this side*? This side of where?"

The man pulled a chair up to the bed and sat facing Lenny. He leaned forward, extended his hand, and said "Lenny, my name is John. We've known each other for a *very* long time."

After Lenny released the man's hand, he glanced away, trying to recall how he had gotten to the healing room and where he might have been the night before. He finally looked back at the man called John and shared his thoughts. "You seem so familiar, but I'm having trouble placing you."

Now it was John's turn to look away. He knew he needed to tell Lenny more, but this part of the reintroduction, when souls—even old ones like Lenny's—initially crossed over once more from earth, was always delicate.

Threads of memory slowly entered Lenny's mind. "I was on my way to a wedding last night, and I guess I don't understand how I got here, much less *why* I'm here. Is there a phone or a way I can let my family and best friend know where I am?"

Not wanting to appear insensitive, but seeing a bit of humor in the statement, John replied, still smiling, "Oh, people who *know* you know where you are for sure. They would know you're with us!"

Us? Lenny wondered.

Not wishing to prolong the anxiety Lenny was obviously feeling under the circumstances, John again leaned toward him, his hands resting on the bed rails. He said softly, "Lenny, you have left earth and have crossed over to the other side, also known as heaven."

Lenny looked into John's eyes, trying to comprehend what he was hearing. "Do you mean I died?"

"Do you feel dead?" John replied with a knowing smile.

"No!" Feeling amazingly detached, Lenny answered, "I've never felt more alive. I don't remember dying. What happened to me?"

John answered slowly. "I'll give you a brief explanation for now, but as you rest and heal, details of leaving earth as well as memories of your recent life on earth will emerge when it is time."

John made no reference to Lenny's previous lives on earth before this most recent reincarnation; it was too soon for that.

Lenny listened intently as John described the events related to how he had departed earth. "Last night a plane crashed in the Midwestern part of the United States of America. Over one hundred souls crossed over—one hundred and six, to be exact. Your physical body died when your head struck the seat back in front of you, and that is how most of the others died. Blunt-force trauma is the leading cause of death in vehicular accidents—especially in a crash where the aircraft strikes the ground at great speed. A small number of the passengers were knocked unconscious at first impact, but later died in the fire. The oxygen in their lungs showed that they survived a few minutes after impact. You were one of the souls who came here to be with us."

"Are all the people who did not survive here in this hospital?" Lenny asked.

"They're all on this side, but they went where they needed to go next according to their own souls' agreements."

"Oh, I see." Lenny did not really understand, but there was something about John's words and tone of voice that resonated with him. It was as if he knew whatever John said was completely true. He was curious about the words *their own souls' agreements*. But he could ask about that later. For now he was more interested in what John had to say about how he had gotten there and exactly where there was.

"In the fullness of time, you will see many of those people, but not until you and they are ready for interaction. Right now everyone needs rest and time to adjust to life beyond earth," John continued.

"How long does that take?" Lenny asked.

John smiled. "As long as it takes. Over here we do not use clocks or calendars or keep records of time the same way it is done on earth. There is no linear time here. As you adjust to your life on this side, you will discover less of a need for calendars and clocks. You will learn to trust your own feelings and learn about a different sort of scheduling."

Unable to imagine life without a calendar or a watch, Lenny smiled at John. "Is it too soon for me to hear more about how you and I knew each other in the past?"

"I can explain it, but to be perfectly honest, there will be a time when you will remember all you want to remember without my help." John spoke quietly. He did not want to tire Lenny with too many facts and details.

"You remind me of one of my professors from my junior year in college. He taught me physics." Lenny was studying John's face intently.

"I recall that person and your mutual fondness for one another," John answered. "But we are not the same. There is a physical likeness but no other connection. However, you and I have had many experiences together. This most recent time when you were born to earth, I agreed to be your primary spirit guide, sometimes called a guardian angel."

The entire discussion resonated with Lenny. "Yes, this somehow sounds very familiar to me. And you mean you even knew my professors and other people I knew and interacted with in my life before I got here?"

"Yes. You see, as your guardian angel I walked every day with you, from the moment you entered earth through your mother's womb."

Lenny's eyes were wide with amazement. "Really? My whole life?"

John smiled and nodded. "Yes, and now I am happy you have returned from earth so we can interact more directly on a daily basis instead of through the veil that was required while you were in your physical body. You see, my friend, you died as far as earth is concerned, which is a very sad occasion for your family and friends who are still on earth, but it's a joyous time for me and many others here. We are happy to welcome you back home."

John paused and once again, and allowed a few moments for Lenny to absorb the information. "Do you see? Death to someone on earth is birth to us here. Others and I celebrated your rebirth here when you arrived."

Lenny seemed to be taking in all John was saying, so he continued. "You and I have shared many lifetimes. And sometime in the future, you will remember them. For now let me just say that in this most recent time on earth, you and I agreed I would walk beside you, guiding you and always offering my support while your soul was on earth."

Lenny's concentration on the words John was speaking was interrupted as two people entered the room. He could hardly believe his eyes. "Meemee and Papa!"

John stood up and stepped aside to allow Lenny's grandparents to approach the bed and embrace Lenny as a newly reunited family unit. He wondered how long it might take Lenny to remember they had walked him home after the crash.

After the very emotional greetings, John pulled up chairs for Lenny's grandparents.

"You both look great," Lenny said with joy, seeing them in such obvious great physical shape.

"And so do you," Lenny's grandmother, Bonnie, replied. "We were both so excited you were coming—but we also knew it would be a terrible time for your mother and father. In fact, we drew near your dad to lend comfort to him when he got news of the crash. Your mother's own parents stood with her when she received the news of the crash, although she could not see them. Do you remember that your granddad and I crossed you over from earth last night?"

Lenny became very quiet. More memory was returning with the mention of his family of origin from his most recent lifetime on earth. The overwhelming feelings of joy now were replaced with growing sorrow as he thought of his parents and younger brother, Bruce.

Recognizing the look of pain on Lenny's face, his grandmother took his hand. She stroked his arm, as she had done when he was a young child, tucking him in for the night. Lenny wept. His grandfather moved closer to his bed.

"I hadn't even thought of my parents or my little brother until now," said Lenny. "How sad they must be, and how sad I am to know I won't be with them again."

John spoke up. "It is a sad time indeed, but it won't be long before you're with them again. In fact even before they join us here, you'll have many opportunities to stand beside them and help them with earthly adjustment to this change and others."

In a faint voice Lenny hardly recognized as his own, he asked, "Will they know that it's me? Will they know I'm with them?"

"On some level they will indeed," John answered softly. "On this side we have ways of sending symbols during dreams and even during conscious waking that communicates to those we love on earth that we are present with them. As you heal, I will help you with this. I will also help you remember some of the signs I gave you before you came home—symbols of my and other guides' presence and support in your life."

Lenny's sobs faded. "I guess I never realized people who pass over to heaven feel emotional pain. I guess I thought heaven meant everything was painless."

"It will be more beautiful than anything you ever imagined, but you're in transition right now. That's why you're here in a healing room. While you're here all of us will help you in your adjustment to your new life on this side. And part of that will involve experiencing full memory of this recent life. You'll first have to come to terms with your new relationships with the people you shared this recent life with. You are still connected to them and always will be, but not on the same level, since you are no longer on the same plane of existence. And it takes time for the full adjustment for both groups—those in heaven and those on earth.

"Working through that will naturally involve some mourning because, as you know, physical separation from those we love carries a degree of sadness with it. Then as the spiritual relationships grow stronger, the sadness is replaced by a much stronger eternal union." John felt it too soon to add the rest of what he was thinking. He wanted to tell Lenny the eternal bonds were much greater and richer than the brief time he had known them in his most recent earthly experience.

John looked up as a woman dressed in white, much like a nurse's uniform, entered the room.

"Lenny," John said, "I want you to meet Yvonne. She's the healer who will help us with the adjustment process I was just speaking about." John stood up, and Yvonne took his seat.

She held out her hand to Lenny, then nodded and smiled at Bonnie and Leonard. “Hello, Lenny. I’m so sorry about what your family and friends on earth are going through. But I must also say I am very glad to meet you…again.”

“Again?” Lenny asked. “So I know you, too?”

“It is true.” Yvonne smiled at him and glanced around the room at the others.

“Are you a counselor?”

“Of sorts,” Yvonne replied. “But here we are more like the energetic healers I am happy to see are becoming more popular on earth today.”

“I don’t understand,” Lenny replied.

“Here we believe in talk therapy, but we also know that adjustment following trauma such as a plane crash will also involve body work. Here we practice therapeutic massage and other techniques associated with energy medicine and homeopathy. So while John and I work with you and help you recall your most recent life story, I will practice many healing techniques in order to help you in your adjustment process.”

Yvonne spoke in a hushed voice similar to John’s, which Lenny found to be utterly relaxing. He felt a heaviness around his eyes. He also felt a deep sense of peace. Lenny had spent his first few hours in heaven and had now met the members of his transition team. He drifted into a deep sleep.

III

A New Life on the Other Side

The following morning Lenny opened his eyes to the sun-filled room. A gentle breeze again lifted the sheer white curtains from the window. The billowing motion was almost hypnotic. Lenny was recalling the events from the day before when John appeared at the door, dressed differently from the day before, in surgical scrubs. Lenny wondered if John was a physician. He had to remember to ask.

"Good morning," said John as he entered the room. "Did you have a good rest?"

"Yes, actually. I don't remember when I slept better and felt more rested."

"Good," answered John as he pulled up the chair beside the bed. He knew memories of life on earth would likely drift in and out of Lenny's mind in the next few days. He had already checked with Yvonne, and she was standing ready for when John summoned her help.

"How long do you think I'll remain in the healing room?" Lenny asked.

"As I said before," John responded, "it really depends on how long it takes for you to regain your strength and become ready to enter into your work here."

"Work?" Lenny hadn't even thought about a career or job. He had not considered how people supported themselves in life beyond earth. His traditional learning about heaven had always made it sound like everyone sat around and lived happily ever after once they crossed over from earth.

Now, after meeting John and Yvonne, this earlier education did not seem to fit. They were obviously productive people who were making contributions to people on earth as well helping souls like him who crossed over to this particular location—wherever *this* was.

"Oh yes," answered John with that knowing smile Lenny was growing accustomed to seeing. "We all are gainfully employed here. We don't receive paychecks because everything we need or could possibly want is available to us. But we do remain productive, and those on this plane are very much involved in helping with earth's evolution, so we are quite busy."

John noticed Lenny gazing off into the distance. He knew that something he had said had triggered a memory—a painful one. He waited for Lenny to speak. He did not want to say the wrong thing or bring up anything that might intensify the pain Lenny would likely be experiencing, which was unavoidable during this early period.

After several moments Lenny spoke in a sad voice. "I was supposed to enter medical school this fall. I had always dreamed of becoming a doctor like Dad and my grandfather. I'm sad to know this dream I worked for, even fought for, will not come to fruition."

John paused before answering. He wanted to pick his words carefully, as some of the information he wanted to give Lenny might be too advanced for the short amount of time Lenny had been on the current plane. "Lenny, it is likely by fall, earth time, you will be in the operating room. You will be practicing with the skills of a very advanced medical professional."

"How is that possible?" Lenny asked. "On earth I would have been just entering medical school as a freshman in late August. I wouldn't have the background, skills, or training necessary to practice medicine."

John looked directly into Lenny's eyes and ventured into the more complicated part of this exchange. "Lenny, you've practiced medicine for many lifetimes. You've been a traditional physician practicing Western medicine, and before that you practiced medicine as a shaman, an Indian medicine man, and performed other types of healing over many incarnations on earth."

Lenny's eyes reflected an enthusiasm, even a joy, that allowed John to relax. Feeling more comfortable with the way the discussion was going, he continued. "You were so drawn to medicine because this is your true archetype. You are a healer. You have great knowledge of the healing arts, which comes from many lifetimes of experience."

"So that's why I wanted so badly to become a doctor. I risked my entire relationship with my father rather than allow him to prevent me from following my dream, and now I understand why."

"Yes," John continued. "One of the obstacles you chose to put in your path during this most recent earth experience pertained to the problems you had with your father."

"How so?" Lenny's question was heavy with emotion.

John remembered the pain Lenny had experienced during battles with his father, Leonard Jr., every time they discussed the subject of Lenny's future. This had gone on for years before he received his father's approval to apply for medical school. If only Leonard Jr. could have known how temporary this conflict would be. Some of the guilt he now had to endure following Lenny's death could easily have been prevented. But John had simply had to endure the paternal conflict during Lenny's last few years on earth. He had supported Lenny as best he could. He knew this problem was part of the contract between Lenny and his father during this last earthly lifetime.

"Conflict between two people," John said, "is always about spiritual lessons for all involved. Some of these lessons are more painful on the earth plane than others." He was thinking of the contract between Lenny and his mother but avoided the topic, knowing it was not the right time to discuss that. The challenges there would surface soon enough.

"Are you saying the arguments and disagreements I had with my father were preplanned?" Lenny felt confused.

"Only from the standpoint that your father needed to learn about allowing others to make choices and decisions based on their own truths instead of his. And you were but one of the many teachers of that lesson for him during his current life on earth." John tried to keep his tone light, as the subject itself was heavy enough.

Lenny looked away, lost in thought. He finally spoke. "And what did I learn?"

"The importance of honoring your own feelings and being true to yourself. You knew deep down you were a medicine man, and the conflict with your father was a test of your ability to persevere in the face of strong adversity."

"So I died because I was finished with earth? Didn't I die prematurely?"

"Yes and no. Your contract with those on earth was complete at that point, from the perspective of earth's vibration. And no, you did not die prematurely. There are no mistakes when it comes to leaving earth. It was your soul's choice to come when you did, as it was for all who departed with you. And every detail about your departure was important, even down to the way you died, the exact second you left earth's plane, and those with whom you died."

Before Lenny could respond, John added a few more comments. "And although you are not on earth any longer, it does not mean you are not connected to your family and those you love. As we spoke about yesterday, you will always be connected to those you love, and for some of them, you are still involved in completing agreements you made with family before this lifetime. You are not finished with earth, despite the fact that you no longer physically reside there."

"Can you say who you're referring to?" Lenny was more than curious. He was worried about impending doom for someone on earth he loved.

John waited a few moments before continuing. "For now let's just say there is nothing bad about any of this. It's all about learning, and soon enough you'll know what I'm talking about. Simultaneously you will know how you can best help those you love with the challenges they're facing—even those still on earth."

The door opened, and Lenny smiled as his grandparents came in for a visit. John left so the family could have some quality time together to get reacquainted. From his office he sent a quick e-mail to Yvonne; he knew another session might be needed, as discussions of Lenny's most recent life on earth had evoked emotional memories. He then hurriedly scrubbed his hands, donned gloves, and entered an operating room where a young doctor had called on him for assistance. On earth the calling sounded like words of prayer. In heaven John could hear the call as the angelic choir singing various verses that spoke of various needs of a patient, a family member, or members of the medical team. The young doctor needed John's hand in saving an infant who was having problems making his way into the earth plane.

As often happened, John had already received calls from multiple family members over a period of several hours pertaining to this case. First the mom had prayed when she'd gone into labor earlier that morning. She'd felt that the baby was in distress, and a nurse had confirmed there were problems as soon as the mom had entered Labor and Delivery at the hospital.

Other relatives had called for help in their prayers when they'd heard there might be problems with the birth. And now, within the last two hours, the young doctor had reached out for assistance and had prayed.

As John entered the delivery room, he could hear the choir of angels, their sweet voices surrounding the young mother, father, and baby with celestial vibration. John knew that the chief of pediatric surgery had assembled a highly qualified and skilled clinical team to assist mother and child. He wished the family could know about a second group of highly experienced professionals who would be working alongside the hospital's team. He and his team would be invisible to the naked eye, but their presence would be felt by more than one sensitive in the room. And it was these invisible hands that would save the child.

IV

Integration on the Other Side

Lenny was not sure how many sessions he had experienced with John and Yvonne, but already he was beginning to recall details of the crash. At first the memories came to him at night during his dreams. And then, several nights after the first dream, he had his first nightmare. Fortunately, because he was still in the healing room when it occurred, one of the nursing staff immediately summoned Yvonne.

She had sat with him until he fell back into a deep and restful sleep. It helped knowing that as soon as he was ready the next day, Yvonne and John would come back and work with him. He had retrieved enough memories now that he could recall the crash and describe it in great detail. As he recalled the traumatic memories, Yvonne performed therapeutic massage using warm essential oils. Of course Lenny had heard of them, but he had not known about the healing qualities of certain oils until now. The smells of lavender, frankincense, clary sage, and many others permeated the room. And sometimes she used a rose fragrance that was particularly soothing.

Lenny found himself becoming more emotional than he had ever imagined he could be during several of his sessions with Yvonne and John. He described the crash in great detail. He cried the most when he saw the little white-haired lady. She seemed so helpless, and he felt so guilty that he had not been able to help her.

Lenny could not help but notice that neither Yvonne nor John ever tried to change his experience. They listened and supported this and all parts of his story. He told them about the sensation of floating above the crash scene and about the joy of being rescued by his grandparents. He wondered if the white-haired lady had been escorted to her next place. By now, of course, he knew that just as he had been nurtured during that time, so had all the souls that had perished in the crash that night. Yet he still felt guilty that he could not save her.

Days passed in the healing room until one day, quite unexpectedly, he found he had cried all of his tears. He could picture the entire crash and the white-haired lady and continually experience peace. Yvonne said they could now enter a new phase of his healing. She explained that their first goal had been to allow him to vent all of his feelings and get his story pulled together both in his mind and in his emotional memory. She helped him see that pulling feelings and thoughts together, which is what therapy is designed to do, would allow him to deal with the memories on a more intellectual level. She also explained that while she would continue her massage therapy, John would now take a primary role in the recovery process. She did not tell Lenny what was happening on earth with all of those who loved him. Soon enough he would see for himself and even become part of it on some level.

Lenny was intrigued by what Yvonne had explained. He had always done well in his psychology classes. He had even toyed with the idea of studying psychiatry instead of gynecology and obstetrics. But it was only a passing thought. He really wanted to follow in the footsteps of his father and grandfather. Between them they had birthed generations of families, and he wanted to continue their legacy of caring for mothers and their infants from pregnancy through delivery.

Thoughts about his future were still troubling to him, but not as much as when he had first arrived. Every day he was gaining confidence that while his earthly life may have ended, he had every reason to look forward to a life here, albeit a different life from what he had expected after college.

Before leaving, Yvonne set up his next appointment for later that same day. Lenny was surprised to learn the next phase of the treatment would be held in a different part of the clinic. Yvonne showed him from the window in his room a very large white stucco building with tall columns across the front. She told him to meet her and John there later that afternoon.

V

Reconnecting with Earth

After taking a short nap, Lenny dressed in jeans and a plaid button-down shirt and headed to the next appointment. Yvonne had mentioned the afternoon session would be slightly more tiring, like his first few sessions with her and John had been. She explained it had something to do with learning more about others who were experiencing distress.

Since Lenny had not thought much about anyone other than the white-haired lady, he wasn't sure why this could be more draining than what he had been through already in recounting the trauma of the crash. Yvonne had not told him he was about to experience some of the distress of his own most recent earth family. She just explained it would be necessary for John to be with him during this phase of his adjustment. John, as his guardian angel, had been with him through all of the really tough and painful times in his most recent earthly life, so it made sense for him to be there for the next step in the process.

While Lenny had not yet realized it, John had been sitting right beside him during the final moments of the crash, and though invisible John had walked with him and his grandparents all the way to the other side. This new piece of learning was about to come into Lenny's awareness. He would need a great understanding of how nonphysical reality worked in order to accomplish what was next for him in this new part of his journey.

Lenny made his way through the large glass doors of the building Yvonne had pointed out to him. As he entered he saw a gently sloping staircase directly in front of him, just as Yvonne had described. He practically ran up the staircase, curious about what might be inside of this large imposing building. Halfway up he saw John emerge from a doorway. Again, John was dressed in what looked like surgical scrubs. Lenny made a mental note to himself to ask John why he was dressed like that so often. Was he currently practicing medicine somewhere?

John came toward Lenny and held out his hand. Lenny took it and smiled into John's big blue eyes, where he always found such comfort.

"Hello, and welcome to another phase of your healing," said John as he led Lenny into a room with a large sign on the door that read "In session." Lenny wondered why this room, unlike the other therapy rooms, required a sign. The room was very large, with an entire side covered by a drape. Lenny could not see whether it was a window or just a wall, as the drapes appeared to be opaque, and there was no light coming through. Facing the drapes were two large, comfortable-looking armchairs with a small table between them. Lenny could not help but notice the box of tissues on the table.

Yep, he thought. *Tissues and therapy go together*—although he thought he was through the emotional parts. He smiled and sat down in the chair John motioned him toward.

"Lenny," John said in the soft voice Lenny had grown to trust, "I want to explain to you what you're about to see..." His voice trailed off as his eyes moved toward the large draped wall. "That"—he motioned with his head as he spoke—"is what we call a remote viewing window."

"Remote viewing? What do you mean by that?" Lenny was puzzled and even a little apprehensive, as John expected of him.

"I mean you're about to view events on earth as they are happening. Events that are related to you, the crash, and all of the circumstances and events surrounding your family and those who knew and loved you in your most recent walking on earth." John stopped and waited for his words to sink into Lenny's mind.

Lenny was confused. The composure with which he had entered the room had now been replaced by a heavy, palpable sadness.

After a few moments, Lenny spoke. "Do you mean I'll see the grief and emotional state of my family from the time they heard of the crash and learned I…" He had trouble saying the word. With help from the therapy he had already experienced, he had been able to avoid much thought of his family's enormous grief. Now, for the first time, he realized part of his own healing could not take place until he knew something about what his mother, father, younger brother, and others who knew and loved him felt. He would also soon learn just how much he was still connected to those he loved on earth. And shortly he would learn how he would still play a major role in all of their lives.

"When you're ready, I'll open the drapes, and you will see your family members as the news of the accident became a reality to them. I know it will be a challenge emotionally, but I think you're ready. Shall I open the curtains?" John reached for a remote on the table, and when Lenny nodded, John pressed the button marked "earth."

Suddenly Lenny, though invisible, was sitting in a car beside his mother. Surprisingly he could read her thoughts as she drove along toward what had once been his home.

VI

Celia Crawford Sawyer

Celia Crawford Sawyer had left her office at the normal time that Friday afternoon. This would be her night off from normal family duties. With her elder son, Lenny, away for his college roommate's wedding and her younger son, Bruce, at a summer camp for the weekend, she would enjoy the entire two days off. Her husband, Len, would enjoy a golfing weekend starting tomorrow with his friends while she caught up on her reading, did a little fall wardrobe shopping, and then enjoyed some well-deserved relaxation time.

Celia was more than a little pleased with her life as a forty-two-year-old married mother of two. As with her own parents, Celia had never looked her age. Born with nearly platinum-blond hair and sky-blue eyes, she had always been taller than the girls in her age group. At nearly five foot nine inches now, she knew she was lucky to have married a handsome young man who stood six foot three—someone she could actually look up to in more than one way, she often joked. She had finally grown used to the idea that she would have a youngster at home for several years to come while her older son was beginning his career as a doctor. Having one son entering medical school in the fall and another starting first grade had not been her idea, but now that little Bruce was finally going to school, she felt maybe having two sons with such an age difference would not be so bad after all.

She had been only twenty-two when she'd become pregnant with Lenny and thirty-seven when Bruce was born. Len loved having another young son to come home to, but it had interrupted her plans for earning her doctoral degree in psychology. She had been a mental health counselor for a few years before Bruce was born and had planned to go on for her PhD when she discovered, to her dismay, that she was once again pregnant. She had been accepted into a doctorate program in a respectable university near her hometown, so things were going to be perfect. No surprise there. Celia had always lived the perfect life. She had indeed been blessed.

But once the test came back and she found out she was pregnant for sure, Celia decided to continue her counseling practice on her current education and credentials and abandon the idea of the doctoral degree. Working and raising a youngster would take all the energy she had, so she quickly settled into a new routine that was actually quite satisfying once Bruce was born.

Always the perfect student, she had met Len in her senior year of college. No doubt he was the best-looking premed student at the university where they both had been undergraduates. Celia's perfect life had not begun there. The eldest of three daughters, she had always admired her parents. Both had been university professors, hard-working professionals, and their three girls had never wanted for anything. Somehow they managed to attend every important event in her and her sisters' school years and had given their children holidays and vacations that made them the envy of their schoolmates.

Following their university graduations, Celia and Len had the wedding of her dreams, complete with a honeymoon in Europe, a wedding gift from Len's grandparents. Both Celia and Len were surprised by her early pregnancy—she had obviously become pregnant with Lenny on their honeymoon. While it did cause her to put her plans for graduate school on hold, the joyous birth of her first son, Leonard Crawford Sawyer, overshadowed any other dreams at that time.

Len was able to obtain medical school loans, and at twenty-one Celia was able to draw funds from the generous trust fund left by her maternal grandparents, who had amassed a large estate thanks to the oil industry. So money had never been an issue for Len and Celia, despite starting a family before either of them became gainfully employed.

Len had followed his father into his highly successful obstetrics practice in their town, and generations of babies had been delivered by the Drs. Sawyer—right up until a few years earlier, when the elder Dr. Sawyer had been killed along with his wife of forty years in a car accident. Despite the emotional toll the tragedy took on the family and the entire community, Len had successfully grown the business. There had been one minor setback involving a patient after Len took over the practice, but they had managed to get through it. And after Lenny began school, Celia was finally able to earn her counseling degree, and continue her own professional life.

Celia was not sure what caused her to reflect on her own professional life that night—maybe it was because she finally had some alone time, for a change. Now that Bruce was in school and Lenny was entering graduate school, she no longer saw herself in a classroom other than the required continuing educational credits she would need to earn each year to maintain her credentials. She was finally enjoying her career in counseling others and no longer felt the need to advance academically. She maintained a private practice, sharing office space and administrative support with another counselor, Ann, whom she had met in graduate school.

Celia had always enjoyed counseling others. She had a general practice and for the most part helped people cope with everyday issues and problems. When clients presented with serious mood disorders or more complicated problems, she referred them to a local psychiatrist who could prescribe medications and treat the more serious cases. Occasionally she grew tired of listening to those who refused to accept change. She had always been a realist who could handle whatever came her way. Maintaining patience with those who had trouble adjusting to life's inevitable changes was a challenge to her. Thus a Friday afternoon with no family duties was always a pleasure after a long week of caring for what she and other colleagues frequently referred to as "the worried well."

While reflecting on how her life had evolved up to that point, Celia's thoughts were interrupted by a call from her husband, Len. He explained his caseload had been especially long that day, with one premature delivery that had thrown his whole schedule off. Tonight he would be working later than normal. He suggested they just have dinner at the country club, since he would likely be arriving much later than the normal family dinner hour.

"Sounds good to me." Celia smiled into the phone. "I was looking forward to a long hot bubble bath and a cold glass of wine."

"Great," Leonard replied. "I haven't had a good workout at the gym for a few days, so I'll try to work that in on the way home tonight too. I'm thinking at this point, I may be as late as eight."

"See you then, darling." Celia was delighted that she now had even more time for herself this Friday evening.

Celia rounded the corner of the street where their home stood, grand and stately, with just the right amount of accent lights on the driveway as well as the walkway. The lighting revealed a giant veranda on their colonial-style home. Her attention was suddenly drawn to the house directly across the street from her own. The sharp contrast between her brightly lit home and the gloomy darkness surrounding the similar style home, once as brightly lit as her own, was uncanny.

Such a waste, Celia thought. She continued to think about the family across the street as she reached for her briefcase and slammed the door on her Mercedes sports car. Closing the garage, she remembered that an entire year had passed since the other family's younger son had been killed in Iraq.

How long are they going to put their life on hold? Celia nearly asked the question aloud as she entered her kitchen and silenced the alarm. Everyone in the community had been there for the family across the street when they'd needed it, but a year? How long would they be surrounded by the darkness that seemed to envelop their home and everyone in it? Barbara, the mother, had not received Celia's offer of counseling well, nor had Bob, the dad, agreed to Len's offer to include him in his Saturday morning foursome on the golf course. It was like they had somehow lost their way when their son died. Thank goodness their older children were grown and had apparently gotten over it, as they never seemed to come around anymore.

"Who would blame them?" Celia asked herself as she tossed her briefcase and handbag on the black granite kitchen island.

Turning her attention to her own life once again, she noticed the clock above the double oven as she moved toward the family room just off the kitchen. For some reason it was off by nearly half an hour. Leonard had called her a little after six, and the clock was set to a few minutes before that time. She remembered glancing at her watch when he rang her. *Interesting*, she thought. She had replaced the battery on the antique clock no more than a month ago.

Oh well, she thought. Maybe it was due to faulty batteries. She would replace them again later, but not before she had a drink and that hot bath she so deserved.

Sport, Lenny's eight-year-old German shepherd, met her as she continued into the master bedroom, whining sadly. She could not imagine what was wrong. It was a different type of sound than she had heard him make before. While normally he would greet the family with licks on the hands and other endearing behaviors, now he was whining and pacing nervously around the room. Grabbing his leash, Celia thought perhaps he needed an earlier walk than usual. He had access to the yard through the pet door in the kitchen, so he was normally pretty independent as far as bathroom habits were concerned. One of the boys typically gave him a long walk prior to bedtime, but Celia thought perhaps today she might need to take him out earlier.

Try as she might, Sport would not go out, even with the leash. "Fine," she said as he continued pacing the floor. "I don't know what's wrong, but whatever it is will have to wait until Dad comes home. I'm too tired to persuade you to go out."

By then he had stopped whining, but the pacing continued.

Turning on the hot bath water, Celia undressed and retrieved her favorite terry cloth robe. It wasn't very pretty, but it was soft and comforting and exactly what tonight called for. Moving back into the kitchen, she poured herself a tall glass of Chardonnay and turned on the music in the den very loud. She loved to sip wine and listen to classical music during a long bath with her favorite salts.

Slipping into the hot water, she turned on the jets of the garden tub to increase the relaxation of the bath. *This is something I need to do a lot more of,* she thought as she took a sip of her favorite white wine and settled in for pure pleasure.

VII

Crashing the Perfect Life

Sheryl Crawford was preparing a simple dinner for herself, anxious to get off her feet after a long workday. The middle child of three sisters, she admired both her sisters for their ability to maintain careers and manage families. Sheryl felt she had all she could handle just holding down her job—although everyone knew she was great at what she did. All three girls were counselors of sorts. Celia, the oldest of the girls, was a mental health counselor, and Barbara—Babs, the youngest—was a child psychologist. Sheryl was a high-school guidance counselor, and while she loved her job, some years were more challenging than others, and this was one of those years. Eating right to keep her slender, petite figure had presented a challenge, and tonight all she could manage to create was a light salad.

Placing her salad plate and iced tea glass on a place mat in front of the television screen atop the kitchen island, Sheryl picked up the remote and switched on the nightly news. Moving through her favorite news channels, she half-listened as she munched on romaine lettuce covered with diet Caesar dressing. Distracted by thoughts about whether she should go to the health club for a swim or just take a long walk around the neighborhood to rid herself of some of the stress of counseling high-school kids, Sheryl pushed her dark-brown hair from her face and rose to place her plate and fork in the dishwasher. Suddenly an image on the television screen captured her attention.

A news reporter was standing in front of a raging fire. She could make out the wreckage of an airplane within the blazing flames. *What a furnace!*

she thought as she moved toward the dishwasher. And then she felt a surge of anxiety in her stomach. She heard the newsman say a jet had crashed on approach to the Omaha airport around 6:00 p.m., less than an hour ago.

Earlier that day she had been sure her sister Celia had mentioned her older son, Lenny, was headed to Omaha for his college roommate's wedding, which was planned for Saturday evening. In fact he was flying there today, Friday, for the rehearsal and dinner with the wedding party. Surely this was not his flight. Sheryl had mixed feelings about what to do. On the one hand, she wanted to switch the channel off and forget about it. *What were the chances?* she thought. *Slim*, she tried to convince herself.

The more footage she saw and the more she heard from the commentator, the greater her panic grew. She couldn't decide what to do. Should she call Celia? What if it was Lenny's flight and Celia learned of the crash from her phone call? What if Leonard was not home from the hospital yet? Calling was not the answer. She knew the right thing to do was to go over to Celia's house. She had to put this fear to bed. She knew Celia would have called her right away had there been any possibility her godson Lenny was on the flight.

Leaving her dishes on the counter, Sheryl hurried to her green Jeep Wrangler and drove the three miles to Celia's home. The radio in the car carried nothing other than news of the crash. They were now saying none of the passengers and crew had survived the crash and deadly fire.

Pulling into Celia's driveway, Sheryl found the garage door closed, preventing her from seeing if the cars were in there. But she could see lights on in the kitchen. *Good*, she thought. *At least someone's home.* She practically ran to the kitchen door and pressed the doorbell. She waited, and when no one answered, she rang it again. Unable to get anyone to come to the back door, Sheryl ran to the front door. She could hear Sport barking. Surely someone could hear that, if not the doorbell. She pressed the button over and over.

"Who in the world is ringing the doorbell?" Celia was annoyed by the disruption. She sank lower in the tub, hoping they would go away. She could hear Sport barking loudly. *Maybe that will scare whoever it is away*, she thought as she sipped her glass of wine.

As the incessant ringing continued, concern crept in. Celia realized someone was not casually ringing the bell. Whoever was there was ringing *frantically*. Something had to be wrong somewhere.

Reluctantly Celia dried herself and grabbed her robe and slippers. Walking through the living room, she could see the outline of her middle sister, Sheryl, through the beveled glass window on the front door.

"Family at the front entrance?" She found that puzzling as only strangers would call at the front door. Sport was still barking loudly. At the sight of Sheryl, he began to whine once more. *So much for a quiet night to myself,* Celia thought as she opened the door.

Before Sheryl could say a word, the look on her face communicated volumes to Celia. Something very bad had happened. Feeling her stomach churning, as it always did during extreme stress, she braced herself for what Sheryl had obviously come to tell her.

Sheryl moved quickly across the living room toward the kitchen and family room. Grabbing the remote but not switching the TV on, she said, "Celia, you told me earlier today that Lenny was flying to Omaha for Jim's wedding, right?"

Celia now experienced full panic in the pit of her stomach. Sitting down on the sofa across from the television, in a voice that was barely audible, she replied, "Yes, he should be there about now. Why? Is there a problem?"

Sheryl moved toward her, still clutching the remote for fear Celia might somehow turn on the set and see the sights on the screen before it was necessary. "Celia, look, I hate to say this, but I saw on the news a few minutes ago that a flight to Omaha had crashed around six o'clock tonight. Do you have Lenny's flight number?"

Without any questions Celia quickly approached the desk across from the sofa. She found the copy of the airline confirmation that Lenny had e-mailed her earlier that day and handed it to Sheryl. "You look. I don't think I can read the small print without my glasses."

Sheryl felt herself growing weak; she leaned against the wall for strength as she read the airline's name and flight number. In bold letters it read "Universal Airways, Flight 045."

Hating the truth she was now facing, she said, "Let's call Leonard at the hospital and tell him. I do think it's Lenny's flight."

"No, it must be a mistake. Let's not call him and alarm him for nothing. How cruel that would be. He would still have to drive himself home. Go ahead and turn on the television. You must be wrong about the flight number." Celia suddenly found strength and tried to take control. She saw the melodrama of the whole situation. She felt like one of her clients, making something out of nothing. This had to be just a horrible mistake, and within a few moments, they would see there was no way it could be Lenny's flight.

"OK." Sheryl had mixed feelings about exposing her sister to the images she was about to see, but she knew if it was Lenny's flight, sooner or later Celia would have to see it for herself. Sheryl hit the power button on the remote control as she and Celia both took seats on the couch.

The images on the screen were those Sheryl had seen earlier. The fire was still blazing, and across the bottom of the screen the flight number and airline name scrolled, confirming the cruel truth of this unspeakable moment in time. There was no mistake now. The commentator spoke the words that forever changed their lives.

"Universal Airlines flight forty-five crashed tonight while landing in a rainstorm. Fire immediately erupted and destroyed most of the airplane. It is believed all one hundred and six passengers and crew have died. Rescue workers are doing all they can to extinguish the fire and determine if there are any lives to be saved." The commentator droned on, relentlessly describing the unspeakable horror of the night.

Sheryl had heard enough. She hit the power button, silencing him and killing the horrific scene behind his image. She looked at her sister. "Should I call Len now?"

Celia was stroking Sport, who had become calm. She looked dazed and devoid of emotion. She stared into space for what seemed like an eternity. At last she spoke. "No, don't call him."

"But we have to tell him. We can't just sit here." Sheryl was worried about her sister. They had been through a lot as a family, losing their parents a few years before and the difficult situation in Len's practice a few years before that.

When Celia finally spoke, her comments made sense. "Call his assistant. Let me give you Keith's number. Keith will still be with him at the hospital and can drive him home. I don't want him driving himself home to this." She pointed to the television as if the nightmare was happening inside the large blackened flat screen. From the desk she retrieved a card bearing internal hospital phone numbers and gave it to Sheryl.

While Sheryl dialed the phone, Celia sat down and switched the television on. She knew she was in shock, but her sensations were different from other times she had experienced devastating news, like the deaths of her parents and her in-laws. She felt detached from the scene as it played out on the screen. They were still reporting the same facts—little chance of anyone having survived the crash and subsequent fire.

Celia could hear Sheryl trying to talk with Keith. They had met on more than one occasion at the Sawyer home over the years Keith had worked with Len and the surgical team, but communicating something this shocking had its own unique challenges.

"Yes, that's right." Sheryl had told Keith the news. Keith could not seem to understand what he was supposed to do at that point. "Please go and find Len, and let him know about the crash. Tell him I'm with Celia. And she would like you to drive him home. Don't tell him this, but to be honest she's concerned about him driving under these circumstances. It's all over the radio, and no doubt he'll be bombarded with the news all the way home."

• • •

At the hospital Len was dictating his final case notes when he heard Keith's soft knock on the door. *That's strange*, he thought. Keith didn't even knock when the door was closed. Why knock now on a fully open door?

He could see Keith standing outside the door. "Come in; door's open," Leonard said. "You look like your day was rougher than mine." He noticed the look of distress on Keith's face. "What's wrong? Is it the Jenson baby?" Leonard referred to a very difficult delivery Keith had assisted with earlier that day.

Keith dropped his eyes to the floor. "No, Len," he answered, calling him by a name only those closest to him used. Looking at his boss directly, he spoke the news he had come to deliver. "Len, it's closer to home than that. Your sister-in-law Sheryl just called. I'm so sorry to tell you this, but Lenny's flight to Omaha has crashed on landing. Celia wants me to drive you home right away."

"So that's it," Len said as he remembered the overwhelming feeling he had experienced an hour before. He put down his dictation and grabbed his coat. Keith followed him as he ran down the corridor out to the parking garage.

"If you won't let me drive you in my car, at least let me drive yours," said Keith.

"You can ride with me if you want to, but I need to drive myself right now," Len shouted. Keith opened the passenger side door on Len's car and strapped himself in for the quick ride to the Sawyer home.

As he drove, Len spoke about the feeling he'd had before. "This afternoon, while I was changing out of my scrubs, a sickening sensation came over me. It was so overwhelming, I had to sit down on the bench beside my locker. For a moment I thought I would faint. Now I guess I know why. It must have been the time of the crash."

"I don't know the exact time, but it's possible, since it had just been reported on the news when Sheryl went to your home to tell Celia. Look, Lenny, I need to tell you that the news is reporting the accident is pretty bad."

With that Len switched on the radio. A local radio station confirmed the tragedy that was unfolding in Omaha.

Keith could barely stand listening to what was being reported, but he knew it was a necessity at that point. For the first time, he allowed himself to think of Lenny. What a great kid. He was a star in every possible way. He was a good-looking young man, made great grades in school, and was slated to follow in the footsteps of his father and grandfather, both the best of the best in gynecology and obstetrics. It could not be true that at twenty-two, his life was over. And yet the newscaster was confirming there was little if any chance that anyone lived through the crash, much less the inferno that followed.

Len drove in silence, his attention on the news blasting out of the car's speakers. And then the commentator announced the time of the impact: 6:05 p.m.

"I knew it!" Len shouted. "I looked at the clock in the locker room, and it was six oh five on the nose when I had that nearly debilitating spell."

Both men stared ahead in silence as they turned into the neighborhood where the Sawyers lived. As they pulled into Len's driveway, he saw Celia running out the front door toward them, and he stopped the car.

"Our son, our son!" she shouted as she threw her arms around her tall, muscular husband. Sheryl and Keith looked on, helpless to do anything. They watched in silence as this tragedy continued its growth. It had already begun consuming the lives of two people they both loved so deeply.

"We've got to call the airline," Leonard said as he embraced his wife. Now Celia had full access to her emotions. She no longer felt detached from the events of that Friday night. Her tears were flowing nonstop, running mascara drawing muddy rivers under her eyes, reflecting the blackness of the situation.

Leading Celia into the family room, Len retrieved the phone from the desk. He glimpsed the envelope from the travel agency containing the proof of the unspeakable event. *That damned itinerary!* he thought. If only it read something different—a different flight, a different day, a different airline, just one digit different in the flight number would make this entire nightmare end.

He switched on the television, and after a moment his fingers punched in the numbers on the phone that scrolled across the bottom of the screen. Following many national and international events over the past couple of decades, he had seen emergency call numbers on television screens before. But never had he thought he would have to dial in and give the name of his family member as one who might be involved.

Not surprisingly he got a busy signal. Slamming the phone down, he took out his cell phone and handed it to Sheryl. "Dial the number on my phone, and I'll dial out on Celia's cell phone!"

Celia pointed to her purse. As he retrieved her phone, he continued giving orders. "And Keith, you start dialing on your phone. One of us is bound to get through if we keep trying. I want to keep the home line open." His voice betrayed his sense of despair. "Just in case…"

Celia looked up from the screen. "Just in case what?"

"You never know," Len replied. "Sometimes people do survive, and the hospital may not know the identity of any survivors for a while. So I say let's not give up hope. I think we should be praying Lenny is a survivor!"

"Prayer!" Celia thought it was not in the cards right now. She had always been a believer, but watching the burning airplane on the screen and knowing her baby boy was dying in the wreckage was causing her to feel anything but optimism—and she certainly had no energy for faith right now.

VIII

Airport Chaos

Friday was a busy day at the office where Jim was working as a student law clerk. He and Roseanne—Ro, as everyone called her—were getting married the following night. He took off early to get ready for the Friday evening events. It would start with picking up his best man, Lenny, at the airport, rushing home and changing, and then joining Ro and the other wedding attendants and family members at the church for rehearsal. They were having the rehearsal dinner at his parents' home. People were coming from miles away, and he and his folks wanted to feed all the family members, not just the wedding party.

It was early summer in Omaha, and the weather had been turning out even better for the week of the wedding than they had hoped. And then today, for some reason, the skies opened up, and torrents of rain had fallen since early afternoon. Thankfully it was supposed to end later in the evening. It would not be great weather for the night's events, but for the big day it would be perfect. Roseanne would be a beautiful bride, and Jim could not have been happier. Things were great and about to get even better, he reflected as he pulled into the airport parking lot, grabbed a ticket out of the kiosk, and parked his car. His parents had given him a new Volkswagen Jetta, and a red one at that—his favorite color. He and Ro needed a new car, and having a sedan would be a great complement to her small sports car.

Carefully hitting the buttons to ensure the doors were locked, Jim hurried into the baggage section for Universal Airways, umbrella in hand, trying to stay dry. With this type of rain, he was glad he had called Lenny earlier that day and arranged to meet him in baggage claim. Not that Lenny would need help with his bag; he could always out lift Jim at the gym. Though Lenny was taller than Jim and all of their friends, Jim, at six foot one, could hold his own in the weight room.

As Jim made his way to the baggage area, he smiled, picturing himself and Lenny in various pictures from multiple parties and events over the years. Jim's nearly jet-black hair and brown eyes were opposite his best friend's blond hair and fair complexion. So many good times, he thought, and now so many more to come.

But luggage was not the issue tonight. With the rain and the new security measures that did not allow anyone to stop a car while waiting for arriving passengers, parking and going in was the only logical thing to do, rather than driving around in case the flight was late. No doubt, with this downpour and summer thunderstorms all over the area, it was bound to be.

He would collect Lenny and then, once they were in the car headed home, call Ro and let her know all was on schedule. Jim was running a little later than he intended, but the way he saw it, with the rain, by the time Lenny landed and made his way to baggage, his timing should be about right.

Entering baggage claim, Jim looked up at the information screen to check the flight's arrival time. It was due in at 6:15 p.m., and it was 6:25 p.m. now, according to the clock over the information screens. The flight still showed an on-time arrival, so he assumed Lenny would be showing up any moment.

Several minutes had gone by when Jim noticed a number of employees wearing Universal Airways uniforms scurrying about, as if there was a problem. Jim tried to get the attention of one of the employees. She motioned him away, saying, "Not now, sir!" as she ran to an escalator, heading toward the departure level of the terminal.

Waiting a few more minutes, Jim noticed the arrival time of Universal flight 45 had been removed. It was replaced with the words *see agent.* Not sure where he was supposed to find one, since there had been none in the baggage area for the last few minutes, Jim decided to call Roseanne and let her know that apparently the flight was running late, so she could plan accordingly.

• • •

Roseanne had left work early that afternoon, like Jim, in order to get ready for the rehearsal and party. After a shower she had switched on the television in her bedroom. She liked to listen to news and weather as she applied her makeup and finished dressing.

Sometimes critical of her own looks, as most young women are at her age, even she had to admit the spray-on tan she had gotten earlier in the week added just enough glow to her normally very white skin. It showcased her bright-green eyes. Brushing her naturally curly auburn hair back away from her face, the way that Jim liked it, Ro could see the television screen behind her in the makeup mirror. A breaking news story interrupted the talk show she had been half listening to.

Turning away from the mirror, she saw a blazing fire, and she thought she heard the newscaster saying something about a crash at the Omaha Airport. She sat speechless and watched the horror on the screen.

Her phone rang. Picking it up, she heard Jim's cheerful voice. His tone and what was being shown on the television did not match. She found herself unable to respond to him.

"Hey, are you there?" Again she heard the smile and affection in his voice.

Finally, she found hers. "Jim, are you…" Her voice trailed off, and she tried again. "Are you at the airport?"

Something about the way she asked the question put Jim immediately on guard. "Why, is something wrong?"

Roseanne began to sob. "Jim, I think Lenny's flight has crashed. I am watching the news, and they're showing an airplane ablaze and confirming it's Universal Airways flight forty-five! That's Lenny's flight. He told us the number on the call last night."

• • •

Local-media representatives descended on the arrivals' area of the airport from every direction. It seemed like everywhere Jim looked, there were cameras, lights, and microphones, everything pointing to a major event happening all around him.

"Oh my God, Roseanne, are you alone?"

"No, Mom is here. But I've just seen it on the news. She can't possibly know yet. That is Lenny's flight, right?"

"God, I wish it wasn't, but he texted just before takeoff. He confirmed the flight arrival time with me again—and apologized that it was so close to the time of the rehearsal, but it was the only direct afternoon flight." Jim felt nauseated over what he had just confirmed.

"What are we going to do?"

"Roseanne, go let your mom know what's happening. And I know you may get some other calls, but keep the line open so I can reach you when I find something out. OK?"

In a voice that was hardly audible, Roseanne agreed to his request and added, "I love you," before hanging up the phone.

As Jim ended the call, he heard an announcement coming from a loudspeaker. "For those awaiting the arrival of passengers from Universal Airways flight forty-five, please go to the Universal Airways business lounge located just inside security on Concourse C. Please identify yourself and provide the name of the passenger you are meeting. You will be escorted through security to the lounge."

The announcement made it all too real. Jim had never even been in the business lounge before, and he did not want this to be his first occasion. But he knew that Lenny's family, Roseanne, and many other people would need to know all he could learn about Lenny, where he was, and how soon they could get to him. Feeling overwhelmed and totally alone, Jim and others in similar circumstances took the escalator up to the departure level.

There was a long line at security. Announcements were being made about other flights, but there was no good news for Jim. Passengers who were there to board other flights were being told the airport was closed and to remain in the terminal until news of their flights' new departure times were made available. The only people going through the security line with Jim were family members and friends looking for arriving passengers from Universal flight 45. Even the press was being corralled and sent to a different area.

Jim presented his driver's license and even showed a picture of Lenny and him together on his iPhone. This was his way of connecting himself to a passenger on the flight that had crashed. He gazed at the picture of the smiling Lenny, with Jim and Ro at a fraternity event from their last semester together. Jim gave all of the details the airline representative requested and waited so a young male employee could escort both him and a young woman to the lounge. She explained she was looking for her mother on flight 45. She was crying softly. Her eyes were red and swollen. Jim noticed she was clutching rosary beads as she walked beside him.

The employee escorted them to the appointed room. The young man, no older than Jim and Lenny, seemed timid and unsure of the tasks that were suddenly thrust upon him.

"Do you know anything? I mean, do you know what happened?" Jim could not resist asking despite the fact that he knew the young man was probably also in the dark. Even if he had some details, Jim knew he probably could not share them at this point.

As expected, the young man replied, "No, I'm so sorry, but we don't know much more than what's being reported by the media. We only know our flight coming from Cleveland crashed in the rainstorm, and—" He stopped just short of saying what else was being reported from the crash scene.

"And what?" Jim asked.

"And that is all we know at the moment."

The young woman spoke up. "And they're saying there are likely no survivors."

Jim suddenly felt the sick feeling in the pit of his stomach returning. This was the first he had heard about the enormity of the crash. Of course he knew the plane had crashed. But unlike Roseanne and those who could listen to the media reporters, he'd had no way of knowing up until this moment that the crash was fatal! This had been the happiest day of his life until less than an hour ago. Now it was becoming a day worse than he could have imagined. What a cruel paradox!

Jim thought of Lenny and the last words they had spoken. He had ended the call with "See ya tonight, Doc!" Already Lenny's friends had begun to refer to him as Doc. Jim had received his letter of acceptance to his preferred law school the same week Lenny learned he had been accepted to the medical school of his choice. The irony of what was now taking place was almost more than Jim could process as he walked into the large lounge, which was in total chaos. He wondered if Lenny's young life was over. Surely he had survived! He was that type of guy. If anyone could make it out of a burning airplane, it was Lenny. He was the epitome of health and fitness, and he was a fighter. Jim suddenly felt renewed hope.

A young woman in a uniform handed him a form and asked him to answer some questions. Who was he looking for, and why did he think this person was on the flight?

What stupid questions! Jim thought. Why would anyone be in this crowded room on a Friday night if they weren't 100 percent sure their friend or family member was a passenger on the flight?

But wait! he thought. *What if I'm wrong?* What if Lenny had missed the flight and was still at home? He may not even know about the crash. Again hope surged through Jim's body.

Walking over to a quiet corner, he hit the number for Lenny's cell phone. It went to voice mail. "Lenny, I'm here at the airport. Did you miss the flight? Call me and let me know where you are."

Next Jim dialed the Sawyers' home. Lenny's father answered the phone with anticipation in his voice. For one brief moment, he was thrilled to recognize the Omaha area code appearing on caller ID. And then his hope died. He recognized Jim's voice. He wanted so badly to hear his son's voice on the other end of the line.

"Dr. Sawyer, this is Jim. I'm at the airport. Have you heard about what's going on in Omaha?"

"Yes, I'm afraid so," answered Leonard with despair in his voice that sounded dark and foreboding. "We're trying to call the airline and can't get through. Can you find out anything there?"

"I've just come into the area where they're taking all who were awaiting passengers on the flight. I just gave them Lenny's name. I'm calling you in hope that he somehow missed it. Is that a possibility?" Jim felt by now that the chances were only slight, but he had to ask.

"I don't think so. Cindy, Lenny's best friend here in Cleveland, was dropping him off, and we haven't heard from her. But I think my next call will be to her. We were keeping this line open in case..." Leonard's voice broke at that point. He fought back tears. He needed to be strong for Celia.

Jim knew what Len had been about to say. He recognized the disappointment in the man's voice when he realized it was not Lenny calling to say he was safe. By then they all knew if Lenny had not called home or called Jim on his cell at the airport, there was a good chance he could not be calling anyone. Jim hung up the phone after Dr. Sawyer's last words, knowing neither of them could complete his sentence.

Jim noticed a man in a gray suit stepping up to the public-address system in the lounge. He appeared official, like he was in charge. He wasn't wearing the Universal uniform like the employees. Jim assumed he was an executive with the airline just by the way the uniformed employees were responding to him.

"Ladies and gentlemen," he began as a hush fell over the anxious crowd. "My name is Craig Johnson. I am the Vice President of Customer Service here in Omaha for Universal Airways. I have information pertaining to Universal Flight Forty-Five."

Jim moved closer to the counter where the man was standing and making the announcement. The VP continued, "I'm so sorry to tell you that Flight Forty-Five, which departed from Cleveland, Ohio, this afternoon at four o'clock, has been involved in an accident while landing here in Omaha at six-o-five p.m. We are currently awaiting news from the emergency personnel on scene as to the whereabouts and condition of the passengers and crew onboard."

The man paused at that point and wiped the beads of perspiration from his forehead.

"Is anyone alive?" a woman shouted from the back of the room. "The news is reporting there are no survivors!"

Just days before, Johnson had just completed training for talking with the press at his airport during a tragedy. Nonetheless, he was stunned when he was called within moments after news of the crash broke and told he would also be speaking to the waiting families. He would be the spokesperson for Universal until more experienced, specially trained personnel from the home office in New York could arrive and take over. He felt ill prepared for talking to the families of the passengers and crew.

"Ma'am." Craig had a soft tone naturally, so it wasn't difficult for him to sound humble. He knew humility was necessary in dealing with families during a crisis. "I am so sorry to tell you that until we get more information directly from our representatives at the crash site, I can confirm only what we know for sure."

"Well, what are we supposed to do?" shouted a man near Jim.

"Please give our team members who are circulating among you now as much information about who you are looking for as possible, and how to reach you. I have to tell you it will be a while before we have more specific information to provide to you about your loved ones. I would like to give you some options. First, if you want to go on home and wait to for us to contact you about your loved one, please know we will be in touch as soon as we know more. If you want to remain with us while you wait for more information, I would ask that you move over to the Gardham South Hotel on the south side of the airport. Our team is setting up a more comfortable area for you to wait. We will have food and beverages there, and members of our family-assistance team will be there to help you with contacting other relatives and assist you in every way we can. This could be a long night. I'll come back with more information once I have something definitive to share."

Questions were coming toward him from every direction, but he was trained to keep moving. He left quickly to make a similar presentation in the room that had been designated for the press briefing. Speaking to the press was not easy, but it beat trying to tell devastated families he had no good news for them.

Jim knew his place now was with Roseanne. Having listed Lenny's parents as the primary contact for information on Lenny's whereabouts and condition, he walked out through security and headed for the escalator. Just as he reached the baggage area, a woman with a microphone approached him, followed by a man with a handheld camera. Jim knew what she wanted, but with one look he told her he would not be giving her a statement about his involvement in the tragedy or anything else that might be on the ten o'clock news! After all, he was supposedly getting married tomorrow. There were already over sixty out-of-town guests at the Parish Inn down the street from the church and more slated to arrive that evening. There were decisions to be made.

Pulling out of the parking lot, Jim drove quickly toward Roseanne's home. He chose not to call ahead, as he had nothing good to say. Upon arrival he saw that his parents had already gotten there, no doubt to help Roseanne's parents with what had to be done with this recent development. Ro's dad had probably called them; Jim hadn't thought to. He hadn't thought clearly for the past hour.

As he walked into the kitchen, everyone looked up except for Rosanne. Sitting at the table, her face was buried in her hands. Wet makeup-stained tissues lay around her. She could not bear to look at the man who would be her bridegroom in less than twenty-four hours—if there was going to be a wedding. Right now she could not imagine their wedding without Lenny. He was not only Jim's best friend and best man; he was a best friend to both of them. Ro was inconsolable.

Jim sat down beside her and took her hand. His father approached the despondent young couple and explained to them that both of their mothers were making calls to let people know the wedding rehearsal and dinner had been cancelled, but for now the wedding was still on. They knew Jim and Roseanne could decide later that evening about the wedding, after they knew more about Lenny's fate.

IX

The View from Heaven

John had remained with Lenny as he watched his family and best friends suffering through the news of the crash and confronting its aftermath. It was understandable that Lenny was still emotionally attached to his earth family, which included Jim and Roseanne and all who were energetically connected to him. Yet there was no doubt that the time he had spent already on this side had prepared him somewhat for the objectivity he needed to maintain. He needed his energy to be able to help support those he loved during the ordeals they were individually and collectively facing.

John sat quietly and waited for Lenny to speak.

"It is so hard to watch the people I love so much suffer. If only they could see me now. If only they could see that while I know they'll miss me and I them, things are really fine. In many ways I've remained with them and they with me. I wish I could help them somehow."

"Lenny, I knew you needed the therapy and some time before you viewed the difficulties your family and close friends were experiencing during your transition from earth. But today Yvonne and I felt you were ready, and I know you are."

"Ready for what? Can I help them somehow? It seems like such wasted emotion. I wish they could see how good I am. And my grandparents, and that all who have left earth are not suffering. It's only those on earth who suffer."

"Yes, it's true what you say. And yet many people who are grieving on earth have rare opportunities to come to understand the close spiritual connection between them and their loved ones who have crossed over."

"What do you mean rare opportunities?"

John sat back in his chair and spoke slowly of things Lenny would one day remember without any prompting from him or anyone. This type of information was common knowledge on this side.

"You see, Lenny, when a soul departs earth, the spiritual connection grows stronger as the physical connection dissipates. Love, like you feel for your parents, your brother, and all your family and close friends, like Cindy, Roseanne, and Jim, has an eternal spiritual component to it. This spiritual component is a portal where you will remain connected on a very deep level." John paused. "Think of the portal as a window, much like the one we're viewing your family through right now."

"And through that window, can they see me the way I can see them?" Lenny seemed to be experiencing some recall about the subject under discussion.

"Sometimes you can reveal yourself to those on earth, if that seems to be the most healing or appropriate sign for the situation at hand. But sometimes there is a different miracle we need to perform to help loved ones on earth experience peace in a more efficient manner."

"John, I feel so bad for Roseanne and Jim. I don't want them to postpone their wedding. I can't believe my transition from earth is ruining their most special day. How do I help them from here?"

"Yes, it is indeed a shame, but you can help them. And in some ways, if what I have in mind works, and it should, we might be able to give them a wedding gift that will give them a whole new outlook on life. It will be far greater than any other gift you could have given."

"John, I want to do whatever you're thinking about. I want to help them. I love them both so much. What about my parents, my little brother, and my aunts?

"Let's take them one at a time. And remember, here where you are, time as you knew it is not relevant." John looked back at the giant window. Lenny followed his gaze. He now understood on some level that this was the portal where he and those still remaining on earth would always be able to connect.

X

Facing Reality

The events playing out at the Sawyer home that evening were not that different from those in the homes of all families of the 106 passengers and crew. At that point all the press could report were the facts as they had them—and those were sketchy at best. It would be hours before details would be known as to the fates of any individuals. Other than the men and women who were involved directly in the response out on airport property, where the crash had occurred, the whole world could do nothing but wait—wait and pray that their loved ones' lives would be spared.

After Len hung up from Jim's call from the airport, he placed a call to Cindy Pervis. She had been like a sister to Lenny since kindergarten, and it was not unusual for the two of them to run errands for one another. Today the errand had been for Cindy to drop Lenny off for his flight, since both of his parents had been working. Len's call went directly to voice mail. Cindy had spent the afternoon in a chiropractor's office for her chronic back pain and was not able to access her phone while news of the crash was breaking.

When Cindy left the doctor's office, she noticed her cell had notifications for three voice mails. She recognized Lenny's home number and wondered why someone from the Sawyer home would be calling her when Lenny was at a wedding rehearsal in Omaha. Hitting the "redial" button, she was surprised when Lenny's father answered the phone in an almost commanding voice.

"Cindy!" he said. "We've been trying to reach you. Did Lenny make the flight this afternoon?"

Not knowing anything that was going on, Cindy was taken aback by his demanding tone. "Well, yes, I dropped him off at least an hour before the departure time. I guess he made the flight. Why? Is there a problem?"

"Don't you know?" Len could not imagine anyone in the entire country that would not have heard of the crash by that time. It had been over an hour since the flight had crashed, and there was nothing else on any news station in the entire country—maybe the world.

"No, I don't know. What is it? I've been in the chiropractor's office since I dropped Lenny off. I just now got into my car and called you."

"Oh, Cindy!" Len realized now that he was telling Lenny's best girlfriend in the world the worst news she had heard in her young life. "The flight crashed on landing in a rain storm around an hour ago. We were just hoping that somehow, just maybe, there was the chance Lenny didn't make the flight."

It took a few moments for Cindy to compose herself enough to respond. "Dr. Sawyer, I watched Lenny go into the terminal, and I have no reason to suspect he didn't make the flight." She held back the tears as she listened to what Dr. Sawyer was telling her.

"OK, Cindy, I'm going to hang up. We want to keep this line open in case Lenny tries to call us. Our other lines are all engaged trying to get through to the airline. Jim just called from the airport in Omaha, and apparently no one knows anything there either. I will let you know if we hear anything from Lenny or anyone at the airline. Take care, and thanks for calling us back." Len hung up the phone, greatly disappointed in what he had learned. His last hopes for Lenny somehow missing the flight were now lost.

XI
The Knowing

Some really powerful feelings were starting to make their way into Cindy's consciousness, including a premonition she had denied earlier that day—more than once. She was beginning to feel a deep sense of guilt. When Lenny had gotten out of her car, he had kissed her on the cheek and reminded her of when he would be returning. She had agreed to pick him up on Sunday afternoon. As he'd walked away, an overwhelming feeling of sadness had come over her. She'd had a horrible feeling that this was their final good-bye! Somehow she knew she would never see Lenny again.

Why? she thought. *Why didn't I park the car and go and warn him?* Sure, she had experienced funny feelings about things before, but this time was different. This sense of loss and sorrow had been unlike any other premonition she had experienced. This had been more than a fleeting thought. This had been a warning. And she had failed to honor it.

Cindy felt responsible for Lenny taking the ill-fated flight. She started the car and let the tears flow. Turning onto the freeway, she decided to go to church and pray. There seemed to be nothing else to do. If only she had acknowledged her fear for Lenny's safety.

XII

The Confirmation No Family Wants

As Len hung up the phone, he noticed that Sheryl seemed to be actually talking to someone. For the better part of an hour, the family had continued to dial with no results. Now it appeared Sheryl had gotten through. He moved closer so he could hear her conversation.

"Yes, that's right. The name of my nephew is Leonard Crawford Sawyer. He is twenty-two years old, and I am sure he was on flight forty-five...No, I am not his parent. Hold on, his parents are here, and they're anxious to hear from you." Sheryl handed the phone to Len.

"Hello, this is Dr. Leonard Sawyer." He spoke with a voice of authority. "Yes, we're certain my son is on the flight. I just spoke with the friend who watched him walk into the terminal when she dropped him off an hour before the flight departed." Len listened intently. "Yes. When you have any information at all, please call us." Sheryl and Celia listened as Len gave their phone numbers.

Hanging up the phone, Len looked at Celia, who was sitting quietly on the sofa. The emotion she had displayed when he'd first arrived had disappeared. He had never felt so powerless. As a surgeon he was unaccustomed to this feeling. His life was about being in control. Now he had none. He thought about the countless times in his career where parents and other family members had paced the hospital room floor and wrung their hands in despair as they waited for news of the life or death of their loved one. Until now he'd had no idea what they were experiencing. How ironic, he thought, that he should have to learn now, after twenty-five years of practice. He now knew what it felt like to be so helpless and powerless.

Sheryl and Keith both sensed the need to give the parents a moment alone.

"Let me make some coffee," Sheryl said, moving into the kitchen.

Keith followed her. "What do you think we can do to help at this point?" he said to Sheryl as she was filling the coffeepot with filtered water from the refrigerator.

"I guess we need to find out who they want us to call for them," Sheryl answered. "I know when Mom and Dad died, we gave a list of names and numbers to Mom's best friend, and it saved us the trouble. But the problem at this point is we don't know what to say about Lenny. I mean, what if he made it and is in a hospital somewhere?" Sheryl thought now for the first time about little Bruce. She knew he was at camp. Someone should go and get him—but not yet, not until they knew more.

"Yeah, you're probably right. I guess it's just that I feel so helpless. I keep wondering what else I can do for them." Like the physician he assisted, Keith was not accustomed to feeling helpless. Nor was he often in situations where he was unable to help his boss in difficult times. But this was entirely different from anything either of them had faced before.

"I think we just have to wait here with them until something else is known," Sheryl said as she pulled out four coffee mugs and assembled a tray bearing cream and various sweeteners for the group.

"I already called my wife and told her what's happening. I need to call her and tell her I'll miss dinner. I think this could take a while," Keith said softly to Sheryl. He then spoke into the phone for a few minutes while Sheryl carried the coffee on the tray into the family room, where Celia and Len were glued to the television screen.

As Sheryl entered the room, Len held the remote in his right hand and increased the volume on the television. "Still no news about survivors." The parents, like people all over the world, hung on every word from the media.

The phone rang. Len picked it up, silencing the TV once more.

"This is Dr. Leonard Sawyer," he said, as though he was taking a call at the hospital, where he actually had some power.

"Mr.—I mean, Dr. Sawyer. This is Kay Simpson at Universal Airlines. I see you called in earlier about your son, Leonard Sawyer." She paused, and Len's heart jumped into his throat.

"Yes, Ms. Simpson, go ahead." Len retained his composure while the others in the room held their breath in anticipation of news about their beloved Lenny.

"I'm calling to let you know your son, Leonard Crawford Sawyer, is confirmed to have been on the flight. While we don't know his condition at the present moment, we are calling to let you know we have matched the passenger list against boarding passes, and we know he boarded the flight." The young woman again paused to allow her words to penetrate. This was her twelfth call within twenty minutes, and she had many more to make.

Len found his voice. "So let me understand what you're saying. You know my son is on the flight for sure, but you don't know if he's alive or not? Is that what you're trying to tell me?"

"Mr.—I mean, Dr. Sawyer, I wish I knew more, but at this time this is all the information we know for sure. We're awaiting word from the emergency officials as to where the passengers and crew are at this point, as well as their condition."

Glancing at the screen, it was obvious to Len that with these crash conditions, only God knew the whereabouts of the passengers and crew. Years of experience in the medical field gave him empathy for the young woman on the phone. She and her workmates had a terrible job to do, and she was doing the best she could to provide families like theirs with information when there was so little known at that point.

"So what happens now?" Len asked.

"Dr. Sawyer, here at Universal we are arranging flights and hotel rooms for family members who want to come to Omaha and learn the details about their family members as we do. Some people prefer to remain at home and wait for us to call while others will want to travel to Omaha as soon as possible. Which would you prefer?"

Len paused before speaking. "Let me talk to my wife and other family members and see what they want to do. Can you give me a moment?"

"I certainly can. I can call you back in an hour, or you can call me and let me know what you want to do." The young woman was very professional. She had obviously been trained for this unthinkable task.

Len reached for a pen and paper and jotted down her name and number. "Thank you, Ms. Simpson. My family and I appreciate your efforts to help us. We will call you right back with our decision, and please..." Len's voice faded to silence.

"Yes?" the young woman asked.

"Just please call us as soon as you can if you find out something about our son."

"We will indeed," the young woman answered.

With that Leonard hung up the phone. He turned his attention to Celia and Sheryl.

"Well, we have a contact inside Universal, a specific name and number. At this point they don't know anything about Lenny other than he boarded the flight. But they have given us some options." The exhaustion of the night's activities could be heard in Len's voice.

"What do you mean *options*?" Celia interrupted before he could explain.

"Well, they seem to understand that just sitting here waiting for information is pretty hard. They're offering to fly us to Omaha as soon as possible and put us up in a hotel." Len's voice conveyed his enthusiasm for the idea.

"Well, call back and let them know I want to go as soon as I can. If my son is in Omaha and injured, we have to go and bring him home!" Celia came to life at the thought of being near Lenny, regardless of the circumstances.

Sheryl spoke up. "Let me take care of Bruce. And you both go on. Let me call Babs. She and Bob and their girls will be back from the lake by now. We can both help with Bruce and look after Sport and the cat as long as necessary."

It was the first time any of the other family members had been included in the discussion. Len suddenly felt guilty about becoming so focused on Lenny that he had completely forgotten about Bruce. He was barely six years old. While it was good he was not home that evening to be in the midst of this turmoil, Len missed him now for the first time.

"Maybe we should take him with us. I hate to leave him home." Len spoke from his heart.

"No!" Celia said. "The baby does not need to be around all of this." To her, both of her boys were still her babies and always would be. The thought of Bruce being exposed to such trauma and sadness, away from the dog and cat, his toys, home, and normalcy, just did not seem right.

"Yes, Sheryl, go ahead and call Babs," Celia continued. "Let me give you the number where Bruce is staying, and go ahead and get him tonight. Do you mind staying with him here? It will be easier on you and better for him. Then he can stay with Babs's kids while you both are at work. They babysit him regularly, so it will seem natural to all of them. Will that work in case we have to be there for a few days?"

Sheryl nodded and took down the number. She began making plans to pick up Bruce. She knew she needed to call Babs about the horrific family tragedy they were now living through. What terrible news to be breaking to people! And they were only one passenger's family. She was beginning to imagine the magnitude of the tragedy, with 106 people onboard that airplane—most of whom had apparently not lived through the crash. She waited to hear more about the plans for her sister and husband's travel.

"Len, with your permission I will go ahead and call Stan," said Keith, referring to Len's partner at the practice. "Don't worry about your cases. We'll handle everything. You just go on and take care of your family." With that he excused himself and left with his wife who had driven over to retrieve him. He knew it would be a while before Len would be able to work. Nothing mattered more at the present than giving Len and Celia the time and support they needed to deal with their family's crisis.

XIII

Travel That No Airline Wants to Book

"OK, we're in agreement then," Len said to Celia as he picked up the phone and dialed the number for the airline. He recognized the young woman's voice immediately.

"Yes, Dr. Sawyer, we'll be happy to make travel arrangements for you. Let me get some information from you.

Len provided her with the specifics she asked about, along with the exact names and dates of birth on their driver's licenses.

"And are there any special needs?" the young woman asked.

Len was struck by the irony of her question. Their need right now, she could not help with. Their need was to have their son back home with them and to live out their normal lives as a family. His mind raced on.

"Dr. Sawyer." The employee interrupted his dissociative state. "Do you or your wife have any special needs we should consider in booking your accommodations?"

"No, my wife and I are both physically fit, so nothing is needed other than more specifics about our son."

"How about at home? Will you need child or pet care or anything like that?"

"No, we have family support here in town. So we just need to get there." Len was anxious to get going.

"OK, I think we're set for you to leave on the first flight out in the morning. You will be on flight sixty-eight. It departs Cleveland at seven o'clock and arrives in Omaha at nine thirty-five. You will have a room at the Grandham Hotel near the airport. When you arrive in Omaha, two members of our airline's family-assistance team will meet you. They will provide transportation to the hotel and help you with any needs you may have while you're there. Do you have any questions about the travel?" The stress of the evening's activities was not yet audible in her voice despite the fact that her shift had started early that morning.

"No, I only want to know about my son. Can you tell me anything else about Lenny?" Len could not imagine waiting until early morning for travel, yet he realized there was likely nothing to do that night but wait.

The woman on the other end of the phone spoke softly but very firmly. "Dr. Sawyer, I am so sorry, but all we know for sure is that your son's name is listed on the flight manifest, or list of passengers, and a boarding pass was scanned at the doorway of the flight with your son's name on it. That is what we know for certain."

"I see," Len said quietly. He knew he needed to tell Celia about the news he was now receiving from the airline. He just did not know how. He tried to control any emotional reaction in his voice.

"Dr. Sawyer, you and Mrs. Sawyer need only to go to the airport a couple of hours prior to the departure of the flight. Present your identification, and our Universal employees will take it from there."

"OK. Thank you for all you have done." Len finished the call and hung up the phone. Before he could tell Celia the latest news, she surprised him with a question.

"Why did you thank the airline employee? You sounded downright grateful to the airline. This is the hardest night of our lives, and you are thanking the people who may have killed our son." Celia had already switched from coffee to wine. The events of the night were obviously taking a toll on her.

Len went over to the sofa where Celia was sitting and sat close beside her. Taking her hand in his, he spoke to her with great tenderness. "Babe, I know you're angry and hurt. I also know they're the closest link to our son right now, and I want to keep the channels of communication open."

Sheryl had been sitting quietly, watching and listening to the painful interactions. "I'm going to give you two time alone while I go and pick up Bruce. I called Babs, and she and I will be able to take care of Bruce and the pets with no problem. I'll call you when I'm on my way back with Bruce."

"Yes," Len answered. "We would appreciate that. Thanks for all you've done, Sheryl."

With that Sheryl took her purse and left the parents to themselves to sort through their feelings. It was the first time Len and Celia had been alone since they news of the crash had broken into their lives, shredding their sense of normalcy. A black cloud of despair was quickly descending over them. The reality that they were likely facing a future without their firstborn son was slowly sinking in for each of them. It was becoming difficult to imagine living through the night, much less the rest of their lives.

Len finally broke the silence. "Celia, we have an early flight in the morning. I think we should pack and try to get a few hours of rest."

"OK, I can pack, but I know sleep is out, maybe for a long time to come." She started toward the bar. "I need another glass of wine. Can I get you anything?"

"No. I learned a long time ago that alcohol and bad news—for me, anyway—don't work too well together. You go ahead." Leonard waited for Celia to return with a glass, a corkscrew, and an unopened bottle of Chardonnay.

Watching him pour the wine into her glass, Celia pondered their situation. "Until they find Lenny, I won't give up. I'm his mother, and I don't feel like he's dead. I think I would know if he was. I feel him now—he can't be dead."

Len sat for a few moments staring into the distance as Celia sipped her wine. "Before I go to bed, I'll check in with Jim and Rosanne," he said. *Those poor kids*, he thought. How were they going to have a wedding without Lenny? And no one knew at that point whether Lenny was alive or dead. Either way, Lenny would not be the best man at Jim's wedding. *What a damned shame.*

"That's fine," Celia said. "I say we let Sheryl and Babs handle telling the family members about the crash. But aside from Cindy, as far as telling Lenny's local friends and our neighbors, let's leave it. No one can do anything to help, so why bother anyone else?" For the first time, she thought about her neighbors across the street. When their son was killed in Iraq, all of the neighbors found out within twelve hours or less. She remembered how everyone pitched in to help with food and anything else they needed. Now she guessed it was their turn to be the talk of the neighborhood and receive everyone's attempts at supporting another grieving family on their block.

"I think we need to call Jim and tell him what we just learned—that Lenny hasn't been found yet," said Len. "They have to be able to go on with the wedding one way or another."

"OK, you call them. I'm going to bed." With that Celia took her glass and the freshly opened bottle and headed into the bedroom. Switching on the news, she lay on the bed and watched the news from a very detached place. The whole thing seemed surreal. It did not seem possible for her son to be part of the story of the crash that was dominating the networks.

Celia finished the glass of wine and poured herself another. Somehow wine always made her feel better. The more she drank, the more her fantasies grew. She hoped to hear from Lenny at any moment. She just knew he would call by morning and tell her it was all a mistake. He had taken a different flight, she imagined, and could not get through on the phone due to all of the chaos.

Celia fell asleep fantasizing about her next meeting with Lenny, when things could go back to normal. They were a good family, after all, and they all deserved to live out their happy lives.

XIV

Father to Father

Len dialed the number for Jim's home. Joe, Jim's father, answered, expecting to hear another relative who had learned of the crash calling about Saturday's plans. When Joe realized it was Lenny's father, his own emotional response surprised him.

"Len, my God! I am so sorry. Is Celia holding up? And how are you? Tell me how to help right now." The sound of Len's voice caused the groom's father to lose his composure. In order to guide his son through the evening's events, he had maintained control over his own emotions. But now talking to Len brought a sense of reality to the situation that created new challenges.

With a voice racked with fatigue from the last few hours of sheer agony, Len responded, "We are saddened beyond words. I just heard from the airline, and it's not looking good for my son. I wanted to check in and let you know, so you could pass it on. How are the kids?"

Joe explained that Jim was over at Roseanne's home still, trying to console her and make decisions about the wedding. Len could tell by Joe's voice that the news was ruining for everyone what should have been the happiest of occasions.

Len expressed his concern for Jim and Ro. "They are going to go ahead and get married, right?"

"When I left Roseanne's place an hour ago, that was the plan. It's very hard for them to decide. There are so many people from out of town who have flown and driven in. It seems a shame to postpone the ceremony, yet it's a tough call to make. They both are so crazy about Lenny." Momentarily Joe recollected an image of the two boys tossing a football in the yard a few weeks earlier. He realized losing Lenny would impact them all for a long time to come. For his son, maybe forever.

"Neither of them can imagine the wedding without him," Joe continued. He knew he had to keep his composure for everyone. He would need to offer support to those who were hardest hit, not to mention his own son and soon-to-be daughter-in-law. Like everyone who was listening to the media reports, this family had begun to lose hope that anyone else onboard the flight was alive. Joe could not imagine anything worse than what Len and Celia were facing. Disappointment about a wedding was a terrible thing, but losing one's child was not comparable.

"Celia and I are booked on a flight early tomorrow morning," said Leonard. "Let me call you when I'm in town and know something for sure. But I should tell you that at this time, it doesn't look like Lenny survived. Go ahead and tell the kids. There's no point in them hoping for a miracle at this point." His voice broke.

Joe felt his emotional control starting to wane. "Look, Len, if there's anything we can do, let us know."

"We appreciate that, but you have enough on your plate. I'll call you tomorrow after we get to Omaha. Please give my best to Jim and Roseanne and your family."

XV

Am I Still a Brother?

Len heard Sheryl's car pulling into the circular drive in front of the house. Like she had promised, she had called to give them a heads up that Bruce was arriving in less than five minutes. Len went to the door to let his sister-in-law and his younger—now likely his only—son into the living room. His heart ached as he watched little Bruce run from the car and straight into his arms. He hugged the boy tightly and fought back tears. Young Bruce looked so much like Lenny at every stage and age. It had always been a source of amazement to Len and Celia. Looking at baby pictures of them both could be downright confusing. If you couldn't see the date on the back of the picture, you couldn't tell Bruce from Lenny. Now this seemed like a consolation they never could have dreamed of before tonight.

Sheryl felt tears welling up in her eyes when she saw the younger son in his father's arms. She realized now that with no word about Lenny's survival, it was not likely they would see the older brother again. Never having been a mother, having Lenny as a godson was a special gift her sister had given her. And now he was gone from them both. She silently mourned her losses—never to be a mother on her own and now losing the beautiful young man who was the closest to a child she would ever know. Her pain would be private, as it always had been. Sheryl would channel her grief into supporting her sister and brother-in-law and young Bruce. She silently committed to this decision and prayed for strength.

"Aunt Sheryl told me Lenny's airplane crashed, and you and Mama are really sad." Bruce spoke very well for his age. Taller than his classmates, he had always appeared to be a year or two older than he actually was.

"Yes, Bruce, there has been a terrible accident." Len spoke softly, with a voice heavy with grief. "Mom and I are going to the city where the accident happened tomorrow to learn more. Aunt Sheryl and Aunt Babs will take good care of you. And we will come back as soon as we can." He had dropped to one knee and was eye level with his son. He rubbed Bruce's small shoulder as he spoke.

"Will you bring Lenny home?" Bruce looked into his father's eyes as he asked.

As a medical professional, Len had watched far too many parents give their children false hope and even lie to them in similar family tragedies. While he understood the intention to protect the child, he also knew that when a child is mature enough to ask a question as straightforward as the one Bruce had just asked, it was best to tell the truth.

"We will if that's possible. But Bruce, right now we don't know for sure if Lenny will be coming home with us or not."

"He is OK, right? Is he in the hospital getting better?" Bruce's eyes were wide with fear for his older brother's welfare.

"Bruce, I'm so sad to say this, but Lenny may not have lived through the accident. We'll know more tomorrow, when Mom and I get to the airport where the accident happened."

Bruce began to cry. Len took him in his arms and held him while he sobbed. "Lenny may have gone to heaven to be with Meemee, Papa, and Mom's parents, Grandma and Grandpa. And we will be OK if he has. Mom and you and I are still a family, with Aunt Sheryl, Aunt Babs, Sport and your kitty, your cousins, and all of those who love you. All of us together as a family will make it."

Sheryl leaned down with tears on her cheeks and spoke to Bruce. "I'm going to stay with you until Mom and Dad get back. Aunt Babs and I will take care of you, Sport, and Kitty. You're going to swim every day with Aunt Babs's girls. You'll see, we'll take good care of you!"

"But I don't want to swim without Lenny. He's my best friend!" Bruce cried out. Len continued holding his son as he sobbed.

"Bruce, he is your best friend and always will be. He will always be your brother. And now Mom and I have to leave early in the morning to learn more about what has happened to him. I need you to trust us. We're all going to stand together as a family. Will you allow Aunt Sheryl to tuck you in if I promise to kiss you good-bye before we leave tomorrow?"

"Where is Mom? Can I say good night to her?" Suddenly missing his mother, Bruce looked around the room for Celia.

"You can see her tomorrow. She went to bed early, so she can get up in the morning for our flight." Leonard knew that even if Celia were awake, seeing Bruce in such a state would upset her even more. He thought it best to allow her to start fresh the next morning.

After one more kiss on his father's cheek, Bruce went upstairs with Sheryl. Sport and Kitty ran up with them. Animals had always been part of the family, and tonight for sure Bruce would not be denied the comfort of his favorite four-legged companions in his room or on his bed.

Leonard turned out the lights and joined his wife in their bedroom. As he had suspected, Celia was already asleep when he got into bed. He noticed the wine bottle was nearly empty. Her pillow was wet with tears, but for now she was snoring lightly. He was sure she had likely wept herself to sleep. And now it was his turn to do the same.

XVI

Travel No Family Wants to Undertake

Celia and Leonard spent some time with Bruce before they left for the airport. The morning news had brought no relief. Despair hung like a curtain over the breakfast table as both parents and Sheryl tried to appear normal for young Bruce. No one spoke of the crash in front of him. He focused on a new video game Aunt Sheryl had given him on his birthday a few days earlier.

There had been no phone call in the night changing the reality of what the family was facing. The front page of the paper now reported a final count. Out of 106 passengers and crew, there were no reports of survivors.

In another section neither Leonard nor Celia had chosen to view, the passenger and crew list appeared. In alphabetical order, the truth of the disaster was spelled out. Sheryl's eyes filled with tears when she saw the name Leonard Crawford Sawyer near the bottom of the list, age twenty-two, hometown Cleveland, Ohio.

The home phone had begun ringing early that morning and rang continuously. Jane Sutton, a friend of Celia's, herself a therapist, was fielding the calls and taking notes from the various callers. It was incredible how many people wanted to know about a funeral when Lenny had not even been identified yet. She knew people meant well, but didn't they know that soon enough the details would be printed in the newspaper?

Sheryl gave Celia and Len a ride to the airport. They had packed lightly. There was no reason to pack many clothes. From what they could tell, they were likely going to Omaha to bring the remains of their firstborn son home for burial. It never occurred to either of them that finding enough remains to identify the victims was already presenting a challenge for the recovery personnel at the accident site.

Celia and Len were both numb by the time they reached the airport. They were relieved that they were able to leave Bruce behind. They no longer felt a need to guard their emotions, as they had at breakfast in Bruce's presence. Now it was just the two of them, and they could allow their raw emotions to surface.

"I packed some Valium and a couple of other sedatives, if you need them," Len told Celia as they entered the terminal.

"Good. I may need some help sleeping. Last night was not easy, and I don't think it will get easier for a long time." Her eyes were red and swollen from the night before.

Arriving at the ticket counter, they waited in line for only a few moments. As soon as they showed their identification, they were given priority treatment. After assigning their boarding passes to them, the agent stepped from behind the counter and walked them to the first-class lounge, where they waited to board the flight.

Celia noticed that several other passengers were being escorted into the lounge. It became obvious that other family members were being flown to the city of the accident on the same flight. There was a general tone of sadness that permeated the lounge as well as the first-class section of the aircraft.

She felt Leonard's hand on hers as the flight took off. Neither of them feared for their safety. After all, what was there to fear? The worst thing had already happened. Their precious son was dead, and they were headed to a strange city to bring him home for a proper burial.

XVII

The Wedding Gift

Jim and Roseanne decided to go on with the wedding. Another friend of Jim's who was already in the wedding party would take Lenny's place as best man. They opted to have a quick rehearsal early on Saturday morning. Len called just as they got started. He had no idea he was interrupting the rehearsal. He called to say he and Celia had arrived in Omaha. He asked Joe to give Jim and Ro their best wishes, as everyone knew how challenging the day would be. He promised to call and let the family know when Lenny had been identified.

Everything else went according to plan. The bridesmaids all arrived at the church at the appointed hour along with the bride. In the room off the sanctuary, they touched up their makeup and picked up the bouquets that had been delivered earlier that day. The groomsmen and groom arrived at the church at the agreed upon hour as well. Only one thing was different about their attire than they had originally planned, and it only seemed right. The ushers and groomsmen, so handsome in their tuxedos, all wore white armbands with wide black ribbon representing their deceased friend, as did the groom.

This acknowledgment of the missing groomsman touched the hearts of family and friends. There was no reason to deny the sadness of the occasion. Everyone in the church knew of Lenny's death, and this was about the only way to honor and include him in the ceremony, in addition to the toast they would make to his short life at the reception.

As Roseanne and her father stood in the back of the church, out of the view of the guests, Marty, her maid of honor did all she could to wipe the tear stains from Ro's pretty face. Her waterproof mascara was working, but only just. Roseanne was grateful she had chosen a veil that covered her face. There was simply no way to be the radiant bride she might have been if only there had been no crash.

At last the music announcing the bride's entrance sounded. On cue, Roseanne and her father started down the aisle. The moment she looked at the altar and saw Jim and the others wearing the armbands, her tears started again. Roseanne simply could not stop crying. Her shoulders shook, and she sobbed openly all the way to the altar.

When Jim took her hand, he was concerned over the coolness of her fingers. The ceremony would be shortened in an effort to move things along as rapidly as possible, but he wondered if she would get through it. He lifted her veil for the vows, and his heart ached when he saw her beautiful tear-stained face and the lines creasing her normally smooth forehead.

As best she could, Roseanne gave her attention to the minister. Some movement in the choir loft above the minster's head caught her attention. As she looked for a moment, she thought she saw another man dressed in a tux looking down at them from the choir loft. Why would a groomsman be standing in the choir loft? The tall blond man placed his hands on the rail and leaned forward so his face was clearly visible. Ro suddenly realized she was staring up into the smiling face of none other than Lenny Sawyer!

Jim glanced over at Roseanne and noticed a look of joy on his bride's face for the first time in several hours. Following her eyes, Jim could not believe what he was seeing. Lenny was there; he had made the wedding after all! Now they both were smiling up at Lenny. They had become oblivious to the minister, who could tell something outside of the wedding vows had captured the attention of the bride and groom. Following their gaze, he quickly glanced behind him up into the choir loft. He saw only the vacant benches.

Both Jim and Ro were slightly embarrassed when the minister was forced to repeat the start of the vows. They forcibly turned their attention back to the minister and repeated the vows as instructed. Once the vows were complete and the rings exchanged, the couple looked up for their beloved friend. He had disappeared as easily and quickly as he had appeared only a few minutes earlier.

The ceremony complete, Jim and Roseanne could hardly contain their exuberance. Within a few minutes, the newly married Mr. and Mrs. James Johnson Ford were walking swiftly down the aisle, aching to get a moment alone. Not for typical reasons associated with newlyweds—they were consumed with the need to discuss with each other what they had both just experienced.

Having planned ahead to have their receiving line at the reception hall, Jim and Roseanne exited the church as planned. After a few parting poses for the photographer, they politely waved at family and friends and dove into the limo that was waiting for them. Finally alone, they could no longer contain their excitement.

"Could anyone else see him?" The color and life had returned to Roseanne's face.

"I don't think so. I think Lenny gave us a gift that was meant only for us to experience." Jim kissed the wedding ring on his new wife's finger. "Have you ever had an experience like that before?"

"No, not as an adult. But you know, my grandmother on my mother's side was able to pick up on things others often could not. When I was a little girl and played with my friend no one else could see, she always defended me when others told me I was making the whole thing up." Roseanne squeezed the hand of her new husband.

"I have never had an experience like that as an adult. If I hadn't seen Lenny myself, I would have a hard time believing it. I mean, I would have believed it if you told me, but it wouldn't have been easy. But not now. I saw him. I will never forget those few moments. He was beaming as he looked down from the choir loft. He loved us so much, and he gave us that gift to let us know he will always be with us." Jim looked out the window as they approached the reception hall.

"You know, I think we need to tell his parents. What do you think?" Roseanne wanted so badly to share their secret but only with people who would fully understand the magnitude of what had happened. This was definitely not cocktail chatter.

"I think the time will come when we can share this with them, but we need to let them get through what they have to endure right now. While we're on our honeymoon in Maui, they'll likely be bringing Lenny home." Sadness had returned to Jim's voice.

"Should we cancel our honeymoon?" Roseanne felt a deep sense of guilt over the thought of flying off to seven days of fun in the sun after what had happened to their best friend.

"I don't think we should do anything different from our original plans. Lenny could not have given us a better send-off than what he gave us at the church. So we need to get on with our plans. I know he would want us to." Jim was determined to hold on to the encouragement he had felt when he'd caught site of Lenny leaning over the edge of the choir loft.

Roseanne wanted more time to discuss this experience, but they were arriving at the reception hall, and the photographer was already there waiting. "I know you're right, but I can't imagine not being at his funeral."

"Ro, from what they were reporting in the news this morning, it's entirely possible we may be back in Omaha before Lenny is buried."

"What do you mean?" Roseanne had avoided watching or listening to the news reports after that first few hours the night before.

"This morning I read that identifying those who died in the crash is going to be very complicated, as the fire caused serious damage not only to the aircraft but to the people as well." Jim tried to choose his words carefully.

The driver had stopped the car, and Ro's father was at the door, helping her out before they had time to say more. Once again the delight of seeing the unexpected guest took over their emotions. This gift now allowed them to enjoy the remainder of the evening. Lenny's love had saved their wedding, despite his physical absence.

XVIII

Joy in Heaven

Lenny enjoyed viewing the reception. It was one of the only scenes where he could view people he loved and felt connected to where there was some level of joy. He knew the black cloud on the wedding had lifted when he was able to let Roseanne and Jim see him. He owed it all to John.

John had explained to him that just as he was able to view the lives of those he loved on earth, under the right circumstances those who loved him could experience him too, with one or more of their five senses. Sitting now alone in the viewing room, he remembered how John had helped him become visible.

"Now, while you focus on their faces, send as much love as you possibly can to them both. See yourself there with them—pick a place where they are likely to see you." John also told Lenny that making himself viewable on earth was not easy, but under the right conditions, with enough love, like most things it was possible.

And Lenny had known beyond any doubt by the smiles on their faces that Jim and Ro indeed had seen him. He loved hearing them discussing their delight over his appearance later, when they were alone in the limo.

Alas, it was time to turn his attention to the more challenging work in front of him. He tuned in to his parents as they arrived at the airport in Omaha.

XIX

Entering the Ripple

The flight arrived on time, and another chapter of the tragedy began to unfold for Dr. and Mrs. Sawyer. They had come to take their son home, and they did not even know where to find him—or if they would.

Upon landing Len and Celia gathered their belongings and stepped off the aircraft into a terminal that was heavy with grief. Two employees holding a sign with their name on it met them. The Sawyers noticed other groups of passengers being met by people with similar signs.

Len spoke first. "I am Dr. Leonard Sawyer, and this is my wife, Celia."

The female member of the pair offered her hand to him. "I'm Lori Priestly, and this is Daryl Grenshaw. We're members of the Universal Airways Care Team." Both Len and Celia accepted their handshakes and waited to hear more about who they were and what they could do for them.

Now the young man spoke up. "Dr. and Mrs. Sawyer, we are so sorry about your son Lenny. We want to help you every way we can while you're here in Omaha for the next few days."

Exhausted from the loss of sleep and the shock of the entire ordeal, Len said to the young employees, "I'm sorry, what did you say your names are?"

At that point both employees presented him with cards bearing their names and contact numbers. There were other words on the cards, but the tension was so high at that point, Len could not focus on them. "Ms. Priestly and Mr. Grenshaw, can you help us learn about our son Lenny?" he asked.

Lori replied, "We've come to take you to meet the officials who can answer all of your questions. What we want to do is to take you to the hotel where those in charge of the investigation are briefing all of the other families. They're the ones who know the most about what's happening with recovery of all of the passengers and crew."

"Well, can you tell us what happened to the airplane? We know there was a crash and bad weather. But do you know anything else?" Celia asked.

"Mrs. Sawyer, there is a full investigation underway. And at the hotel, there are officials who can tell you what they know." Daryl was leading the way now, and they were headed toward the baggage area.

A car was waiting outside for them as they left the terminal. Celia allowed the others to lead her. The normal independence that was part of her personality was no longer dominant. She did not want to go to the hotel where other grieving people would be as helpless as she felt. But she did not know what to do other than follow.

The foursome made the short journey to the hotel in silence. The driver had shut the music off as soon as they joined him. Celia was relieved. The music was the same kind Lenny had enjoyed. Everywhere she looked was a reminder of her handsome son. Hearing his favorite music only made things worse—if that was possible.

The employee team checked the Sawyers in to what Celia considered a second-class hotel. She planned to let Len know of her disappointment in the accommodations. This hotel was not on the same par as what she would have selected. But of course, like everything going on for the past several hours, nothing was of her choosing. They took the elevator to their room, and as soon as they entered, Len noticed her disgust. The room was shabby, without the luxury his wife was accustomed to.

"Look, honey, let's stay tonight, as it's easier to be here and get as much information about Lenny and the accident as possible. If you just hate it, tomorrow morning I'll try to find us a better place to stay."

Celia knew he was trying to cope too. Everything was just so damned depressing. She started to feel as powerless as Len had felt the night before. Some considered her a very good therapist, yet she was unable to help herself. The sadness was overwhelming everywhere she turned, and having to spend even one night in a hotel so beneath her standards would certainly not help her feel anything but more helpless.

Celia was happy to see that even this cheap hotel had a small refrigerator, which she assumed functioned as a minibar. She needed a quick drink. To her surprise, the refrigerator was empty. Had they emptied it to keep the guests from drinking? Oh well. She would buy her own drinks as soon as she could.

Feeling physically worse than he had in the entire time since he'd learned of the crash, Len exited the bathroom as Celia was closing the door to the minibar. Reality was setting in for them both. They had arrived in Omaha, and there was still no sign of Lenny.

"Don't you think we should go on downstairs and meet some of the officials who can help us find Lenny?" Len headed toward the door.

"Yes, although there is a part of me that would rather not. If we can avoid the next step, somehow it doesn't seem as real. But I know we have to get on with it. Let me call Sheryl. I promised to check in with her as soon as we got settled. I want to make sure Bruce is doing OK."

Celia took out her cell phone and quickly spoke to Sheryl, who assured her Bruce was coping well. Sheryl explained he was playing with friends and only occasionally asking questions about Lenny and the crash. The calls to their home from friends and well-wishers had been kicked off by Lenny's name appearing on the passenger list in the morning newspaper. She and Babs had everything at home under control, as much as possible.

XX

Meeting the Earthly Officials

"OK, let's go." Celia followed Len out of the hotel room.

The despondent parents boarded the elevator and followed the signs in the lobby to the area designated as the family-assistance center. The same two airline employees who had met them at the airport approached them as they entered the room. They helped the Sawyers obtain badges and explained this form of identification would allow them access to areas for families only. They explained that the press and others would be prohibited from entering these areas.

"The first family briefing is just getting started," said Lori as she pointed them toward a table where other men and women were sitting. By the tissues in front of the two women Celia sat down beside, it was obvious they were grieving family members. There was no time for introductions, as a man with gray hair, dressed in a blue business suit, stood up at a front table and introduced himself.

After nearly an hour of listening, or rather trying to understand what all was being said, Celia and Len were ready to leave. The discussions were so technical and businesslike. There were just too many unanswered questions. The only facts known at that point could have been learned just as easily by listening to the media reports. In a nutshell, the main speaker reported it this way: Universal Airlines flight 45 had crashed while approaching the runway in a rainstorm. Due to the fire that erupted after the crash, no one had survived.

Len and Celia had heard enough. About the time they were leaving, a different speaker stood up and addressed the group. Listening to him introduce himself, Len and Celia were glad they had remained to hear him.

"My name is Henry Brennan. I am the county medical examiner in charge of identifying the passengers and crew onboard Universal Airlines flight forty-five. I would like to begin by expressing my sorrow to all of you whose family and friends were in the crash last night."

At last someone who realizes what this is about, Celia thought. This was about pain and suffering, not just a technical investigation. He was the first of the speakers who did not refer to her son as a victim. He used words like *passengers* and *crew members.*

"Now, as many of you know," Brennan continued, "the fire and impact force have made our job of identifying the passengers and crew very challenging, to say the least. At this point we have begun the process of positive identification, as some of the people were more easily identified than others. After this meeting members of our team will be contacting each family to begin the process of collecting information. This information will be used to help identify each of your family members as quickly as possible."

The term *information* must have been code for DNA and so forth, Len thought. The thought of this process was another blow to him. He had not considered that his son might be so badly damaged, he would be unrecognizable. But of course, with all of that fire, he should have realized it could be that bad. Celia had cried throughout the time they had been listening to the men speaking. He wondered how much she understood about what the medical examiner was saying.

When Brennan finished talking, another man approached the microphone. Len had heard enough about the technical investigation and felt his wife probably had too. He noticed the direction the medical examiner headed when he left the room.

"Are you ready to go?" Len leaned down and whispered to Celia.

Without answering, Celia stood up. Together they left the room, with officials still talking. At that point the Sawyers were interested in one thing. There was a reason they had come to Omaha. Len wanted to find the medical examiner and make that happen. He was tired of feeling powerless and as though he had lost all control of his life.

"I want to talk with Henry Brennan. I saw him walk out that way." Len led Celia out of the room through the door he had seen the medical examiner exit. He wanted to find Brennan and talk doctor to doctor. He wanted to provide the DNA or whatever the hell they needed as to help find Lenny, get his son, and go home.

XXI

Taking Control

Henry was just outside the meeting room speaking on his cell phone when Len and Celia approached him. He quickly ended the call. Len introduced himself and Celia as parents of one of the passengers who had likely died in the crash.

Henry offered his hand to Len. He reached for Celia's hand, but she seemed frozen, unable to respond to his gesture.

"Look, I'm a physician in Cleveland, and I carry a heavy caseload. I realize you have a lot of families to deal with in addition to ours. But I'm wondering if there is any way we can expedite the identification process, get our son, and take him home."

Henry felt a heaviness in his heart for this father. As a dad himself, he felt for Len and all of the families involved. But he had to help them all understand this was one time when status of any kind would not move anyone to the front of the line. They were facing a long, drawn out process, and it was not even close to being over.

"Len and Celia, I am so sorry to meet you under these circumstances. Can I buy you and Celia a cup of coffee?"

"Sure, we would appreciate a moment with you, if you can spare it." Len felt he might make some progress at last.

The threesome walked over to a coffee shop and sat in a booth in the back. It was quiet and conducive to a private discussion.

"Len and Celia," Henry began as soon as the coffee was served. Others around them were ordering lunch, but no one at this table was able to even think of food. "First I want to say I can't begin to understand what you're going through. I am a father of three boys, and I can't imagine how my wife and I would survive if something happened to one of them."

"Thank you for saying that. It all just seems impossible that yesterday at this time we had two sons, and now we have one." Celia spoke about her loss for the first time. "It just seems unreal. I mean, it doesn't seem possible. And we want to see Lenny, identify him, and carry him home with us. Can you help us do that?"

As Len had suspected, Celia had not understood the extent of the damage to the passengers in the aircraft. She had not realized what they were up against. He knew it would be better if Henry tried to explain it to her.

"Celia, you heard me talk about information being required, right?" Henry said.

"Yes, and I know we can provide you with what is needed." Celia regained some energy over the prospect of doing something to help find her son.

"Well, yes, many of the families who have already arrived will be able to give what is needed to help with the process of identification. However, there was severe damage done to each of the victims." Henry had to remember he was speaking to parents and needed to be as sensitive as possible. "I mean passengers and crew members who died. There will be no visual identification of anyone. And—" Henry stopped as he saw Celia look away. She was trying to process what he was saying. The visual images of what he was describing were pretty horrific.

Celia looked at him. "And?"

"And the devastation inside the burned aircraft contributes to the difficulty too. You see, the degree of hot fire and general conditions of the cabin interior will not allow for any visual identification." Henry stopped short of telling them how bad the destruction really was. The incinerator-like conditions in the cabin had produced near total destruction.

"I see." Celia comprehended more fully what they were up against. "So you mean I have seen my son for the last time?"

"Yes, I am afraid so." Henry met Celia's eyes at that point.

"So what do we do now?" Celia asked.

"I can arrange for you to provide information necessary to identify him this afternoon. Then we'll just have to wait." Henry took a sip of coffee. The reality of the situation was no doubt taking its toll on these parents, like so many other family members.

"So do we then go home?" Len asked.

"That depends. If you stay for a few days, you'll get a great deal more information about what the investigators are finding out. They'll also arrange a visit to the crash site in the next day or two, and they may be able to identify some of the personal effects—uh, I mean personal belongings of the deceased passengers and crew. So if it were me, even with a busy practice back at home, I would stay for a couple of days."

Henry knew he had a lot more to do and many more people to talk to, and as much as he hated it, he simply had to go to the next meeting with the government investigators.

"Look," said Brennan, "I need to keep some other commitments. But I want you to take my card, and if you want to talk to me again, call my cell phone. It will ring directly to me."

Len could only imagine how grueling Brennan's schedule might be as the chief medical examiner for the county where this nightmare had occurred. He was grateful for the professional medical courtesy Henry was extending. This was such a cold process. The term *personal effects* and his son's belongings just did not seem to go together.

"Thanks, Henry." Len stood up and held out his hand. Celia was crying again, and both men understood. The latest news about the destruction of the aircraft and all in it due to the crash conditions had been such a shock that Celia had no energy to communicate with anyone.

Henry touched her on the arm with a brief gesture of compassion. With an increasingly heavy heart, he walked away.

Sitting back down at the table, Len noticed Lori and Daryl were approaching them again. He tried to let them know with eye contact that this was not a good time, but they missed his signal and came to the table.

"Is there anything we can do for you right now?" Lori asked both of them.

Celia shook her head. She was unable to speak or even to behave politely.

Len stood up again. "Lori and Daryl, may I have a word with you?" He pointed toward the doorway where they had entered.

Both employees silently followed Len out of the door of the coffee shop.

"Please forgive my wife. The medical examiner just told her she won't be able to identify our son visually. He also told us how bad the crash conditions are. You have to understand that losing our son is one thing. Not being able to bring him home for a proper viewing and burial presents another entire level of loss."

Daryl spoke first. "I am so sorry, Dr. Sawyer. We'll give you some time alone. You have our cards. Would you call if you think of something we can do for you?"

"Yes, I will call," Len said, although, he could not think of what they could do for him and Celia. He knew they were trying to be helpful, so he added, "And thank you. Please forgive my wife for seeming rude. She is normally not like that."

"We realize this accident is like nothing anyone could have imagined. We could never judge your wife or any family member for anything they say. It's a terrible time." Lori spoke with a softness that touched Len deeply.

"Thank you, and we will call if we need help," he said.

With that the employees walked toward the hotel lobby. Len was relieved, as he knew Celia would not be very accepting of anyone's help for a while. He could not imagine the role the airline people were playing. He knew they were doing the best they could under the worst possible conditions.

Returning to Celia, Len sat quietly with her for a few minutes and waited while she ordered a bottle of Chardonnay with two glasses. Then she spoke her thoughts.

"OK, so let me get this straight," Celia said softly. "No Lenny, alive or dead. Did I hear correctly?"

"I'm afraid so." Len knew facing the truth was the only way to move forward. He waited before he continued. "We do have some decisions to make, even under these circumstances."

"Like what?" Celia poured herself a glass and started to pour one into the glass in front of her husband.

"No." Len put his palm over the glass. "I don't feel like a drink right now."

"Fine. I just can't imagine *not* having one right now." Celia took a long drink and leaned back in her chair.

"Look, Celia, as I started to say, we can go ahead and get the identification process underway, as Henry suggested. Then we can go on home and wait until they let us know they have Lenny. Or we can stay here and wait until they've identified him. So what do you want to do?"

"Stay here in this rat hole with all of these other grieving people? Doesn't sound like a choice to me. How do we finish up and get going? I want to go home, to be there with Bruce and try to support him right now. Poor kid; he loved Lenny so much."

"Henry mentioned we could call him, and he would help us. Want me to give him a call?"

"Yes. Let's do whatever we can and go home."

Len retrieved Henry's card and rang his cell, as Henry had invited him to do. As he expected, the call went to voice mail. Len left a short message asking for a return call and placed his phone back in the holder on his belt.

Celia was sipping her wine slowly. "Should we get a different room for tonight?"

"We can. Let me check with Charlotte and have her find us something a little bit nicer." Charlotte had been Len's administrative assistant for nearly ten years at the office he shared with Keith and his partner.

Charlotte answered the phone in her normal cheerful voice, which quickly changed when she recognized Len's voice. "Dr. Sawyer, I am so sorry about Lenny. We were all devastated when Keith called us last night after the news came out that Lenny was in the crash."

"Thanks, Charlotte. We're in Omaha trying to get through the red tape so we can get Lenny identified and bring him home." Len did not have the energy to say more about the complications involved in the identification of the passengers and crew.

"I understand. How is Mrs. Sawyer?"

"As you might expect, it's pretty rough, and we expect that to be the case for quite a while. I'll tell her you asked about her. Charlotte, I need a favor. The place the airline has put us up is not exactly what we would have chosen. Can you find us a nice place near the airport for a couple of nights?"

"Couple of nights?" Celia expressed her dislike for the prospect of staying longer than one night with a sour look.

Ignoring her comment, Len carried on with his conversation. "Find something as nice as possible and close to the airport if you can. And I guess I'll need a car, if you can arrange that too." Len noticed the wine bottle was already half-empty. He had not had a sip.

"Sure, Doctor, I'll give you a call as soon as I have confirmation numbers for you. Oh, and please know all of us here are praying for you, Celia, Bruce, and your entire family." Charlotte ended the call.

Her last comment struck Len as ironic. Celia and Bruce were now his entire family. Until yesterday at 6:05 p.m., he'd had a family of four. Now it was three. His parents had died a few years earlier, and he had no siblings. Thank God Celia had sisters. At least they could help her and Bruce in the months to come. His own pain was so great, he wasn't sure what he could do for his wife and son. But he knew he would try.

His thoughts were interrupted when his cell rang. "Dr. Sawyer," Len answered.

"Len, this is Henry. I got your call and took the liberty of telling the airline reps you want to get started with the identification process as soon as they can arrange it. Go ahead and call the airline people who have been assigned to you, and let them help you with the paperwork. Feel free to check in with me in a day or so, or let me know if you run into any roadblocks." At that point Henry felt he had done all he could in order to be helpful.

"OK. I appreciate the advice, and we'll let you know if we need more help."

Len was inclined to stay longer at that point. Celia was a different story. And he could not bear to think of being separated from her. Being away from little Bruce was starting to weigh on him. But he also knew the overwhelming grief in the places he and Celia would be visiting could not be good for a six-year-old. *Hell*, he thought. It wasn't where he wanted to be either, but right now he had no choice. He had to try to get his older son home—if there was anything left of him.

"Hon, look," Len said to Celia, "Henry says the airline people are the point of contact for us for everything right now, including getting started on the process of identification of Lenny. I'm going to call them."

Without further delay he found Lori's card and reached her right away.

"Dr. Sawyer." Lori saw his name on caller ID. "How can we help you?"

"I was speaking to Henry—Dr. Brennan, the medical examiner—a few minutes ago. He told me you and Daryl can help us get set up for beginning the identification process."

"Yes, Daryl and I are just out in the lobby. Let me make a call, and we'll be there in a few minutes. They've just started making appointments for families to provide information and evidence. You'll be one of the first, as over half of the families who are coming haven't arrived yet."

"Great. We'll be here in the coffee shop."

Len noticed the Chardonnay bottle was empty.

"I am exhausted." Celia yawned and took her last sip of wine. "I want to go up and lie down."

"The airline people are coming to take us to the office where we can give what's needed for the identification process. Don't you want to do that before you lie down for a nap?" Len reached for her hand. He was sure she would not want to know how she looked at this point. The alcohol gave Celia's fair face a flushed look. Red, tear-stained cheeks and a nose that continually ran produced a very different appearance from her normal natural and well-groomed looks.

Once he had thought Celia had an alcohol problem. Yet each time she became pregnant, she had no problem avoiding her daily wine. So Len thought that to be a good sign. In the last couple of years, he had started to become a little concerned again, but even if she drank a little heavily, it had always been under control around the family. Maybe after the worst of this, he would suggest she stop or at least cut down. But not now. However she coped with the loss of their eldest son, he would support her. He knew she would be there for him too. They had been together for a long time, and they knew how to support one another.

"I guess you're right," Celia said. "I'll wait until we get that done. Do you think we can go home tonight?"

XXII

No Control After All

Before Len could answer, his cell phone rang. It was Charlotte. "Dr. Sawyer, I don't have very good news for you concerning different accommodations for you and Mrs. Sawyer."

"Oh, what happened?" Len would have liked some good news at that point.

"It seems that with the crash, all of the hotels in Omaha are filled with press and government officials in addition to the airline and family members who are in the city. And I can't even find you a rental car. I am so sorry. Even if you're willing to stay in the suburbs on the other side of town, I wouldn't be able to get you a car. And they say the commute to the airport in the traffic could take over an hour or more each morning." Charlotte did not want to disappoint Len, but these were the facts.

"I see." Len felt less in control with every bit of news anyone gave him. He was not accustomed to being dependent on others under any circumstances, and now he was not only dependent, but even normal things like rental cars and a nice hotel room were not available to him.

"Ok. Thanks, Charlotte. I know you tried. That's all I can ask. I'll check in with you tomorrow and let you know our plans. I know Keith is making plans to handle my caseload. Thanks again. Good-bye." For the first time, Len thought about his wife's clients and caseload. He had not thought to ask her if her partner had been contacted. Before he could ask, he noticed Daryl and Lori entering the coffee shop.

Len noticed the pair seemed more nervous than when they had met that morning at the airport. He supposed it was due to Celia's attitude toward them.

"Dr. and Mrs. Sawyer, we made arrangements for you to begin the identification process at three o'clock this afternoon. We have a little time. Do you want to freshen up before we go over?"

Len caught Lori glancing at his nearly drunk wife as she asked the question. He wondered if a quick trip upstairs, with maybe a splash of cold water on her face, would make a difference in Celia's looks or attitude.

"Celia, do you want to go up to the room and freshen up?" Len tried to appear nonchalant about the suggestion.

"Do I look like I'm in need of something?" Celia was in need of a nap, but she suspected there was no time for it.

"Oh no." Lori was embarrassed because that was precisely what she meant. She regretted that it must have been obvious. The dark streaks of mascara running down Celia's cheeks caused Lori to feel for the grieving mother. "I just meant we have a few minutes, if you need some time. But we can go now if you would like."

"Fine, then. Why don't we go on over to the medical facility and get started?" Len stood up and touched the back of his wife's chair.

"Dr. Sawyer, it's not exactly a medical facility we're going to visit," Daryl said.

"Oh?"

"No, you see, the medical examiners have set up facilities at the hangar where the temporary morgue has been set up."

"A hangar?" Now Celia spoke up. "Did I hear you say the morgue is in a hangar?"

"I am sorry, Mrs. Sawyer, but that's the way it's being organized. The large airline hangar is easy to keep secure and near the site of the crash. And it is plenty large enough for everything that has to take place."

More surprises, Len thought. "Let's just go, wherever it is." He pulled Celia's chair out and helped her up. She was somewhat unstable. It was partly the wine, but the sheer exhaustion was a problem for both of them. He felt unsteady on his feet without the help of alcohol.

All four people boarded the minivan that was waiting for them outside the hotel. On the way to the hangar, Len decided to tell Celia about the lack of available accommodations in the area.

"Celia, when Charlotte called back, she told me there are no other rooms and no rental cars anywhere near this area. In fact all of the hotels in Omaha are taken up by press people, airline reps, government officials, and others. I guess we're lucky to have a room at all."

"Len, the word *lucky* does not fit anything about this ordeal."

The Universal employees could not help but overhear Celia's comments. They had discussed among themselves how unfortunate it was that of all the hotels near the airport, the one that had the largest number of rooms and fit the needs for the families in some ways, was not the nicest or most modern. But it was all they had, under the circumstances.

The ride to the hangar was brief. Lori and Daryl helped the emotionally fragile couple out of the minivan and led them to the front doors of the hangar. The security guards checked their badges at the door and allowed them all to enter.

Lori and Daryl showed them to a private room where a folding table had been set up with some medical supplies on top. There were three or four metal fold-up chairs beside the table. They waited for only a few minutes before a woman joined them. She introduced herself as a staff member from the medical examiner's office. She walked them through the process, and within a few minutes, they had completed the necessary forms.

The questions were brief. It was the first time Len was forced to think of his son's physical appearance in great detail. He had avoided the newspaper write-ups with names of the passengers. It seemed if he did not have to focus on Lenny, he could somehow avoid the truth of his death. It just seemed impossible that his older son was dead. The guilt was nearly insufferable. His mind occasionally drifted to the arguments they'd had over Lenny's desire to go to medical school. If only he had known what was in store, he would have allowed Lenny to do whatever he wanted. He was such a great kid!

His thoughts were interrupted when he heard Celia asking questions about the identification process. "Can you help me understand what happens now? I mean, where are they in the process at this point?"

The technician thought about how best to answer the question without being too graphic. "Well, at this point the recovery personnel are working through the wreckage of the airplane, and as they recover human remains, they bring them in here. Then we have a huge team of medical personnel who have come from all over the state and in some cases out of state in order to make positive identifications of the people who perished. We also have many labs involved to help expedite the process where smaller samples are involved. Then, as each person is identified, the medical examiner's office contacts the family and confirms the positive identification of their loved one."

"So how long does all of this take?" Celia asked.

"Well, it depends on many things." The woman was trying to be direct yet sensitive. "But one thing is for sure. As soon as your son is identified by any means, you will be notified, so hopefully not very long."

"OK, thank you for your time." Len, already standing, helped Celia out of her chair.

Lori and Daryl were waiting for them as they walked out of the room.

"Would you like to get something to eat on the way back to the hotel?" Daryl asked.

"Can we just have room service?" Celia asked. "I'm not hungry, but a bowl of soup or something warm would probably be good for us."

"Sure. You can order room service and food from the restaurant in the hotel. Universal is paying for it. So just sign your name, and it will all go on our master bill." Daryl had intended to tell them before, but it had been pretty clear they were not open to much information during the original meeting.

"And what about wine? I like to have a glass of wine before I go to bed each night." Celia thought she should at least get clarification on this issue while they were on the subject of hotel charges.

"Actually, Universal does not pay for alcohol in the rooms. But we can pay for a drink during dinner when we're with you for a meal." Daryl spoke very softly, as he knew the subject of liquor was a sensitive one with many families.

"So how does this work?" The sarcasm in Celia's voice was obvious. "If I want a glass of wine, I either eat a meal with you, or I run a personal tab at the hotel? Is that how it works?"

"Yes," Daryl answered. "I am sorry."

Neither Celia nor Len replied.

The ride back to the hotel was quiet. Before the employees left the couple, they explained the next day's activities, which had already been established. Len committed to attending the early morning family briefing. Celia would decide the next morning. Len was doubtful, but he did not want to push her.

Back at the room, the Sawyers ordered room service. Len assured the hotel he would pay for the wine. Neither of them finished the soup they ordered, but they knew they needed to try to eat something.

Len called home and spoke to Sheryl and Bruce. It was difficult, but he tried to be positive with Bruce. He answered directly when Bruce asked about Lenny. "No, my precious son, Lenny has gone to heaven. He won't be coming home with us."

Celia motioned for Len to give her the phone. "Hello, darling. Mommy misses you so much." Listening to her young son cry was really difficult. "I know, and I miss Lenny too. Dad and I will be home soon. Now get some sleep. I love you. Here are your kisses."

With that Celia went to bed. Len heard her crying into her pillow. He knew crying would be part of their lives for a long time to follow.

Turning back to business, he next called Keith. All was well, and the cases were being covered. The accident was headline news all over the country, and patients and medical professionals alike were expressing compassion for the Sawyer family and all those involved. "I'll check back in tomorrow," Len said before ending the call.

The following morning Len went to the family meeting room alone. Celia was hungover from too much drinking the night before. This mixed with the incessant crying was taking a toll on her—as well him. He knew she was doing the best she could. They both were.

Much to his satisfaction, Henry announced they had been able to identify nearly twenty of the deceased the day before. He explained they were optimistic that more progress would be made in the next several hours. And he explained that later the next day, the officials would lead them on a visit of the site of the crash, since it would be ready for people to view.

Also, Len learned, some of the belongings of the passengers and crew were to be displayed for families to observe.

The official in charge of this part of the meeting explained the belongings were not ready to be released. However, families could make claims on anything they recognized, and after the investigation process was further along and the items were no longer needed for that purpose, the items would be returned to them. He explained the belongings would be held in safekeeping, and the process for making formal claims and receiving the belongings would be explained in detail later.

XXIII

Assistance from Heavenly Leadership

Lenny was certain the next two people who needed to get messages from him were his parents. He knew his appearance at the wedding had provided a sense of hope for Ro and Jim. He needed to let Mom and Dad and little Bruce know that as difficult as it was for all of them to experience this separation, it was only temporary.

He and John were discussing options as they learned about the activities being planned for the families to view the site and personal belongings.

"One of the ways some families have received effective connection from this side has to do with the belongings of the loved ones. That might be a way to make direct contact right away." John had turned his attention the scene where the recovery personnel were sifting through the charred remains of the airplane and its cargo. As he observed the workers, he mused over what a crash represented from the earthly perspective. It was like an abortion of sorts. Individual travel plans had been laid out, complete with an expected time of arrival, when suddenly it all ended, and life as the people knew it died. Even for survivors of a crash, their lives were never the same. He was grateful there were countless ways to prove to those left on earth that despite how it might appear, life did in fact continue, just on a different level or plane of existence.

"OK, but there is so little to work with that's recognizable. Do you think we can make something happen with what's left of our suitcases and other things we were carrying?" Lenny was now watching the same scene.

"There are many things we can do to help sensitives know we're sending messages. It's worth a try. Some people will still be able to feel the energy of their loved ones as they are exposed to the personal items where there was strong emotional attachment, even though the visual is greatly changed. It is all about energetic connection. People on earth often forget there are four other human senses in addition to sight. And when emotion is as strong as it is between you and your parents, we have what it takes to work another miracle." John smiled and knew Lenny was remembering the joy and comfort the sighting had provided Jim and Roseanne.

XXIV

Standing on Sacred Ground

Early on the second day in Omaha, Len was successful in getting Celia up and dressed in time to join the other families. Lori and Daryl picked them up in the van, and the driver took them to the dreaded hangar once again. Several buses were lined up, doors open, waiting to take the families to see sites only they would find comforting to view. Airline employees and various helping professionals stood by to assist the families in boarding the coaches and finding seats.

Celia could not remember the last time she had ridden in a coach. She had asked for a private limo, but none were available for families to rent for this purpose. The government officials even had control over who could visit the crash site, when they could go, and how they were transported over there. She wondered if she and Len would ever have control over anything in their lives again. She felt her standard of living had been so compromised.

Len had hopes that today would help them move forward. He hoped so much that they could see something that belonged to their son. Two days in Omaha and still no word that Lenny had been identified—not any part of him. Holding Celia's hand tightly, he took a deep breath as the coach lurched forward and pulled onto the freeway.

After a brief ride, the coach entered the gates of the airport property and drove into the roped-off territory, heavily guarded by police and other uniformed personnel. Len squeezed Celia's hand. Standing at attention as they caught sight of the coaches, the men and women in uniform saluted the families as they drove by.

Celia spoke for nearly the first time that morning. "I guess these people really do care about us. Maybe it's not just a job for them after all."

"Hon, you know they do. This is not a normal day for them either. There's nothing pleasant about this for anyone here today." Len quickly placed a kiss on her cheek and wiped away her tears with a tissue. The helpers had taken the time to supply the coaches with tissue for the families' convenience.

The sight of the aircraft wreckage in the distance commanded the attention of the coach passengers.

"Not much to look at," commented a man in front of them, Gregg Peterson.

"Not much indeed," Len responded. Gregg was one of the few family members he and Celia had met and talked with briefly. His wife and son had been killed as well. They too had not been identified as of yesterday's briefing.

Len pondered Gregg's situation. What if he had lost his son *and* Celia? He had also learned one entire family of five had died in the crash—a mother, a father, and three children. He had no idea how any of the families would be able to survive this ordeal. The collective grief was overwhelming.

Surprising to Len, the sight of something physical and tangible that was part of the accident felt strangely consoling. Prior to then, other than a few pictures he had glimpsed on brief news clips, Len had little to connect him to the place his son had died. But now, being near the aircraft wreckage provided much-needed visual proof of their new reality.

Dear God, he found himself praying silently. He asked for strength for both himself and Celia. He continued to pray for all of the families. He knew they would need nearly supernatural help to get through the events of this day and the days that would follow. He realized this was the first time he had prayed since first learning of the crash. Len was a man of faith. Prayer ritual, up until a couple of nights ago, had always been a major part of his life. That, like so much of his routine, had been interrupted since Friday night.

The coaches stopped farther from the wreckage than he had hoped. The families were told they could walk around the aircraft wreckage as long as they did not attempt to enter the areas that were taped off.

After helping his wife down the bus steps, Len waited for Gregg. Len wondered why he was alone. He knew Gregg's only child had died along with his wife, but surely he had a family member or friend who could be with him during this nearly unimaginable time.

In silence the three grieving people walked toward the rear of the wreckage. Then Gregg walked away from Len and Celia. It was as though he felt a need to go solo during this part of the process. Len understood his need to be alone.

Celia stumbled. Len placed his arm about her waist to steady her. They found themselves in a full embrace, crying audibly over where they were and what they were viewing. The tail section nearly destroyed by fire—the only part of the aircraft that was recognizable—and a few bent pieces of metal were the only proof they could see with their own eyes that confirmed the crash and the death of their son.

Len continued to hold Celia as her shoulders and entire body shook with raw emotion. His thoughts drifted back to Cleveland. How many times had he seen parents hold each other this way when they had learned from him that their child did not survive the birth process? Oh, sure, he'd had empathy for the parents, or so he'd thought, but up until this moment, he'd had no idea what those mothers, fathers, and family members were experiencing.

"I can't take this anymore." Celia had broken the embrace and was walking toward the coach. "What else is there to see? This is just a horrific experience."

"I know. I don't need to see any more of the wreckage, either. But hon, I want to stay and walk through the hangar where the suitcases and other items are being displayed. Do you mind if we wait for that?"

Len knew this was a day that could never be repeated. As badly as he wanted to return home to Bruce and move past these grueling sights and discussions, he knew this brief and final connection to his older son was necessary. There was just so little to see, to touch, much less hold on to. No matter how hard it was, Len was determined to do whatever it took to survive this unimaginable process—whatever the emotional toll.

XXV

Energetic Connections

Len and Celia joined a long line of people, probably two hundred or more, walking silently into a large room in the hangar. Len could see long tables, each bearing a metal stand with a number written on cardboard, looking like the numbers fast food restaurants often use for matching food orders to patrons. There were many long tables—he counted seventy, at least.

As he had expected, most of what was on display was badly burned. The smell of charred leather and fabric combined with jet fuel was an assault to the senses. The vast hangar, with its high ceilings, allowed for much-needed ventilation and plenty of room for the tables and people to be spread apart. Len appreciated the hangar more than he had imagined. He could see how its size and location made many things possible.

Some of the articles were easily recognizable. Others looked like burned rubble that would have been thrown in the trash under different circumstances. Uniformed personnel were stationed about the room to make sure no one touched the suitcases, garment bags, shoes, children's toys, stuffed animals, and unidentifiable items on display. As grim as this process was, with so little left of those souls once aboard the aircraft, every item likely meant something to someone. In spite of its condition, it was worth saving—if at all possible. Table by table the grieving exhausted family members filed by in hopes of associating something with a loved one.

As Len and Celia approached the table bearing the marker "#33," Len experienced a pulling sensation, like arms drawing him to the table. Dropping his wife's hand, he stepped back a few steps, and the sensation dissipated. Intrigued, he stepped again toward table thirty-three. The pulling sensation happened again.

Looking past the badly burned items on the table, Len saw the outline of scores of people. He could not see faces. In fact what he was looking at appeared to be wispy, almost smoky outlines of human forms. As the scene drew him in, the pulling sensation continued.

"Len, are you recognizing anything of our son's?" Celia noticed that table thirty-three captivated Len.

"It's not what's on the table that's causing me to stop here. It's a feeling I have that I'm somehow connected to something at this table." Len didn't know how to explain any of the phenomena that were drawing him in. He continued to stare at the wispy forms.

"Celia," he continued. "Stand here." He moved her into the space where he had been standing. "Do you feel anything?"

"Like what?" His wife seemed equally intrigued.

"A pulling sensation—like some invisible arms are holding on to you." Len knew his words were inadequate. But he felt a need to include her in the experience.

"No, I don't feel a thing except exhaustion." Celia had no idea what he was talking about.

"Well, when you gaze behind the table, can you see wispy figures?"

"What kind of figures?" Celia was staring at the same area as her husband but saw nothing but a blank wall.

"Celia," her husband said, his voice lowered. "I think I can see the souls of some of the people whose belongings are here on the table." Crazy as he knew it sounded, Len felt a need to try to explain what he was experiencing.

"Sir, may I ask that you move along?" The voice of a uniformed young woman interrupted Len's words. "If you think you'll want to claim something here, just make a note on the form you were provided. Write down the table number and describe the item. Your notes will become part of the formal process for claiming belongings later, when they can be released."

"OK, thank you." Len smiled at the thought of writing down what he saw. They might put him away if they knew what he was seeing and feeling. He knew what he was experiencing was real, but he had no schema for understanding it, much less describing it.

After the guard walked away, the wispy forms disappeared. And with the forms went the pulling sensation that had captivated Len. Due to the fire that had destroyed most of the cargo bin where his son's luggage had been boarded, Len was not able to recognize the large dark-green suitcase that belonged to Lenny. It had been badly worn before this flight, and now it bore few identifiable markings. Despite the wear on it from all of the trips back and forth to college for four years, Lenny would not part with it. It was part of the luggage set his grandparents had given him on his birthday the same year they died in a car accident.

While the distinctive markings of the luggage had been burned away, the emotional attachment between Lenny and the suitcase could not be destroyed. He stood behind it, hoping his parents would recognize it. His father felt the connection and perhaps later would still be able to claim it—just not today.

Many of the passengers had stood beside Lenny at the table. They too had attachments to items that were on display there. Like Lenny, they wanted their families to sense their presence. While some were unsure if the connection had been made, Lenny knew his dad had felt his presence. He was sure of it. And there would be more invisible connections to come.

XXVI

Returning Home without Lenny

Len and Celia let the employees know they wanted to return home the following day, after the visit to the wreckage and the hangar. The day had been long, but somehow they managed to meet a few more family members that evening before turning in. They met another couple who had lost both of their daughters on the flight. Both Len and Celia hugged the parents when they learned of their loss. Looking at the pictures of the teenage girls caused Celia and Len to want to go home to Bruce. They knew his presence in their lives would help them, and they talked about this after they said good night to the other parents.

Boarding the aircraft was very difficult. Not because they were afraid of flying but because they were going home without Lenny. Somehow this felt like failure on their part, although rationally they knew it made no sense. But to go home without Lenny made them feel somehow they had let Bruce and the other family members down.

But there was still no word and no reason to think staying another day or two would make a difference in finding Lenny—if there were any parts of him left to find. May as well go home and wait, Len and Celia thought; at least they could be in the comfortable environment of their own home, with Bruce and other family.

As they pulled into their driveway, they were pleased to see Bruce playing basketball with his teenage cousins and another young boy from the neighborhood. Babs's twin girls were good babysitters, as they were both athletic and played with the kids they watched. Not unlike Lenny, the sixteen-year-old girls swam and ran track. Having them look after Bruce was a bonus.

They all stopped and waved when they saw the car. For just a moment, Celia felt that life might be normal again somehow, someday. There was something about seeing kids at play, smiling and tossing a ball around, that was consoling. Kids were resilient. Celia and Len had discussed on the way home how they both would do all they could to give Bruce as normal a childhood as possible. But neither of them were naïve about the challenges they were facing.

Bruce leapt into his father's arms as Len got out of the front seat. Just as quickly he was in Celia's arms on the opposite side of the car.

"Hi, darling," Celia said, kissing him on both cheeks. "Mommy missed you very much!" She was glad for the dark glasses she was wearing, so no one could see her red and swollen eyes.

Sheryl greeted Len and Celia at the kitchen door. "Glad you guys are back. Bruce missed you. And Babs and I were worried about what you were probably going through."

"Well, whatever you might have imagined we were doing, it was worse." Celia sat down at the kitchen table without removing her shades. "And the worst part is that Lenny remains unidentified." Bruce and Len remained outside with the basketball, so she knew she could tell her sister what was going on without her young son hearing.

"Oh, Celia, how awful. I guess I never thought about that. When Mom and Dad died, as hard as it was, we were able to do the normal kinds of things families do. I had no idea what it might be like to have a death in the family and be held in limbo." Sheryl put the kettle on for tea as she continued to talk.

"Who would ever think about that unless you had to?" Celia responded. "Did Bruce cry very much while we were gone?" She wondered how much he realized about what was happening.

"No, having the kids to play with and talking to each night while you were away seemed to occupy his time pretty well. But as much as I tried to keep the television off, last night, before I could turn off the evening news, the crash footage came on. The news reminded him of Lenny, so naturally he started asking questions again."

"Well, we'll just try to keep him occupied as much as we can. Of course we'll answer his questions, but I hope to shield him as much as I can from the raw pain of it all. I want to talk to Babs about what she thinks we should do. I never knew her specialty in child psychology would come to be so important to us. Our lives were always so normal until now." Celia looked out the window as she spoke.

"She told me to call after you were home and settled. She was concerned about the twins and how well they could hide their own feelings while around Bruce. We were both relieved to see they knew how important they were going to be in helping out with Bruce, especially now, without Lenny." Sheryl regretted saying that last part as soon as the words left her lips. Her sister had enough of her own fears about the future. She did not need to be reminded of how all of their lives were now changed.

"I just don't know what happens now," said Celia. "I mean, we don't have Lenny, not any part of him, for burial. Do we have a service of some sort? I honestly felt envious of families who were able to leave town having had their family members identified. At least they had something they could do. A direction to go in, plans to make—albeit plans no one wanted." Celia knew she could tell her sister these things that were on her mind that she would not want to say to Len. She and her husband were both shielding each other as much as they could from private fears and thoughts.

Sheryl had been thinking about that very same thing—what to do next. "Look," she said. "Let's call Gleason's when you and Len are ready."

Gleason's was the funeral home that had done such a good job for them when their parents had died. Their dad had passed a year before their mother. Both had died of cancer. And during both experiences with the staff there, Celia and Sheryl had come to feel comfortable with them.

"But without anything to bury, I'm not sure what we would discuss with them." Celia wished they could meet with them and start planning something, but what?

XXVII

Spiritual Messengers

"Look, Cel." Sheryl used her childhood name for her older sister. "I don't want to distract you from making plans, but some interesting things happened while you were out of town."

"Like what?" Celia inquired.

"Well, you know we always have crows around, but every day since you left, one crow has flown into the yard alone and sat in the same spot in the oak tree outside the kitchen window. Bruce pointed it out the first morning after you left."

"Crows are not that unusual around here. Why would he even notice?"

"He noticed because it was a single crow. We see them in groups of three or more around here, and Bruce is such a smart kid that he noticed it was one crow alone."

"Was Bruce scared?"

"No, not at all. He came straight in the house and pointed it out. The crow just sat there looking at us through the window. It stayed a good fifteen to twenty minutes. Bruce then asked me to help him read about crows on the Internet." Sheryl could not help but smile over the child's nonstop curiosity. "We pulled up a good bit of information about crows and how animals often give messages from people who have died."

"Well, how did he react to all of that?" Celia was intrigued.

Sheryl had always had an interest in the occult and found it comforting to look for signs or omens from the animal kingdom when tragedy occurred. She had noticed a good bit of bird activity in her own yard after their parents had died.

"Actually he wanted to read about crows both nights when you were gone. I helped him, as he seemed to get consolation from the thought that somehow Lenny was sending us a message."

"A message about what?"

"We read that often crows appear to families after someone dies to let them know they are OK. I know this is strange, but if you could have seen how it helped Bruce when we were reading about it, you would understand why I was eager to share it with him." Sheryl knew her sister did not share her interest in the occult.

"Well, coincidences happen all the time. If you're looking for that sort of thing, you can find it." Celia was now looking through the pad where names and phone numbers had been collected for them while they were away.

"Oh, yes, I wanted you to see who called. Most people wanted you to know about their concern and are anxious to hear about the funeral." Sheryl wished she could take that last part back.

"Oh, are they? Well so am I," Celia snapped over her shoulder as she headed upstairs for a short nap. She did not have the energy to look through the names of the well-intentioned callers.

Sheryl was happy to learn Bruce had already told Len about the crow by the time he came in for a cold drink. Bruce and the twins had remained outside.

"So Bruce tells me he had a new bird in the neighborhood." Len poured himself a drink. The ice-cold soda reminded him of his many discussions with Lenny about consuming too many soft drinks. He regretted every memory he had of trying to put restrictions on his older son. He knew he would have problems in that area with his younger son too. He wondered if he would be able to manage his guilt about Lenny in such a way that it did not interfere with how he raised Bruce. He knew time would tell, but he had oh-so-many regrets.

"Yes, it was uncanny. While you were gone, we saw the crow daily." Sheryl stopped at that point. She was hoping Bruce had said more to his father. And he had indeed.

"So, sounds like Bruce has expanded his vocabulary. He told me about how a crow often comes to a family after a death to let them know the soul is OK." Len's eyes drifted outside, to where the younger ones were once again shooting hoops.

"I didn't want to put strange ideas into his head. I didn't know what to do but help him understand the words he was having trouble understanding. I hope you're not upset." Sheryl felt embarrassed over her behavior.

"Oh no, don't beat yourself up. Bruce will see and hear a lot in the next few weeks and months, as we work through the rest of this horrible thing we're dealing with. If he asks questions, we have to answer him the best way we can. There will be enough confusion he'll have to deal with, where none of us will know how to answer." Sadness had returned to Len's voice.

"Look, I'll leave now and let you have some family time." Sheryl grabbed her small suitcase and handbag. "I'll get the twins and take them home. We can all talk tomorrow. You know how to find me if you need to."

With that Len headed out the door with her. Spending time alone now with Bruce was what he wanted to do. He had no energy for checking in with the office. He would have the rest of his life for that. Family was all that mattered now—however much of that was left.

XXVIII

Visual Proof

The ringing phone woke Celia early the following morning. She realized Len had already gone downstairs to care for Bruce, who had always been an early riser. Pulling on her robe and slippers, she went downstairs for coffee. Entering the kitchen, she could tell by Len's tone that something serious was happening.

"OK, so what have you found?" Len was talking in his doctor voice—very businesslike. "How did you make the identification?" Len caught sight of Celia and nodded his head.

Ignoring that he was engaged in a call with someone else, Celia began to question him. "They found him? They found our son? Oh, thank God! How do we get him home?"

Putting his index finger to his lips, Len motioned for Celia to be silent and allow him to finish his call. "OK, so when is the service…? Tomorrow afternoon. I see. OK, we will contact the airline people again and arrange to get there…Yes, I have your number. I will call you if I have more questions before we get there. Thanks, Henry. You've been really helpful." Len paused to listen to more from Henry. "You, too. I know it hasn't been easy for you." He responded to the medical examiner's kind wishes for good luck with the rest of the journey, and he meant what he said. He knew the grim task of talking to hundreds of people in the aftermath of something so tragic would be life-changing for Brennan also.

"Tell me what Henry said. Have they found our son?" Celia had forgotten about the coffee.

"Yes, apparently last night they were able to make several more identifications of passengers and crew members. Lenny was one of those." Len's voice broke as he said the last few words.

Celia felt overwhelming compassion for her husband and herself. Who would ever think the best news they would get when they got up in the morning would be that their son, although dead, had been identified? She wrapped her arms around her husband's broad shoulders and wept along with him. Some of her tears were for the relief she felt. Some of the ordeal was nearing the end. They could bring their son home and lay him to rest finally.

"So should we start making arrangements?" Celia was anxious to move on.

Here we go, Len thought as he searched for the right words. *I'm going to disappoint her once again.* But he knew he had to give her all the news. After all, they had to take the next steps.

"Hon, it's not quite that simple." Len paused as he sat down beside Celia at the kitchen island. "Lenny was pretty bad. I mean…" He searched for the best words. "Most of our son was destroyed by the fire. A small amount of his left arm was identified, bearing the watch we gave him for graduation."

Silence permeated the kitchen of their once happy, perfect home. Finally Celia broke the silence.

"*Most* of Lenny was destroyed? If all that's left is a small amount of his arm and his watch, sounds to me like *all* of our son was destroyed."

"Yes, Henry confirmed that to be true." Len knew there was no way to soften the visual image Celia, not unlike him, was experiencing. "He asked about the Tag and the inscription on the inside. I told him we gave Lenny the watch for his college graduation."

"Was the inscription readable?" Celia was perplexed about the way this was all coming down.

"Apparently. Henry asked me if our son was following in my footsteps with his career choice. And without telling him what an ass I had been to discourage my son from his right to choose his own profession, I told him yes. He then read me the inscription and told me the rest of the story."

Len was reliving the final blowup he and Lenny had had before he gave in to Lenny's pleas for his support in applying to medical school. After he had agreed, Len had chosen the inscription on the watch. Thank God. That was one good memory of interacting with his son in the last year.

Impatient, Celia pressed Len for more details. "So we're going to receive part of our son's arm to place in a casket?"

"Celia, I know it sounds horrible. Hell, it is awful. And yet some people may never be identified. And some people may not get a watch or anything proving their family member died that night. I hate to use this word, but we are among the fortunate ones."

"Don't use the word *fortunate* when you talk about this unspeakable thing that has happened to our family. It just doesn't fit." Celia left her coffee untouched and headed upstairs.

Allowing her some time to get a shower and accept on some level the news that had come to them that morning, Len finally approached Celia in their bedroom.

"Hon, we need to decide if we want to go back for the service they're holding. Henry explained what's left is mostly very small—I mean in terms of being able to identify people physically. And that may take weeks, even longer. So the airline and the other officials want to hold a memorial service day after tomorrow. We could travel up tomorrow, talk to Henry about Lenny's remains, attend the service, and bring the watch home ourselves."

Len wasn't sure it was a good idea, but then having Lenny's watch sent home didn't seem like a good idea either. What if it got lost somehow? They had lost enough.

"How soon do we have to decide? Can I have the rest of the day to think about it?" Celia was sitting at her makeup table. She was looking at the dark circles under her eyes. No amount of makeup could help her right now—and maybe not ever. Her child had been killed in a senseless plane crash, and now all she had left was the watch she had given him for graduation. What had happened to the rewards for living a good life? No one had ever been better than her son Lenny. And look what had happened. Gone before his life had even begun.

"Well, we need to travel up tomorrow, so we have to call the airline to get a flight. Can you tell me by this afternoon?"

Len hated to leave Celia, but he had made up his mind. He was going to the service to honor and represent his son with all of the other families who would be there to mourn their family members. So many strangers had died together that evening. Having met only a few other family members, Len already felt a bond with them. He needed to be there out of respect for all of those who perished and their families. And besides, he owed it to Lenny to connect with him in every way possible. There were so few opportunities now.

"OK, I'll think about it." Celia was brushing her long blond hair. She could see gray hairs, which seemed to be multiplying by the minute. She knew her youth was gone. Like so much of her, it had died with her son that rainy night in Omaha.

XXIX

No Such Place as Closure

Len reached for his wife's hand as the aircraft came to a stop in Omaha. Never having flown there before the crash, Len wondered if he would always feel the same way toward that airport as he had both times he landed there since the crash. It didn't seem to be any different from the first time he had arrived, on the day following the crash. The overwhelming sense of dread and sheer panic in the pit of his stomach made it difficult to breathe. Len stood when the seat belt sign was switched off and tried to smile at Celia in a gesture of support.

Celia was again wearing her large dark glasses to cover her red, swollen eyes. But nothing could hide her puffy cheeks. Reaching for her bag beneath the seat in front of her, she stood and felt the strength of her husband's strong, solid arm supporting her as she walked slowly down the aisle of the aircraft.

The familiar airline team members were waiting as the grieving couple exited the secured area of the terminal. After grabbing the small bag they had packed together for what they hoped was the last trip to Omaha for a while, Len and Celia followed the employees to the van that was awaiting them.

Looking back from his seat in the eight-passenger van, Daryl spoke. "First we want to take you to the hotel and get you checked in. You arrived in time to make the afternoon meeting where the government investigators and others working the accident will brief everyone on the latest information about what is known. After that we can take you to..." His voice trailed off as he realized the magnitude of the subject he was about to broach.

"You're taking us to see Henry, I mean the medical examiner, so he can tell us about Lenny and what they know about his death?" Len picked up where the sentence had stopped. *Hell*, he thought, *why beat around the bush?* As disappointing as it all was to hear about, at least they had something of Lenny's to take home; he was hearing some families might not get anything—much less *anyone*—to take home.

"Yes, that would be our next stop unless you would rather wait until after the services tomorrow morning." Daryl spoke more softly now, realizing once more that this was not like taking someone to the mall or anywhere normal, for that matter.

"No, I mean yes," Celia said with more energy than Len had seen her have that day. "As soon as we can, we want to see Henry. I want to make sure he knows when we're coming, so there will be no delay."

"Actually, we've already made the appointment for this afternoon at five o'clock, right after the briefing, since we knew this would be a priority today. And we knew we could always reschedule if for some reason you couldn't make it today." Lori spoke reassuringly.

"Thank you for that. And yes, it is urgent." Len spoke politely, knowing the young people understood on some level how important, despite how sad, a positive identification of their son was to them.

"Yes, we know this will be part of your closure—"

"You know what?" Celia cut sharply into the inexperienced young woman's well-intentioned statement. "You think getting a watch back, knowing there was a small amount of my son's arm attached, gives us closure?"

"No, I mean we hope knowing your son was onboard for sure would help you in your healing."

"You have no idea what you're talking about." Celia cut the conversation short and reached into her handbag for another small pack of tissues. She seemed to never have enough for this ordeal.

Feeling embarrassed by his wife's behavior was a new part of Len's life he had not yet become accustomed to. He knew his emotions were as raw as Celia's, but the loss had not stripped him of his empathy for others. And he hoped it never would. These airline people were in a horrible position, obviously inexperienced, and he saw no reason for them to be experienced. Thank God they did not have to work crashes on a regular basis—no one would fly the airline if that were the case! He genuinely felt for the employees.

"OK, let's follow your plan for today, and maybe at the end of the evening you can tell us about what to expect tomorrow." Len was glad to move the subject forward.

XXX

16-D

Neither Len nor Celia felt they learned much at the briefing that afternoon. The facts still remained that terrible winds and rain over the airport at the time of the scheduled landing had contributed to the crash. No one yet knew why the pilots had decided to land in the weather, regardless of the information given to them just prior to landing.

Henry then stood up and reported on the number of identifications that had been made. There were several passengers who remained unidentified at the time. All of the crew had been identified as of earlier that morning.

Len sat silently and reflected again on how lucky they were to know for sure that Lenny had been identified. As hard as it would be, they could finish the last step in the process and move on to the next stage of their lives.

Celia seemed to get some comfort from some of the other families she had met on their first trip that she saw again at this meeting. There were a few familiar faces and names, which resulted in embraces and pleasantries. But there was no way the atmosphere of the evening could have been described as anything but sad and painful. The visit with Henry would not provide any more comfort.

Len knew conducting painful discussions with families, like the ones Henry and his team members were having, could never be pleasant. And having to meet in an aircraft hangar in such cold, sterile surroundings did not help the situation.

Len did feel, however, that everyone they met were as respectful as anyone would hope. As he and Celia entered the hangar with their airline escorts, everyone stopped their work and stood at attention in a mock military gesture. Henry came out of his makeshift office and ushered them in, showing them to a table where the three sat down for the grim task at hand.

"Before we begin, I just have to tell you again how sorry I am about Lenny. I don't know how well I would do if I were in your shoes." Henry looked at both of their faces as he spoke.

Celia spoke first. "It is the worst thing I have ever been through. We both lost our parents within a short time span, and we thought that was hard. But at least we had funerals, and at least for my parents, who both died of cancer, we even said good-bye before they died. This is so much worse."

"Celia, I've seen a lot of loss in my professional life and, like you, on a personal level, buried my parents. But sudden, brutal circumstances like a plane crash, where the crash-and-burn conditions leave so little evidence of human life, is hard on all families. And in your case, when I have so little to give you of your son for burial, I am dumbfounded as to how to even begin."

Henry spoke softly, with humility in his tone that the parents found comforting. Knowing he would give the information straight but that also he got it on a human level felt right and framed the discussion with much-needed compassion.

"So Henry, in the earlier call, when we learned how our son was identified, we heard his watch was found on a small part of his arm. Can you give us more of a picture of where his remains were found?" Len wasted no time in getting to what he had come to learn.

"Yes, that's right." Henry picked up a seating chart of the aircraft type involved in the crash. Taking a yellow pencil out of his pocket, he touched its pink eraser to an aisle seat.

"According to the flight manifest, this is where your son was sitting." Henry paused to allow the parents to absorb the visual of the aircraft and where their son was believed to have been sitting when he died.

"So the seat beside him was vacant?" Celia asked.

"Yes, the records show Lenny was sitting on the aisle, and there was a female passenger seated by the window. The seat in the middle was open, as the flight was not completely full."

Henry knew it was important to use their son's name, so he did so as often as he could. So much of one's identity is lost in a horrific mass tragedy, and for all the families he tried to make the discussions as personal as possible.

"Shall I continue?" Henry was aware Celia was dabbing around her dark glasses with a tissue. After checking with Celia, Len asked him to continue. "The recovery personnel mark the scene with small flags where they find any evidence of a passenger or crew member or identifiable personal belongings, as in the case of the small part of Lenny's arm bearing the watch."

The pink eraser once more settled on the diagram where Lenny had apparently died. "From the seats over the wing back to the tail section on the left side of the plane, the fire was totally destructive. However, in the debris there were several items discovered as the wreckage was examined, believed to belong to passengers seated there. In more than one case, there were human remains found—ever so slight, but evidence all the same, indicating who the item may have belonged to, as in your son's case. Specifically, skin from his arm was matched to the DNA evidence you submitted when you were here a day or so ago." Again Henry paused to allow this graphic discussion to sink into the minds of the parents.

"So where is the arm fragment?" Celia had removed her dark glasses, making her bloodshot eyes visible.

"On ice," Henry answered. "In a container with Lenny's name on it, so it can be transported home for burial, if that is what you choose."

"There aren't many choices, but what happens if we don't take the arm fragment home?" Celia was curious about this morbid part of the process.

"We would keep it and bury it here, with remains of others who died on the flight," Henry responded in a modulated, factual tone.

"That's ridiculous. Of course we want any part of him we can get." Celia picked up her glasses and placed them over her eyes.

"And his watch? Can we have it today?" Len was ready to move on—he had heard all he needed to hear, and he knew he and Celia needed time to process the horror of it all.

"Yes. Although all personal belongings are part of the investigation, if the investigators release them, we can send them home." Henry then reached under the table and retrieved a small gray bag bearing a white label with black printing that read "Evidence: Leonard Crawford Sawyer, 16-D."

Celia gasped at the sight of her son's name on an envelope labeled "evidence." For a moment both parents froze at this, the first direct physical link to Lenny's presence on the plane. Sure, the e-mail confirmation that Lenny had left behind bore his name and the flight number, date, and so on. But that had all still been hypothetical. This...this was real. They were sitting in an airline hangar designated as a makeshift morgue for a crash in Omaha, Nebraska, and now being handed an evidence bag bearing their son's name on it and a seat number—the seat he had died in. And inside this little gray bag was the last gift they had given and ever would give their elder son.

The threesome sat in silence, with the hideous bag lying on the table, untouched since Henry had retrieved it. Sensing the gravity of the moment, Henry stood and walked behind the two parents, who sat beside each other. He placed a hand on each of their shoulders.

"Let me give you a moment. There's no rush. Take as long as you want. Just let me know when you're ready, and I'll get my assistant to bring in the forms you need to sign, showing that you're taking the watch home. I'll be outside discussing a few things with the team. So take your time." With that Henry left the room, closing the door behind him.

"We don't have to look at the watch now." Len finally broke the deafening silence. "We can just sign the papers and take it with us and open it tomorrow night after we get back to Cleveland."

"No, I need to see it, to touch it, to hold it. I need to touch something of my son's, since I can't touch him." Celia was sobbing now.

"OK, hon, if you want. Let's open the bag and make sure it's Lenny's. We'll know by the inscription." Len wanted badly to see it and read the inscription that had brought such joy to his son only weeks before he had died. But he knew Celia's emotions were at a breaking point, and he felt her needs were more important than his at that moment.

Nodding her head, Celia reached for the bag. "Go ahead, darling, you open it."

Len's hands shook as he tore into the gray bag. And there it was, the TAG Heuer Titanium. Quickly removing it from the clear plastic bag that held it, Len turned the face over so he could see the inscription, which read, "To our next family doc, Dr. L. C. S."

Celia leaned forward and put her arms on the table; burying her face in her arms, she sobbed audibly. Len sat back in his chair and allowed his best and most recent memory of his son to come forward in his mind. It was graduation morning. Lenny had already been accepted to the medical school of his choice. But until that day he hadn't fully understood that his father was finally happy for him. His father would now fully support his decision to follow in his and Leonard Sr.'s footsteps.

Len allowed the memory to flood his very being now. Lenny had come down for breakfast to find several balloons bearing "Happy Graduation" messages, attached by ribbons to his seat. And on his placemat there was a small bag. Len could recall the surprised look and sheer joy that appeared on his son's face when he read the inscription. Len knew the watch was a great gift, but the words on the back of it were the biggest gift of all.

"Let's sign the papers and go to the hotel. I need a drink." Celia brought the moment back to reality.

"Yes, let me get Henry. I'm ready to get out of here, too." Len opened the door and summoned one of the employees to help them complete this part of the business.

XXXI

The Final Good-Bye

The following morning, Lori and Daryl, along with the familiar van driver, appeared at the appointed hour, ready to drive the parents to the next step in the process of the nightmare they were living. On the way the employees explained what the morning events would include.

"We're meeting at the hangar, where all of the families will once again board coaches and depart for the site of the memorial. Because the crash occurred on airport property, the memorial cannot take place there in the middle of a live investigation. It was a challenge to have the investigators stop long enough for the site visit. However, there is a large field adjacent to the property where the flight went down that will be used for the service. We will be able to view the site of the accident from there, without interfering with the investigation and recovery that are still taking place."

"Fair enough," Len said. "We know this is a way to come together as families one more time and say good-bye as well as we can under the circumstances."

Boarding the coach, Celia and Len were happy to see Gregg, and this time he was not alone. He introduced them to his companion, Belinda, the sister of his wife who had perished in the crash.

"Let's make sure that after the services, we exchange e-mails and details," Len said to his new friend. "I don't want to lose track of you once we all go home."

"I would like that, too," Gregg answered.

Len felt for him. Len knew that he himself was lucky. He had his wife and his younger son. This man had lost his family. Len wondered how he would make it himself if he had no one to go home to. His thoughts were interrupted when the person in charge of their coach took to the public-address system to speak.

"Excuse me for interrupting your conversations, but if you can give me just a moment, I would like to explain today's events to you so you'll know what to expect." Len did not recognize her. He wondered where all of these people came from. They were all so helpful and seemed to know how to do what they were doing—like the airline people, he hoped they didn't have these jobs all the time. Surely they had jobs that were more pleasant.

"Shortly we will arrive at the area where we'll hold the memorial dedication. It is the intent of the local authorities to find a more suitable location, not quite so close to the airport, for a permanent memorial stone and a place for all of the families to gather in the future. However, for now, we chose this open field due to its proximity to the site of the accident. When we arrive you all will be provided flowers. There will be a brief service, and then each name of the deceased will be called, and as many members of your family as you would like can walk forward and lay the flowers on the temporary memorial stone. After all names are called, we'll have clergy from each of the religions of those who died say prayers. After the prayers we will lead you back to the coaches and return you to the hangar. At that time you can return to your hotels or go back to the airport if you're flying out this afternoon."

"Are you sure this is a good idea?" Celia whispered to Len. "I mean, they don't even have the stone for the actual memorial yet."

"I know what you're saying," Len responded, "but I think the intent is a good one. Sooner or later we all have to go on to what's next for us. And from what I was hearing at the hangar as we boarded earlier, it may be a long time before the final few passengers are found. This ceremony is a way to help people come together one more time before going home and facing our lives as they will be now."

It made sense to Len to try to help move people in a direction. There was just no reason to live in limbo any more than necessary. He could not help how often his mind presented pictures of parallels between his professional life and what was happening now in his family life. How many times had he presented families with earth-shattering news, turned his back, and gone on to lunch or whatever mundane thing was next for him? He now wondered how they moved on. Who assisted them? Who offered to help them move on to what was next? Medical school had provided him with none of the lessons he was learning now.

The coach came to a stop at that point, and once more the families of the deceased filed off and moved in the direction they were being led.

XXXII

The Flyby

Lenny knew this was a big day. He had been briefed the day before, as all of his fellow passengers and the crew had been. Today was the first time all who had crossed over that night after the crash would meet again for one last good-bye. John had explained it was another part of the passage.

When the flight had crashed, they had all gone to where they were supposed to go next for their souls' evolution. But today they would join together as one large group to form a final connection with one another as well as bid farewell to those left behind, most of whom would be in attendance at the memorial service at the site of the crash. John explained that the souls' presence would be felt better by their group energy than by single efforts.

Lenny had come to have confidence in John's leadership. From what he could see, the crow they had sent to Bruce, Lenny's presence at the hangar when his suitcase was on display, and of course the wedding visit were all signs that his messages were getting through to the other side.

As Lenny dressed that morning, he chose jeans and a blue button-down shirt, like he had worn the night he crossed over. When he arrived at the location of the gathering, he was surprised and delighted that the aircraft appeared as good as new. Stairs had been pulled up to the door, as there was no terminal building to connect a Jetway to. He noticed that Captain Judie and First Officer Sam were climbing the stairs, flight bags and suitcases in hand, along with two other pilots he did not recognize.

If they had been on the flight before it had crashed, he had failed to see them.

John made his way over to where Lenny was standing and offered his hand and a big smile of encouragement. “So today is a big day. Are you ready?”

“Yes, I think so. While I didn’t know anyone on the flight, there are some people I know I’ll recognize. It will be good to see them under better circumstances than that night I saw them last.” Lenny was picturing the white-haired lady with the broken neck. He had often thought of her and hoped she had died quickly, with little suffering.

“Well, today you will have a better memory of them than you were left with the night of the crash. This memory of seeing them going their own ways, continuing their personal journeys, just as you are doing, is intended to help you in healing the memories of that night.” John’s eyes shone with the sparkle that had always engendered trust, and today was no exception.

“Yes, I know this will help me. I wanted to ask you, are there extra passengers and crew members on the flight?” Lenny was still puzzled by the two extra pilots he had seen boarding earlier with Captain Judie and Officer Sam.

“Well, it all depends on what you mean by extra. Today all of the souls onboard the night of the crash will be accompanied by their guardians, just as you were that night.” John gestured to the large crowd that was gathering near the bottom of the stairs of the aircraft.

“Oh, now I get it.” Lenny looked back toward the cockpit. “So when I saw the two pilots who were flying the aircraft the night of the accident boarding earlier accompanied by two other pilots, the two I did not recognize were their guardians.”

“Exactly. When you were in human form, you were tuned in to a different frequency and could not see the others—or me. Just as I was with you through the crash and later walked with you and your grandparents, who came to cross you over, guardians accompanied all people on the aircraft that night and all of their earthly lives, for that matter. Now that you’re on this side, you’re no longer limited by the five senses associated with life on earth. Your energetic radar is clearly coming back to you.”

John knew Lenny was starting to adjust to the new life and would enjoy the events of the day immensely.

Lenny heard the angel choir singing; the public-address systems for making announcements on earth were replaced by angelic choirs in heaven. He was starting to understand that when humans prayed on earth, angels heard the prayers and responded by calling all of the appropriate heavenly beings into line, so as best to respond to the prayer. The calling took the form of a choir singing and was really quite pleasant.

"So the angel choir is starting up due to the prayers our family members are putting out on earth right now, as they prepare for their part of the service. Is that how you see it?" Lenny wanted confirmation about some of his new insight.

"Precisely. They pray, and the angels orchestrate the response to the prayers through their singing. I think it's time to line up and board the flight so we can arrive at the appointed hour." John touched Lenny's arm as they moved toward the stairs.

Once on the flight, Lenny strapped in to his seat on the aisle of row sixteen. John strapped in beside him. *Funny*, Lenny thought. With twice as many people onboard, the airplane looked perfectly normal. Funny how that worked. Lenny smiled to himself. Then just as he was settling in for the ride, he saw the white-haired lady, who was not white-haired at all. Smiling at him, she waited for him to stand and allow her to reach her window seat.

Lenny could not help but notice the white-haired lady was actually a striking brunette who exuded confidence and style, as did the handsome man beside her. She clung to his arm as they continued their lively and obviously private conversation. Relaxing a little now, Lenny leaned back and turned his attention to others on the flight.

This was a different event than he had expected. And so far it was more uplifting than what he had imagined. Captain Judie made the typical announcement welcoming the passengers onboard, and much of the preflight activities were the same as on the original flight, except the flight attendants were not conducting their typical safety announcements. Lenny smiled at the irony of that. He realized everyone had survived and always would, so there was no reason to demonstrate safety equipment and earthly life-saving maneuvers.

As the flight took off, the sound of the choir rose. It was quite beautiful, and Lenny knew all who were praying on the ground were receiving comfort on some level. He decided to inquire more about the activities planned for the day.

"I know today we're going to fly over the folks as they gather to pay their respects once more before going their separate ways, much the way we will as passengers and crew today after the flight. So here's my question. Will my parents and the other family members see us?" Lenny was unsure how this part might go.

"Yes. Let's say they will know we're there in a symbolic way." John gestured with his right hand toward the bright-blue sky outside the window. "You'll see, and you will have no doubt that they know we are there."

Captain Judie's voice came back on the public-address system and told them all to look to the right beneath the aircraft. She had turned off the seat belt sign, so everyone could move about as necessary for better vantage points.

"We are flying directly over the memorial service, so if you look carefully, you will see your family and friends who are there. We will get as close as the HFRs—the heavenly flight regulations—allow, so you can get a good glimpse." A short while later, she came back on. "OK, we are approaching the site, so good luck in viewing your folks." Judie had confidence in her voice. Lenny knew why she had been such a respected pilot, as had her copilot, Sam.

Lenny caught sight of his blond parents within a millisecond. Their height had always made it easy to see them in every crowd while Lenny was still on earth, and today was no different. Lenny noticed his parents and everyone at the ceremony were looking up and pointing toward the sky.

"John, you were right. They can see us! They're pointing, and as sad as they are, many are smiling up at us—they're happy in the midst of their pain!" Lenny was beside himself with joy. He could hear the others on the flight squealing with delight. The joy on the flight was unmistakable—the goal of the day had in fact been accomplished. And now he saw the brilliance of it all. And just to give every passenger and the flight attendants one more chance to see their families, Captain Judie and copilot Sam flew over a second time, which added to everyone's delight.

The flyby—or, rather, the double flyby, thanks to the flight crew—gave the families hope that life could have joy again and that all was not lost. Similarly, those on the aircraft would now finally go their separate ways on their souls' journeys, but like the families, they had positive memories to sustain them. They shared a bond, having crossed over from earth that night at the same time. And now the memory of their association contained more than grief and loss. Many would meet again down the road somewhere. And the original memories of the crash would be balanced with joy and hope for them as well as the families temporarily left behind.

On earth, once the families returned home from the memorial service, a photo of the flyby would be mailed to each of them. A public safety employee assigned to help manage the traffic that day had snapped several pictures of the symbol that appeared over the site. Captain Judie and her copilot Sam had left an indelible mark in the minds and hearts for those on the ground and in heaven to enjoy—a double rainbow, a symbol of hope and promise.

Part 2
The Crisis

Grief is in two parts. The first is loss.
The second is the remaking of life.

—Anne Roiphe

XXXIII

Facing New Lives

Three weeks had passed since Lenny died in the crash. Len and Celia had completed all of the rituals that were possible at the time. They had gone to the city where the accident happened to learn all they could about the crash. They had attended the memorial service organized by the airline and government officials and did their best to have a funeral with the cremated remains—all that was left of their precious son's left arm.

Now the challenge that confronted them lay in trying to rebuild some kind of normal life, whatever that meant and however long it took. They both knew they owed it to Bruce and each other to do their best at building a quality and meaningful life with the one son they had left.

Their family had shrunk so much with the loss of both sets of parents within a two-year period before the crash. And now without Lenny, the family was smaller and so much less than they ever could have imagined.

During the weeks that had passed since the crash, the media paid a good bit of attention to the cause of the accident. Nearly every day there was a reference to the investigation in the national press. While the government officials continued to remind the interested public that the investigation would take time, there was not a lot of new information being reported. Len knew it was just a short while before the subject of what happened to the airplane that unspeakable day in June would be of little interest to most of the public. It would soon lose importance to everyone other than the lawyers, the airline, and the families whose lives were forever changed.

From the very beginning, reports indicated that the pilots had landed in weather conditions that made it virtually impossible to maintain control over the aircraft. Despite the references to potential mechanical problems and other factors, already experts were predicting the final report would show the cause of the crash to be plain and simple human error—pilot error, to be exact.

Back home in Cleveland, Len had taken another week off from work. He wasn't ready to see patients yet, much less deal with the rigor of the surgical routine of a successful practice. He had promised Celia he would help her with some of the business that needed to be done in sorting out Lenny's final affairs. How they would do this was still a mystery. Len was still not able to wrap his head around the word *final* for someone who had not even lived to see his twenty-third birthday.

Despite his own confusion, he knew he had to do it for Celia. He also knew that when the time came, it would be good for him to return to his routine. He remembered after all of the losses he had been through, work had always been the stabilizing force in his life. He also knew the loss of his parents and his in-laws had been very different from the loss of his son. Yet work had always been good for him. He was confident it would be again. Celia, on the other hand, was the one he worried about.

He hoped that when Bruce got ready to go to kindergarten at the end of summer, this might be the turning point for Celia in adjusting to life without Lenny. Right now it was pretty bleak, but it had been only three weeks. She had already announced she did not intend to return to her counseling practice and had let her partner know. Len had tried to convince her to take a leave of absence. She did not listen to his advice. On the day they arrived home from Omaha, she started letting everyone know, including her longstanding patients, that she did not intend to return to her practice. He overheard her dropping the news into conversations with well-meaning friends who called.

Aside from helping Celia with her requests and expectations, the one call he intended to initiate before returning to work was one he had wanted to make right from the start. He had to call Howard Stoddard, one of his closest friends since freshmen year in medical school. Howie, a name he still went by with family and friends, practiced medicine at the same hospital, but due to his specialty he and Len seldom saw each other. Howie had become a heart surgeon and, from what Len had heard over the years, was a damned good one—maybe one of the best in the country.

Howie had left a message for Len the day after the crash. Len saw it on the list of calls Sheryl had taken during the time he and Celia were just too devastated to talk to anyone other than family. Howie was almost a brother, and Len knew he needed to find some quality time with him for a private discussion that would last more than a few moments. He had seen Howie briefly in the reception line at the funeral. The tears in Howie's eyes made it impossible for the men to do anything other than embrace.

But now the time had come to place that call to his friend. Howie's father, Walt, was a retired aircraft accident investigator. Before his retirement he had participated in over one hundred investigations. For the last twenty years of his career, he had been a lead investigator for the aircraft manufacturer he had worked for and had presided over several major investigations for the company. Len knew even though Howie's dad was retired, he had remained very active in the community. Len had seen him at a hospital fundraiser only a few months before the crash.

Since Celia was still sleeping, Len decided to go ahead and place a call to Howie's office. He was in luck. This was the day Howie saw patients in his office. When Len identified himself to Howie's receptionist, there was an unmistakable hesitation in her voice. Everyone in the medical community knew about Lenny, and, like her, even people who did not know the family knew the story.

"Oh, yes, Dr. Sawyer…" Her voice faltered. "I'll have Dr. Stoddard call you as soon as he finishes with the patient he's with." The receptionist had a twinge of sympathy in her voice. Len was becoming accustomed to the tone.

After pouring himself a second cup of coffee, Len picked up the newspaper. His eyes scanned the headlines. There, on the lower right corner of the front page, he saw the latest article on the crash. It contained no new information, as Len suspected. It rehashed the facts that had been presented the day before and the days before that. As he turned the pages, he barely saw them, much less concentrated enough to read the small print. He wondered silently if he would ever again care about what was going on in the world. He laid the newspaper aside.

The sound of the phone startled him. He had no idea how long he had been sitting in a trancelike state, staring out the kitchen window, looking for the crow that no longer came. Without thinking he answered in his professional tone, as if he was at his office or the hospital.

"Dr. Sawyer speaking."

"Len, it's Howie. Thank God you called. I've thought about you every day for the last three weeks. How are you and Celia holding up?" Howie's concern for his friend came through the phone line.

"Howie, thanks for calling back. I know you're busy. I hope you don't mind taking my call on your office day. I know how packed these days always are." Len's need for connection with his good friend was evident in his tone.

"Don't apologize, man. You know I would do anything for you and your family right now. I wanted so much to spend time with you before now, but I know you must have been overwhelmed with all you had to do. God, I'm just so sorry about Lenny!" Howie could not contain the emotion that broke through his composure.

"Yeah, I saw you had called right away. Celia and I were just trying to hold on and get through those first few days. I wanted to talk to you but just had so little energy. Dang, I still don't have any energy, but I wanted to reach out to you. I wanted to ask a favor."

"Anything!" Howie suspected what his friend wanted, and he wanted the same thing. He had talked to his dad almost daily since the crash. Dad had focused on the information that was being given to the press, and he had his own discussions with other retired investigators behind the scenes. He still had his connections in Washington, DC, and they were as strong as ever. Howie's father knew how much like brothers Howie and Len had become over the years. He had placed a call to his son as soon as he'd heard about Lenny. Like everyone who knew the Sawyers, Dad also wanted to help in whatever way he could.

"Look, I know Walt, I mean your dad, has been retired for many years, but I would love to just sit down with him and ask him some questions. Celia and I went to Omaha and even attended a few meetings where the government people and other investigators spoke about what was known at the time. But I feel so powerless just sitting around waiting to find out what really happened to that airplane." Len felt hopelessness rising in his voice.

"Len, Dad is waiting for me to call him and arrange a time for you to meet. At this point, of course, not a lot is being released as far as formal information, but I can tell you investigators, even retired ones like Dad, have their own ideas about the crash. They can't help but have opinions after so many years of living with their own investigations. This stuff haunts them twenty-four seven, until the final report is written. Their hunger for solving the puzzle doesn't let up just because they're retired."

Howie paused as he tried to put himself in Len's shoes. He couldn't really feel what his friend had to be feeling. But with so many years of practicing medicine, he had learned how important information was for families who suffered the loss of a loved one. That was one of the many things he learned from his dad that was similar in both their professions. When people lose control over their lives the way they do in these situations, information is the lifeline between them and gaining a little bit of power back over their lives.

"OK, look, I'm off this week, and I just need to find a time that works for your dad that will also work for me and the family. We're pretty much at loose ends right now, and I'm trying to be as available for Celia and Bruce as I can. I am almost certain that Celia is meeting with her sisters, Sheryl and Babs, tomorrow night. They're starting to organize the thank-you notes that need to be handled. Thank God they're actually writing them for her, but Celia needs to help them get started." Len felt a little bit stronger just knowing he could talk to someone with some technical knowledge. He needed a break from the emotional discussions, if that was possible so soon after the loss of a son.

"Let me put a call in right now. You check with Celia, and if Dad can do it, let's set it up. What time is good for you?" Howie knew just sitting with his dad over a beer would help his friend. His dad could help them understand the investigation process, and that alone would be helpful. It would be for Howie anyway, if he were in Len's shoes, God forbid.

"How about tomorrow night at seven? I know the girls will have help taking care of Bruce while they work." Len reflected on one of the things that had been great for them: people were coming out of the woodwork to help with their one remaining son. Mothers of Bruce's playmates were calling and offering to let the boys play together so he and Celia could have some time to get things done, though letting him sleep over at their houses was not happening. Neither Len nor Celia could be away from him for more than a few hours at that point. He knew they would have to get over that, but for now they were not fighting the need to overprotect Bruce. He was all they had left, and they were clinging to him, poor kid.

Howard knew he could probably reach his dad right now if he called within the hour. His dad had a standing tee time at the club on certain days, and right now he would be having coffee with the guys, if he were keeping his normal schedule. "Let me hang up and try to reach him. I'll call right back."

Len hung up quickly. This was a meeting he needed. He was still unaccustomed to the helpless feeling. This was unchartered territory for him. Like his father, Leonard Sr., he had always felt he could get things done for his family. That had been true up until the crash. Now he felt like he had lost all of the resourcefulness that had once been second nature to him.

Looking up from the unread newspaper, Len watched as Celia entered the kitchen. He wondered if she would ever regain her normal habits of showering and applying makeup before seeing others. He had always admired that about her. She had always been attractive and proud of her appearance. Like so many things, this had changed too. He hoped it was only temporary.

"Who was that on the phone?" she asked as she poured a cup of coffee.

Hesitant to start the inevitable daily if not hourly discussion of the crash and Lenny's death, Len knew he needed to include her in his plans to pursue his own search for answers. "I was talking to Howie. I want to meet with his dad and hear what he thinks about the cause of the crash."

"I thought he was retired." Celia stirred her coffee slowly as she took a seat opposite him at the kitchen island.

"Yes, he is. But for as many years as he investigated accidents, I feel like he probably at least has an educated opinion of what happened at this point.

"Opinion would be about all he has. He won't know anything more than other members of the public, right? I mean, what would he know that isn't being told to the families?"

"Well, you are right technically, but on the other hand, I'm sure he's formed an opinion, and I want to know what that is. I have some questions I want to ask someone who understands how these things work." Len chose his words carefully. He knew it would upset Celia to know how much he needed to have a discussion that went beyond how much she hated the airline and everyone associated with it. Len was starving for some logic to come from somewhere. It sure was not happening at home.

"When are you meeting with him? I need to go too. I would like to ask some questions too. I'm going with you."

Here we go, Len thought. He had to structure things so they could have some time apart from one another. This was his first attempt, and it was not an easy thing to do.

"Look, hon, if you want some time with Walt to ask some questions, we can set that up," he said. "But I was planning on meeting with him while you and the girls are working together. I want to have a meeting with him and Walt on my own—you know, just guys talking about technical stuff."

"Sheryl, Babs, and I can change our schedule. I know they'll understand." Celia was not going to give in easily.

"Celia, I am not going to argue with you. I need this time with the guys, and I promise I will let Walt know you want to talk with him too. But for now, let me have this first meeting on my own."

"Fine, but I do want my own meeting." Celia took another sip of her coffee and looked away, hiding the start of her daily tears.

The sound of the phone broke the intensity of the discussion. Len was relieved as Celia left the room. He was equally happy to see Howie's number on the caller ID. He picked up. "Howie, did you reach your dad?"

"I did indeed. Seven works, and Dad is looking forward to spending time with you. Do you want to meet us at the club, or do you want me to swing by and pick you up?"

"You mean Briarwood, right? Is that where your dad still belongs?"

"Yes. Let's have a drink at the Benton Room there to get started. We can decide if we want a meal after that. Will that work?"

"I'll be there. I really appreciate this. I can't thank you enough. I'll see you then." Len hung up the phone. Walking up the stairs, he noticed the door to Lenny's bedroom was open. It had been closed since the night of the crash. Walking into the room, Len saw Celia sitting on Lenny's bed staring out the window. Glancing around the room, Len could not help but think about how normal it all looked. If he did not know better, he would think the young man who once lived there would be returning to it any minute. If only! Len could not help but sigh. Sitting down beside Celia, he took her hand in his and waited for her to speak.

"I am so ashamed." Celia continued to stare out the window as she spoke. "I had no idea what they were going through."

Len knew where her gaze was directed. He also stared out at the dimly lit house across the street.

Celia broke the silence. "We didn't know. We had no way of knowing until Lenny died what Brad and Jane were going through. When their boy died in Iraq, I thought they would eventually be themselves again. I kept waiting for Jane to come back to bridge night at the club. Now I realize how ignorant I was about their pain. Who did I think I was all these years? I counseled scores of people about grief. Is it any wonder I'll never be a counselor again?" She looked directly into her husband's eyes. The determination to give up her counseling practice was unmistakable.

"I think you're being too hard on yourself. I think about my own medical practice and how many times I judged people for their reactions to the deaths of family members. The only thing that helps me now is to know I'll be a better doctor because I finally get it. What a shame I had to lose my own son to understand and appreciate others' grief." Len returned her look.

"Well, that's the difference between you and me. You want to help others again. I don't. I just want to take life one day at a time and try to live without my one son in order to raise the one I have left."

Something about the way she spoke had a final ring to it. Len knew Celia had made up her mind, and he knew it was futile to try to get her to envision a future without their elder son. It was too soon for both of them.

The couple sat in silence for an indeterminate amount of time before their attention was diverted. They heard their younger son starting a favorite cartoon in the DVD player in his bedroom next door. Len patted Celia's hand and went to check on Bruce.

XXXIV

Probable Blame

Len and Celia found there was much to do in closing bank accounts, canceling the apartment lease, and countless other tasks related to the end of Lenny's life, despite its brevity. One of the hardest yet most rewarding parts of this time in their own lives was fielding the endless calls from Lenny's friends. Len and Celia knew their son was special; they'd just had no way of knowing how many people felt that way about him during his short life on earth.

The time between the initial call and the meeting came quickly, with all the tasks to be done. The mood of sadness lifted slightly for Len each time he remembered the meeting scheduled with Howie and Walt. He was not aware of anything that helped Celia's mood. He was concerned about her drinking but determined not to bring it up. There would be a time to address it, he knew that, but the time was not right now.

After Sheryl and Babs arrived, Len got his keys and a notepad and prepared to leave for the meeting. He was grateful that the sisters had offered to help. He knew Celia did not have the energy to write thank-you notes to hundreds of people. And he certainly did not.

Len drove the six miles to Briarwood with a mix of apprehension and anticipation. In a hurry to get the discussion started, he allowed the valet to take his Porsche at the front door, something he rarely did. Getting out of his car he reflected on how little he would care about getting a scratch on his sports car. Much like Celia's inability to care about her looks, Len had lost his interest in his car and other material things that once he had attached great significance to.

Walking into the reception area, Len saw Howie and his dad seated at a table off to the left of the large bar area. Both men were tall and had similar Roman noses and high cheekbones. Both had full heads of hair, but unlike his son, Walt's was snow white. Len was once again reminded of how much he missed Leonard Sr. His father had been strong physically as well as emotionally and always took control of all situations. By contrast, Len felt constantly embarrassed over his inability to regain emotional control, let alone provide leadership for his family following the crash.

As Len approached the area where his friends were seated, he noticed a large group of men who seemed to be enjoying pitchers of beer and good stories marked by much laughter. Len wondered if he would ever be part of good times again.

Howie motioned for him as he caught sight of Len approaching. Walt stood up and smiled as Len came to the table. Walt extended his hand, the look on his face expressing his feelings of sorrow.

Before Howie or Walt could speak, Len began. "Thanks for coming. I really appreciate your taking time out of your life to try to help us." He stopped at that. It was physically impossible to say more with the gigantic lump rising in his throat.

"Not at all," Walt responded in a hushed voice. "Anything I can do to help."

"What are you drinking, Len?" Howie asked.

Relieved for the temporary diversion, Len found his voice. "Any lager on tap is fine, thanks."

Howie motioned for the server and ordered a round.

Walt leaned forward across the table and started the discussion. "Look, Len, I know you want to talk about the crash from a technical perspective, but before we begin that, I want to let you know how sorry I am about Lenny. As you know, I've been around these things all my professional life, and I'm always affected by these tragedies. When I heard your boy died in the crash, this thing became personal. I want you to know how terribly sorry Barb and I are for your loss."

As the beers were delivered, Len leaned back in his chair, allowing the server to set them in place. He hoped his reaction to Walt's words was not apparent. Up until then it had never occurred to him that professional investigators made any personal connections with the people killed on flights. He had assumed it was business as usual when one of these things happened. While Howie had known Lenny since he was a baby, Walt had never met him. Yet Len felt the sincerity in his voice.

"I appreciate your sympathy. We've had a pretty rough time of it over these last few weeks. I guess most people like us don't ever think of losing a family member this way, let alone your kid. Seems like these things are always happening to other people but not to us." Len was feeling more emotion than he had expected in what he'd thought would be a factual meeting.

"Yeah, I think that's pretty typical. No one ever thinks these things will happen to them. I've been following this accident investigation pretty closely. Of course I always do. It's the nature of the beast. As an investigator I'm driven to solve the puzzle from the moment a plane goes down. Retired or not, you want to figure out what happened, even though you're no longer part of any investigation officially."

Walt looked away and stared out the window, as if wanting to escape the personal nature of the discussion, if only for a moment. Looking down at the table, he continued, "I can tell you this one is pretty clear. I don't see much mystery as to what happened. But it's the why behind what happens in one of these that boggles my mind." Looking directly at Len, he took a long sip of his beer.

For the second time, Len tried to hide his surprise. "So you think it's pretty clear that what's been reported by the media from the beginning is correct? I mean that the pilots killed themselves and all the others on the flight with their own stupidity? I guess I was hoping the cause of the crash would be more forgivable than that." The disgust came through in his tone.

"Len, on one hand I wish it was more complicated too, as I hate to blame anything on people who aren't here to defend themselves. But the truth is, even if that's what the final investigation shows, that it was the pilots who messed up, I think we have to look at *why* they were allowed to make mistakes that could have such a disastrous result." Walt's passion on the subject was creeping into his voice.

Silently Howie was hoping his dad would remember he was addressing a family member here. This was not just a discussion with other professionals in his field. He hoped some of that compassion in his father's voice when they'd first met a few moments earlier would return.

"I don't know what you mean by *why*. How do you explain two professional pilots climbing on an airplane, flying to their destination, and choosing to land in weather conditions where clearly they would lose control over the aircraft? In short, how do professional people mess up so badly that they just plain kill innocent people who placed their lives in their hands?" Even in a dimly lit room, Howie and Walt could see the veins in Len's forehead. Some of the anger he had been holding back for the past few weeks had finally surfaced.

Walt took a long draw on his beer and leaned back in his chair. He appeared to be planning a thoughtful response.

Howie hated this moment. He wanted to break in and lead the discussion in a different direction altogether. But he didn't know how without giving away his grave discomfort. He sipped his beer in silence.

Finally Walt spoke. "Len, you had it right when you called them professionals. All I'm trying to point out is that both the captain and the first officer were excellent pilots. One of my buddies knows the chief pilot at Universal. He said Captain Judie and First Officer Sam were among the best pilots they had. Like you, Howie, and me before I retired, they took their jobs seriously. I hate to see you or anyone attack them without knowing more about why they chose to land under the circumstances that turned out to be fatal."

When no response came from Len, Walt continued. "When the facts all come out, and they will, I think we will see there were likely factors that affected their judgment. No professional pilot gets on an airplane one day and decides to take his or her life along with the other crew and passengers—except in an act of terrorism, and we know that's not relevant here. There's more to this than just the words *pilot error*. The reason the government investigators refer to the findings of the investigation as *probable cause* is because it is always more complicated than just a few mistakes on a couple of people's part. It's a shame, but from the beginning the press reports these accidents with such a negative spin, they might as well call their reporting of events probable blame!"

"What kind of factors?" Len was genuinely curious.

"There are all sorts of factors that will be considered and eventually disclosed. Like fatigue—we don't know yet if they had proper rest breaks. We also don't know what types of demands were being placed on the pilots to land the plane and keep it in sequence for the flights scheduled after the equipment—uh, I mean airplane arrived at that airport. All of these things affect their decisions. There could be any number of facts affecting the *why* behind the choice to land in those weather conditions. One thing we know for sure is that the crash did not occur because the pilots wanted to die that day!"

Len felt the familiar anger arising in his belly again. Without trying to check his emotions, he banged his fist on the table as he spoke. "Then someone else needs to be punished for my son's death. If someone in a management position at Universal put pressure on the pilots to fly without proper rest or land regardless of the danger, they should be held accountable! Those pilots had the power to choose. My son and all of those others onboard had no say in the matter. No one should be allowed to make such a lethal mistake!"

Howie sank down as low as he could in his chair. There had been few times when he regretted his six foot four height, but this was one of those rare occasions. Wishing he could disappear as this discussion appeared to be heading in a tragic direction, he suddenly wished for a cigarette. While he had not smoked since medical school, a deep draw on a Marlboro Light would have felt really good right then.

"So what's the difference between a doctor who's been on duty too long and makes a mistake and kills a patient and what you're saying about mistakes made by professional pilots?" Walt's words seemed to freeze the air around them.

The three men sat in silence. Howie respected his father, but this was too much of a direct attack on his best friend. He understood his father's logic, but his timing for this comparison was unforgiveable. Surely he was aware of how sensitive this entire subject of medical mistakes would be for Len long before the Universal crash.

Len leaned back in his chair. He looked down at the floor, unwilling or perhaps unable to speak at that moment. The silence at the table was downright painful, especially for Howie, who wanted to say something to console his friend. He wanted to soften his father's words, but he knew this would not change the truth. The comparison was accurate. He regretted that his dad hit on this fact at this moment, but he could not change the reality of it.

Though not willing to share his thoughts, Len was now forced to fully acknowledge this truth of what Walt had laid on the table, but he was also incapable of discussing its relevance to his own life at that moment.

Motioning the server in their direction, Howie spoke up. "Another round?" Both men nodded.

Walt now spoke, wanting to move the discussion back to the crash. "Len, you know it's true. When I think of the accident where Lenny died, as I said, I think we will learn the pilots had been pushed to the limit of their duty requirements. I have seen this all too often. The corporate bean counters put way too much pressure on the pilots to land and keep the airplane moving, without regard for weather, mechanical problems, and other reasons that can delay a flight. And then throw in improper crew rest breaks, and you wonder how the skies are as safe as they are."

Now it was Walt whose tone revealed a high degree of emotion directed at those whose actions were often related to a tragic crash, though they were invisible to the public. Not unlike countless families whose lives had been drastically changed on emotional and psychological levels by their losses, like most professional investigators, Walt's life was impacted too. For thirty-five years he had devoted his life to helping move the field along, and it always felt like a setback when another one of these avoidable tragedies happened. It had all become personal to him somewhere along the way. The pacemaker in his chest was a testament to that.

Howie sat silently sipping his beer, wishing he could help somehow. Not unlike his friend Len, as a respected physician, feeling powerless was not a familiar experience for him.

"Look, Len, I don't see this as an uncomplicated problem at all," Walt went on. "I see it as a very complicated one. You see, it's the safety of aviation today that in some ways causes the problem. These things happen so seldom that most people in planning roles play the numbers game. It's like betting on the chances it won't happen and then being prepared to pay out the insurance claims whenever it does. It's the proverbial double-edged sword." Compassion was easing back into his tone.

"An insurance claim is the last thing Celia and I are concerned with at this point. We can't even go there in our minds right now." Sadness had returned to Len's tone. How well he knew that each of the families had ample time to take whatever approach they chose about lawsuits and settlements. As a physician he knew too well the world of legal issues when death and human error become entangled.

Sitting in silence, the three men entertained their own private thoughts on the subjects of death, accidents, and the personal nature of this most recent aviation tragedy.

Finally Len spoke up. "So if investigators like you have known about the preventable nature of so many accidents for such a long time, why in God's name have you not done something about it? From where I sit, I think far too many people sit on their asses and don't care because it's not their kid, their wife, their parents, or anybody they even know!" Frustration, if not out-and-out anger, near rage, had made its ugly way back into the meeting.

"So that's what you think? You think these accidents happen because people in my profession don't care? I suppose you also think doctors are the only people concerned about saving lives and ending human suffering. You have no idea how dedicated other professionals are when it comes to these things."

Len did not respond, so Walt continued. "I remember a whole string of accidents in the United States during the '90s where all onboard the flights died. While they weren't all our jets, enough of them were. We were pushed to the maximum with the investigations." Walt stopped long enough to sip his beer and reflect on those difficult years in his past. "I remember wondering if we could live through that time. It took its toll on my investigative team and me, physically as well as emotionally. I also wondered if our company could survive. When All Airways went down in Orlando, killing all the passengers and crew onboard, the press accused us of a cover-up. Nobody wanted to solve that mystery more than we did. Nobody was more determined to find the problem and fix the airplanes more than we were. Hell, we were flying on those airplanes and our wives and kids were too, just like passengers all over the world." Walt's voice level was rising. Years of frustration in a highly stressful profession in a complicated industry were showing in his voice and face, and he felt it in his chest.

"I remember that one. It was the rudder, right?" For a moment Len was caught up in the discussion, as though it was impersonal. Someone listening in would have thought he had an interest in the subject of aviation accidents, like much of the flying public, devoid of personal emotional investment.

"Yeah, it was the rudder system. When we finally figured it out, we retrofitted the planes that were in service and corrected the design on the future ones."

Changing the subject back to the present accident, Len leaned forward and asked, "So what happens now? If it's as simple as this, do we just wait for the airline to own it?"

"Well, there will be a thorough look at other factors that contributed to the accident. But yeah, pretty much. At some point the report will be finished, and then the families will be offered settlements. I guess you and Celia will need to choose a plaintiff's lawyer; I would go with one of the big firms. They'll take their chunk of it, but they know pretty much what your settlement should look like and will keep you from wasting a lot of time and unnecessary splits with ambulance chasers."

Walt had seen many families of victims of crashes taken advantage of over the years by small-time lawyers who were somebody's brothers-in-law or otherwise moved in on the family during times when emotions clouded their decisions about whom to place their trust in. Educated people knew even these small-time players would eventually turn over their cases to one of the big guys but not before negotiating their own shares of the proceeds. The pie could be divided in only so many ways, and the extra strife of having too many lawyers involved caused additional harm to families who so often had little interest in the money part. He always wished families would become more aware of the issues on this subject before they signed with attorneys. He hoped Len would heed his advice.

"I guess I was hoping for something more than just human mistakes. Seems like if there had been a mechanical malfunction or something more complicated, it would be easier to live with. I guess I need some time to process it all. It's just so much to take in, at the same time trying to come to terms with the loss of my son." Len was repeating himself, but the discussion had shed little light on the subject—or at least nothing more than what he already suspected: human mistakes on the part of two pilots, an airline, and an industry.

"Of course you need time. It takes longer than most people think. I don't believe there are shortcuts for coming to terms with this type of tragedy." Walt reflected on the countless stories of people he had read about in the press. He remembered hearing stories about families who were torn apart by the losses, over fights about money, and sometimes the fights even involved children orphaned by the crash. He secretly prayed for all of the families of these tragedies, and his son's friend was at the top of the list.

"I do appreciate your time tonight. I need to get home to Celia and Bruce. We've got a long road in front of us, trying to build a life without Lenny. I guess I'd better get started." Len felt defeated as he rose from the table. His voice and his entire countenance showed it.

"Len, stay for a drink with me. You and I haven't had any time to talk since the crash happened. Let me buy you dinner." Howie stood up with his friend.

"You guys stay and talk some more if you want." Walt stood, taking his windbreaker from the chair. "I have an early tee time tomorrow, and I need to get some rest."

"I really need to get home to the family." Len turned and headed toward the door. Howie followed closely behind him.

Walt had disappeared into the men's room. Howie could finally speak privately to Len. He caught up with him as he passed the bar, near the exit.

"I'm embarrassed, to say the least, that the old man was so insensitive. I never expected him to bring up so much of his own past. I guess I forget sometimes how much tension he carried around all of those years from the stress of his work. And I guess until tonight, I had no way of knowing how much of it he still carries. I thought he had worked through a lot of that. But regardless, he was out of line bringing up the comparison of mistakes in our profession, and I apologize."

Len turned toward the bar, holding on to the brass rail as though he needed it for support, staring off into the distance. After a few moments, he turned to Howie. "Maybe he said some things I needed to hear. I mean, of course I had no idea about some of the problems he mentioned that go on behind the scenes in aviation, but the part about the similarity between the two professions hit home with me."

"OK, so much for an intellectual comparison at a later date, but you're entitled to grieve for Lenny right now. I think Dad forgot that. My old man, if anyone, should know this was not the time and place for that discussion. I'm sorry his own personal emotional involvement in this subject clouded his judgment. I hadn't counted on that."

Walt exited the men's room and waved good-bye as he headed out. Both men waved in return, but neither made a move toward the door.

"I shouldn't have done what I did that night. I was coming down with the flu, and I knew it. But doctors don't call in sick." Len leaned forward on the bar now, elbows supporting him, chin resting in his hands. "I was tired, and I was just plain ill. I have lived with that for a decade and will the rest of my life."

"Look, Len, don't go there right now. That is the past, and you don't need to live there anymore. That was a long time ago." In his wildest dreams, Howie had not expected the night to end with this review of his best friend's past medical mistakes.

"A long time ago to us maybe, but not for Tim and Brenda Waters. The moment I knew Lenny was gone, I wondered if the Waterses thought about an eye for an eye and that sort of thing."

"Wait a minute." Howie regretted mixing these subjects more by the minute. He never expected his father's comments to bring up the Waters kid and the malpractice suit that had nearly driven Len out of medicine and had dominated the local press for over three years in their city. "You and I both know Lenny died along with a lot of other people, and I don't think God works that way. This is going a little beyond an eye for an eye. You can't be serious. I don't think anyone could be happy you lost Lenny, including the parents of the kid who died during delivery!"

Almost as if he didn't hear Howie's rebuttal to the comparisons he was making, Len continued, "I always wondered what it might be like to try to forgive someone for making a mistake that took the life of your kid. I guess I'll find out myself what the Waterses have gone through for a decade now. Guess it's my turn."

"OK, let's have another beer." Howie motioned toward the table where they had been sitting. "I don't want you to leave and go home to Celia thinking about all of that. You came here tonight to learn about the accident. I'm disappointed in the way this discussion turned out, but the last thing you need is to take this home to Celia."

Using his wife as an excuse for buying more time with his friend, Howie knew, was pretty transparent. He didn't want Len to have an even worse night than he might have because the old man had been just too damned insensitive. If only they could start the meeting over.

Turning to leave, Len put his hand out in a gesture of goodwill. "Don't worry. I'll be careful not to bring any of this up to Celia. It wouldn't be well received, as she still has more bitterness about the malpractice case I went through than I do. I'll just give her the highlights of the discussion with Walt about how the investigation is going."

Grasping his friend's hand with both of his own, Howie said good night. The men walked out together in silence, both lost in their own thoughts. Howie was disappointed and downright angry with his dad. Len was pensive and unable to stop thinking about the irony of it all.

XXXV

Tunnel Vision

Len found himself driving very slowly toward his home after the meeting. He needed time to process the emotions the evening's events had brought to surface in him. His friend had been right in that Celia would not be interested in helping him deal with his feelings about events prior to the crash—especially the events surrounding the Waterses and their son who died during delivery in Len's own hands. If anything had come from the talk with Walt, it had to be that now his obsession with the crash and the loss of his son was sharing space in his head with another couple and the loss of their son.

Len had been successful in keeping his mind mostly on Lenny and the crash in order to better support the family and keep his own sanity. But tonight he lost the battle. Lost in thought, he suddenly felt the power beneath the accelerator of his Porsche. As he pulled onto the freeway, he felt a rush of adrenaline and pressed the pedal harder. His senses began to lessen, all but one—the feeling of the power in the accelerator of his Porsche paired with an intense desire to end the pain in his life, to end life itself.

Glancing around him, he noticed there were few other cars on the road—less chances of involving an innocent party, he thought. The power beneath his right foot increased as his mind continued to narrow on one thought. He saw the concrete median in his peripheral vision. *A little more speed now*, he thought as the adrenaline continued to race through his veins. Power and control back again, at last!

A voice inside his head took over his mind as quickly as the lethal thoughts had blocked his ability to think rationally. *Wrecking your car and taking your life is not the way out! I will decide when and how you leave earth. There have been enough deaths that were preventable—this senseless loss of life has to stop now!*

Len instantly lifted his foot from the accelerator and allowed the car to slow to legal speed. He steered his once most prized possession toward the nearest exit. The thought of how close he had come to ending his life to stop the pain frightened Len. Up until now he had known every negative emotion a man could feel. But now he was experiencing a new one. He felt shame that even for a moment he had been so selfish as to consider ending his pain by ending his life. Len knew he had to get back in control of himself somehow. A young boy sleeping in his bed at home and a woman to whom he had pledged his life needed him. He owed them more than a coward's way out.

But Len was not ready to go home to them yet. He needed help, and he knew it. Continuing to slow his speed, Len turned on a side street. He drove his car to his favorite place, where he knew he could contemplate things without interruption. It was still early enough that the doors to St. Thomas's were unlocked. Len crept up to the altar. Kneeling and making the sign of the cross, he prayed for the second time since the crash.

Kneeling in total surrender, this time he prayed for forgiveness followed by the special prayer that Leonard Sr. had taught him to pray when he learned his son had chosen to become a healer, a physician. It was the prayer of St. Francis. The near brush with death, albeit by his own hand, had called forth a sense of humility Len had not experienced before the crash—deeper humility than he had ever felt in his life. As he had thousands of times before that night, he began, "Lord, let me be an instrument of thy peace..."

After a while, not sure how much time had passed, Len rose from his knees and sat down on a pew near the altar. He allowed the memories that had been walled off for years now to flood his mind.

XXXVI

Parallel Universes

Brenda Waters had experienced a good bit of discomfort during her entire pregnancy. Barely five feet tall, she had been plagued with morning sickness during her first trimester. When she was not throwing up, she was suffering from acute nausea. Assuming the second trimester would be better, Brenda took a temporary leave from her job as an elementary school teacher.

During the second trimester, she developed gestational diabetes, causing her to take a permanent leave of absence from teaching. Unable to work, this first-time mother was bored and depressed each time she went for her routine checkups during the entire nine months. Not unlike other first-timers Len had seen before, she was most anxious for her delivery date to arrive. But when it did, labor pains did not.

Len saw her early that day in his office. Tim had come in with his young wife, hoping Len would give them good news. They were both anxious to go to the hospital and for Brenda to give birth. They were ready to meet their son, Timothy III, and get on with raising him and enjoying a normal family life. The young couple's relationship had been a good one, despite Brenda's health challenges.

After the examination Len sent them home to wait a little longer. The baby was already quite large, and Len had his suspicions it was due to Brenda's diabetes. Other than that, nothing else appeared to be wrong. Len knew several specialists who could help with the baby after delivery if he had problems. Just a little more time was needed for the birth to take its natural course.

Later that day Len received an urgent message from the baby's father, asking him to return the call. As soon as he could, Len placed the call to the anxious first-time dad. Tim asked if Len could help Brenda move along in her delivery. He described her as being very uncomfortable. He further explained he was unable to get rest as long as she could not, and he had used most of the time off his company would allow him for the pregnancy. He practically begged Len to induce labor.

As well as he could, Len tried to explain it was not time to take measures to speed things up. Brenda had just hit the projected delivery date, and going a day, even two, beyond that was considered normal, especially for a new mother. Len was allowing his better judgment about the baby's welfare to take priority over the father's discomfort. But this anxiety was not unusual. He knew things would be fine. Besides, Len felt unwell himself, maybe coming down with a bug that several others on the hospital staff were dealing with. He knew he could call on a couple of his colleagues should the birth, or any others for that matter, be imminent. He knew this birth might be complicated, so he wanted to be at his best. He felt that it would be better for them to wait for even twenty-four to forty-eight hours since the baby did not seem anxious to be born on the projected delivery date.

It was shortly after midnight when the hospital called. Len awoke on the first ring, partly due to the sore throat that was setting in—he wasn't able to sleep. He learned that Labor and Delivery had admitted Brenda twenty minutes earlier. Her blood pressure was dangerously high.

"And the baby?" Len knew fetal distress was also a risk when the mom was experiencing problems like Brenda's.

"Fetal heart monitor indicates baby is fine right now." The experienced delivery nurse knew the situation could get dire; the tone of her "right now" indicated her concern.

"OK, I'm on my way." Len heard the nurse's last question before hanging up.

"Should we start the Pitocin?"

"Yes." Len gave the dose and the intervals before putting the phone down. He had been speaking in a low voice throughout their conversation, trying not to awaken Celia. But with his last words, she sat up in bed, as though on cue.

"Len, dearest man, I know you want to be the one to deliver all of your patients' babies, but you know you are not well. And you were so late getting home last night. I don't think you should go in." Celia let her concern come out in her voice.

"I know, but this has been a special case all the way through, and I'm worried as much about the mother as the baby. I want to make sure she's OK, even if I don't stay to deliver her. I just need to make sure she's stable. If the baby doesn't come pretty quickly, I'll come home and take a day or two to fight this thing." Concerned that his flu would be bad for the patients, Len really meant what he said.

"OK, if you promise." Celia held her cheek up for her routine good-bye kiss before fluffing her pillow and lying back down. She fell back to sleep instantly. She had no way of knowing it would be her last night of good sleep for three years to come.

XXXVII

Timothy Brown Waters III

What happened after that was pretty much a blur for Len. Months of depositions and hospital records would reveal he had made a mistake in his actions. The dose of Pitocin he ordered and the intervals he prescribed for the team in Labor and Delivery to administer contributed to fetal distress. While Brenda came through fine, the baby did not. Little Timothy Brown Waters III was born at 2:13 a.m. on July 18 and lived for exactly seven minutes before he was pronounced dead by the team who had tried desperately to revive him.

When Timothy was born in obvious distress, Len's teammates remained with Brenda and Tim as the baby was swept away to the neonatal intensive care unit. Len remained as focused as he could, despite the fact that his own temperature, he would later learn, was well above normal. It was not his first time being involved in what would become a fatal delivery. But the conditions had always been different. This was the first time his own decisions and actions would be called into question as the actual cause of death.

No amount of time would ever remove from his memory the looks on the faces of the young parents when he returned to the room where they waited and prayed for their young son. The look on his own face when he entered the room confirmed their worst fears. He did not try to hide the tears in his eyes as he tried his best to explain what even he, in that moment, did not totally understand.

"Brenda, Tim, I'm so sorry. The baby, your son, did not make it. I have asked for all of the records so I can try to explain what went wrong..."

Brenda's mother, who had joined the couple while they were awaiting news of the baby's condition, cut his words short.

"Why don't you leave our family alone? I think you've done enough. I've called for our priest. There's nothing else you can do." While she spoke quietly, Len could feel the anger in her tone. Worse yet, he knew she was right. Brenda and Tim's son was dead, and with him died the connection Len had once felt with the young couple—at least on their part. He simply had no place in their lives now, and he had to accept it.

Sensing the family's need for privacy and Len's need for emotional release, not to mention support, Shelia, the nurse who had assisted him that night, touched his arm and gestured with her head toward the door. Frozen, unable to think, with barely the strength to stand, Len excused himself and followed her into the doctors' lounge.

"What went wrong?" Physically he had been wrecked even before the ordeal had started that night. But now he had a sickening feeling that somehow he personally was responsible for Timothy's death.

"Look, Dr. Sawyer, we will hold all of the records for the admin team to start their investigation first thing in the morning. There is no point in your hanging around here. As soon as possible, you need to go home and get some rest. You haven't been yourself tonight. I could tell you weren't well when you walked into the delivery room." Shelia knew she was right. And she knew what Len was facing would not end that night or for many more days and nights thereafter.

The events that had started that night had not culminated in the death of little Timothy—far from it. After the investigation was completed, lawsuits were filed against Len and the hospital; the legal case took three years to settle. Thank God during that time, both Len's parents were still alive, and his father was finishing his last few years in practice. He felt deeply for his son. How many times had he made mistakes? And how lucky he had been that no one ever died from them. Leonard Sr. was proud of his son that he had not run from the truth when it came out. He tried to help him see that learning from our mistakes is all we can do, and besides, others were learning, too.

Len accepted responsibility for the death of young Timothy with humility and genuine sorrow. The hospital was seen as partially to blame, which alleviated some of Len's guilt. As a result of the investigation, rules were put into place that would not allow a doctor to be on duty as long as Len had been on the night the baby had died. While nothing was said about Len's personal health issues that contributed to his fitness for duty, he knew that had he been 100 percent healthy that night, he would have made better decisions.

XXXVIII

Turning Toward the Future

Unsure of how long he had been sitting there, Len suddenly became aware of a man sitting to his right, several feet away. Catching Len's eye, Father Benjamin smiled and moved beside him.

"I didn't know you were here. How long have you been sitting there?" Len extended his hand to his favorite priest in the parish—maybe his most favorite priest ever.

"A few minutes, maybe fifteen or more." The priest, who had presided over Lenny's memorial service just a few weeks earlier, could not have been more delighted to see Len in church, albeit not on a Sunday. Father Benjamin had noticed this very faithful family had not been to church since the service, a week after Lenny's death. He was biding his time before he tried to visit. He was grateful Len was there and made it easier to check in on him and the family in general.

"I'm glad you're here. I've been praying for you, Celia, Bruce, and the others in your family. I hoped you would return to church when you're ready." Father Benjamin was definitely the type of priest who would not push a family toward religion. And with Celia's current state, this was a good thing for them all.

"It has been hard, as I'm sure you know. We're having a difficult time figuring out how to go back to our old way of life, including going to church as a family, without one of our boys." Len knew he could tell Father Benjamin anything he was feeling, and there would be no judgment from the priest.

"Maybe that's part of the problem. Len, when a family loses a child, it's not the same as losing another family member." Father Benjamin had also presided over the double funeral of Len's parents not too many years before the crash. He knew the family was likely confused as to why the death of a child was very different from their other losses.

"I never understood before," said Len, "but I'm beginning to now. When my parents died, the car accident was shocking and horrible, but after the funeral, while we missed them terribly, Celia and I went back to work, our boys went back to school, and life went on. And then when both of her parents died of cancer within a short time, it was the same way. We grieved, but life went on." He looked off into the distance, as though he was reliving the sequence of events.

"Precisely. You see, when a parent loses a child, this is what psychologists call disordered mourning. Deaths of grandparents or parents are considered normal to the human brain. We grieve and feel intense sorrow, but who we are is not fundamentally changed. But for parents who lose a child, even the way you define yourselves changes. It will take time for you and Celia as parents to come to terms with having only one son now. All of the plans and ideas you had about your future involving Lenny died, too. And for your one son left, his life has also changed drastically."

The priest hesitated with his next words but then decided to continue. "The thing parents have to figure out is how to grieve the child who died while providing a healthy environment for the other children who still need them as parents. I've seen far too many parents who aren't able to do that, and the children left behind suffer—and, of course, the suffering of the parents then is intensified."

"That's amazing that you should say that. Next to being crazy with grief over losing Lenny, what you just described is the fear that chases me day and night. How do Celia and I go on with our lives and give Bruce a good childhood, like the one we gave Lenny? All the while, though, our hearts remain broken."

"It's healthy that you're already looking straight ahead at that question. You already know the life you knew with Lenny is over, and the challenge now is to grieve that loss while allowing a new life to come in.

Accepting change is the struggle, but at least you know you cannot live the way you did when you were the parents of two boys." The priest stopped and allowed his words to sink in to Len.

With no comments from Len, he continued. "Trying to live the old life is the trap. You have a new life to live. And the more you embrace that, the less likely it is you will suffer unnecessarily. You have to grieve Lenny, and you have to find a way to do that while simultaneously reaching out to Bruce and Celia, sharing your feelings, and encouraging them to do the same. Shared grief is more bearable and actually healthier." Father Benjamin stopped when he saw a look in Len's eyes signaling he had touched a raw nerve.

"Now, that is interesting," Len volunteered. "I came here tonight to allow myself to reflect on the very painful parallel between what happened to Lenny in the crash, which appears to be due to mistakes made by the pilots, and how my own mistakes led to the death of a child several years ago."

"I wasn't here in the parish at the time, but one of the other parishioners has mentioned something about the court case. I was having coffee with one of the women's groups a few days after the accident involving Lenny. The woman recalled that your family had dealt with many tragedies during the past several years, including the death of the infant you mentioned."

"Yes, I had been on duty way too long, and I was coming down with a bug. I shouldn't have gone in that night. I think I misjudged my own frailty." Len would never stop blaming himself.

"So, like the pilots, there were complications that led to the tragedy?" The wise priest could see the process of healing unfolding right in front of him.

"Yes, and I'm not sure if that realization hurts or hinders my own coping ability." Len felt more confused than ever.

"You're entering the dark night of the soul, my son. As humans we all have suffering in our lives that will change us. How we change is our choice. The suffering is not our choice, but how we emerge from the pain is our decision. It is our decision whether we will learn to love more deeply in the future or succumb to the tendency to hate those who made mistakes—which is interesting, since in Lenny's accident the pilots died too."

"That's something I've thought about a great deal. Do the parents of little Timothy have an easier or more difficult challenge because I'm alive? Is it easier to heal when you have a living perpetrator to hate?" Len felt foolish asking what felt like the question of a juvenile, but it was one of the real questions he had been turning over in his mind.

"I think in time, your own experience with having made a fatal mistake will give you a different perspective—and I hope it will help you in your healing. My sense is your enemy here has no face and has no body. When major accidents happen like this, involving an organization like an airline, there are often hidden variables that led to the human error." Father Benjamin had counseled more than one family in situations where human mistakes had resulted in loss of life. He had some idea of how complicated the healing could be.

"When I spoke with a retired investigator," Len said, "he told me that often when pilots make mistakes, it can be attributed to the people running the corporation. So I see where you're going. Like the hospital took some of the responsibility in my case." Len was seeing the parallels again.

"Exactly, and you can get through this without having the name of a specific person to forgive. The larger issue involves accepting that human beings in all walks of life, including in businesses, make mistakes out of unawareness about how their decisions impact others—which is what I think of as unconsciousness."

Len was nodding his head. Father Benjamin continued.

"*Consciousness*, the way I'm using it, means someone realizes all humans are connected, and any business practice where even one life is put at risk for profits—whether it's an airline, a hospital, or any institution—reflects a lack of consciousness. Hospital rules that do not allow a doctor to be on duty longer than is safe would be the same as airline leadership being more concerned with pilots' duty regulations and their practices that risk the lives of human beings."

"So if there is no one to forgive, what do I do with these horrible feelings I have? I want to kill *someone* for allowing my son to die this way."

"At some point you decide to direct that same energy it takes to hate toward a cause or something that helps you feel like you're helping the unconsciousness that is on earth today. Healthy healing has to do with how you use that energy. You know Christ said to 'take up thy cross and follow me.'"

"So my cross is about forgiving a big business for its lack of consciousness?"

"And forgiving yourself for being human. The pilots were human too."

Len knew he needed to get home, but it felt good to have a discussion that led to something other than rehashing the loss of his son and the events that led to it.

"I need to get home. It's all so painful—to go home and to stay away from home." Len withheld the details concerning his earlier impulse to die, which he realized now was yet another way to avoid going home.

"This is a process, and you need to allow yourself time. When you were going through the protracted court case, did you see a professional?" Father Benjamin was hoping to point Len in a direction, for one was sorely needed at this point. Prayer and forgiveness of himself and his own humanness were part of all of this and part of the spiritual journey, and the emotional and psychological side needed to be addressed as well. While tonight, the priest felt, his parishioner had made progress, he knew too well that the process would involve several steps ahead and many steps backward for some time to come. He felt Len was ready to approach his healing with as much intelligence as possible—thus the question about professional help.

"Actually I saw a local psychiatrist. He helped me a lot in coming to terms with my own mistakes and whether or not to remain in my profession. I guess I hadn't considered how he might help me with grief, since what we worked on was centered around my career." Len realized he had not once thought of the psychiatrist since the crash. Maybe it was because Celia's current feelings about therapy had become so negative.

Len stood up to leave. "Father, it's getting late, and Celia is probably ready for me to come home and let her know what I learned from the investigator. I can't thank you enough for your time. You will see us, or at least me, in church again. I just need a little more time. Our son Bruce, however, will be coming with my nieces. Thank God for Celia's sisters. They're the best for helping us with him right now."

With that the men embraced and said good night. Len set off to spend time with Celia and Bruce, feeling determined to follow the advice of Father Benjamin. It made sense to share his grief with his son and wife. They had all lost life as they once knew it, and the three of them would build their future together, no isolation allowed. His moment of hope was slightly tinged with concerns over Celia's situation, but he was determined to help her, Bruce, and himself the best way he could.

Father Benjamin remained in the sanctuary for a while after Len departed. He reflected on their discussion and another he'd had the day after the crash. While he would later share with Len his interactions with Lenny's best friend, Cindy, he was sure now that he had made the right decision by holding back at this point. Len had enough on his mind, and there was nothing to gain by telling a father that his son's best friend had experienced a premonition about the crash and his son's death.

The evening after news of the crash was dominating their entire community, Cindy, who had been a faithful member of the church community her entire life, went to see Father Benjamin. She knew he also knew Lenny and the entire Sawyer family and trusted he would continue to be connected to them all, long after the crash was front-page news. When Cindy came into his office that Saturday evening, she was nearly inconsolable. She described the feeling that had come over her as she'd watched Lenny disappear into the terminal building only twenty-four hours earlier.

Amid sobs and countless tissues, Cindy described the guilt she was experiencing and had since she'd learned about the crash. She was just certain that had she parked the car and run after Lenny, somehow she could have saved him—and maybe all of the passengers and crew. Father Benjamin listened patiently as he thought about his response.

Finally, when he felt Cindy had gotten her story out, Father Benjamin tried as best he could to help her understand that this accident was not her fault. He did his best to help her see that when something this large happens, involving so many deaths, not to mention lives that would be forever changed, there were likely countless others who had similar premonitions—none of which were about prevention.

Father Benjamin explained to her that over time, she would be able to understand that many times a knowing like she had experienced would go a long way in helping her and others adjust to the losses due to the fact that on some level she had known about it before it began. Not that Father Benjamin was a fatalist, but having supported so many parishioners in the aftermaths of similar tragedies, he had begun to believe the hope for long-term healing would be based on looking ahead and not back. The crash had happened. Lives were forever lost, others forever changed, and he would be there for Cindy just as he would for Len, Celia, and all of them.

Dropping to his knees in front of the altar, Father Benjamin prayed for peace for them all and for all of earth. These types of tragedies come into the world in a matter of moments, and many, many years can pass before the losses can be fully integrated.

XXXIX

Meanwhile, Back on the Home Front

Things had not gone well with Celia the night Len met with Howie, Walt, and, unexpectedly, their priest. The girls had finished their work earlier than expected, largely due to Celia's inability to control her alcohol consumption. When Len arrived home, he found Celia passed out on the sofa with two wine bottles on the coffee table in front of her. He saw a note to call Babs. She had apparently picked up Bruce after his play date with a young boy down the street and taken him home with her for the night. Going into the kitchen to phone out of earshot, Len dialed her number hurriedly.

"Babs, I'm sorry I'm so late." Len felt responsible for leaving Babs and Bruce alone for so long. It had not been his intention to do so. He had gotten carried away with his own needs, and now he regretted it.

"No worries, Len. Sheryl and I know you need some time to yourself. You've been with Celia for twenty-four hours nonstop since the accident, and you both need to have some time apart." Babs, like Sheryl, had such a level head, as Celia also once had—before the crash.

"Well, what happened? Did she get drunk pretty early, or was that after you left? I found her passed out when I returned just a few minutes ago." Len was genuinely worried about his wife's drinking, and now it was starting to show.

"After we got together and started organizing the notes and discussing how we wanted to divide them up, she started to get really upset about the crash, and her bitterness increased as she continued to drink. I could see it was not going to get better, so I went ahead and got the number of where Bruce was staying. I knew I needed to keep him with us for the night. He didn't need to see her that way."

"Thank you, Babs. I've been putting off the discussion I need to have with her about her drinking. I was trying to find the right time. But now that we're home and we have to find our way back to some kind of routine, I plan to address it. As soon as she's sobered up tomorrow, I will sit down with her. Let me come by early and pick up Bruce. I'll take him out to breakfast and out for a little while. Then if the girls can watch him tomorrow afternoon, I'll come home and have a talk with her. I do not want Bruce to see any part of her drunken behavior."

"I think that's a good plan. Tonight, before Sheryl and I left, we hid her keys in case she got up and wanted to drive somewhere. They're in the linen closet upstairs in the hallway, under some blankets. We knew she wouldn't look around too much since she was too drunk. Honestly, Len, I had no idea she had such a problem."

"That's the issue. She always liked her white wine, but this is new behavior. She has always taken such pride in her looks and her work. She never got intoxicated like this. She would never have allowed anyone, even me—much less the rest of the world—to see her with her hair uncombed and wearing no makeup. Twice I've seen her go out to get the paper in the morning in her robe, without her slippers, her hair a mess, and smelling of booze from the night before. But passing out like she did tonight with people in the house, even her own family, is new. I promise I will address it. And thanks so much for all you're doing with Bruce. I have no idea what we would do without you and Sheryl."

"Look, Len, we may be a small family, and recently smaller than we were a few weeks ago, but we are family, and we will live through this. We have to raise Bruce and my girls without Lenny, and we're going to do it the best way possible. And getting Celia to straighten up with the alcohol is a great place to start for now. Let me know how tomorrow goes—and remember, I am here for you. There is no hour too early or late to call me." With that the two said good-bye and hung up.

Len spent the next morning with Bruce. Kids were so resilient. Len could not get over how happy his young son was to see him. The girls had taken such good care to protect him and dote on him that most of the time he seemed unaware of anything being much different. With Lenny being in college almost since Bruce was born, as close as they were, it did not seem unusual for him not to see his big brother. Thankfully this made the daily routine for him much more normal—more than for his grieving parents.

After dropping him off with Babs's girls, Len headed home to face Celia. He rehearsed what he planned to say to her. He was surprised when it came out very different from what he had intended.

By the time he returned home, Celia had showered and dressed. Aside from the puffy face and bloodshot eyes from the hard drinking the night before, she looked OK. Gone was the beauty she had enjoyed, but Len was more concerned about her health and their family life than her looks. He tried to start the conversation from the health concern angle.

"You're looking well today, babe," he said, kissing her on the cheek as he entered the kitchen.

"Thanks, darling. I'm sorry I was already asleep when you came back last night. How was your meeting? Did you learn anything new?" She seemed to dismiss her situation from the night before as having turned in early. Len decided not to press.

"No, I didn't learn anything we don't already know. Looks like it will be ruled pilot error in the end. Walt seemed to believe the corporation may have pushed the pilots to land regardless of the weather conditions, hoping they could beat the worst part of the storm."

"Well, you're right. There's no news there. I'm glad the pilots died in the crash. Otherwise I would kill them myself."

Len was unable to control his anger, and the conversation erupted into a full-scale heated argument. Thank God Bruce wasn't there to hear it. Len knew Celia had no way of knowing all that had transpired the night before, including his own review of his experience with making a fatal mistake. But never had he seen this violent side of his wife, despite their many years together.

"People make mistakes, Celia. Did you forget my mistake that robbed a family of their firstborn son?" Len could not hold back his anger.

"I was wondering when you were going to try to explain what happened to my son in the context of your own career. This is not the same, and I won't have you try to make it the same. That airline and those pilots killed my Lenny, and somebody is going to pay!" With that Celia left the kitchen.

Len left the house and placed a call from his car on his cell phone. His frustration and anger at his wife made it impossible to confront her about her drinking. Not today anyway.

XL

Barrett C. Klein, MD

"Dr. Klein's office. Deanne speaking. May I help you?

"Yes, hi, Deanne. This is Len Sawyer.

"Dr. Sawyer. It's been a while." Deanne remembered Len from the many visits in their office a few years earlier.

"It has indeed. Say, is Barrett in the office these days? Or is he spending more time at the hospital clinic? I saw his services had been extended for more outpatient care at the clinic." Len so hoped Barrett was still in private practice. He dreaded seeing someone who would not know him and his past the way Barrett did.

"Well actually he's seeing only a few private patients these days, but I know he would make time for you. He has an opening a week from Wednesday. Will that help?"

Len tried not to show the disappointment he was feeling at having to wait a week to see Barrett, but he knew he was lucky to be able to see him at all with the way his work had grown. He was a well-respected psychiatrist and very involved in supervising new professionals at the new facility at the hospital.

"Next Wednesday will be fine. What time?"

"After your workday? Around five?"

"Actually I'm on leave, so whatever time works will be fine."

"Well, in that case, I have an opening tomorrow at nine o'clock in the morning. I assumed you needed to come after work, the way you did before. But we've just had a cancellation for tomorrow, and I know Doc would want you to have it. Shall I put your name in the slot?"

"That's really good news, Deanne. Tomorrow, then. I will be there." Len had something to look forward to. Living with Celia right now was anything but pleasant.

"Great, Dr. Sawyer, and before I hang up…" Deanne's voice dropped off.

"Yes? Are you there, Deanne?"

"I'm sorry about Lenny. I've been praying for you and your family."

"That's very much appreciated right now. We need all of the prayers we can get. I will pass your sentiments along to Celia."

Len was once again touched by the kindness of people who barely knew them. If only Celia could be open to all of the goodness in the world, maybe she could get past this angry behavior, fueled by the alcohol, and be her old self again.

With that the phone call ended. Len went back to Babs's house and retrieved Bruce. For Len, dinner and a movie with his son were in order. He would check with Celia to see if she would be willing to get out of the house. He knew she would likely decline. But at least he would keep trying. The last thing he felt like doing was sitting through the newest animated movie at the neighborhood theater. He had a son to raise and one to grieve. And doing both as best he could was what he had to do right now. The words of wisdom from Father Benjamin played through his mind.

The next morning Len drove to Barrett's office with many thoughts going through his head. He had dropped Bruce off with Babs's girls. They were planning all sorts of fun things for the day. Bruce did not seem to notice that once again his mother was sleeping in, which was the new expression used to sensitively describe being too hungover to rise before noon.

Taking the elevator to the fourth floor, Len turned left toward the office he had spent so much time in several years ago. After the baby died and the malpractice suit got going, Len had gone to Barrett at the suggestion of one of the attorneys who was working the case. Barrett had a reputation in the medical community as a straight shooter, with a special place in his heart for docs who were being sued.

Although reluctant at first, Len often wondered how he would have made it without that weekly visit to a fellow professional who turned out to be a great friend in the end. Now Len was glad he and Barrett had followed the code of ethics and ended the relationship when the appointments ended. While he felt they were great friends, and they even attended the same church, they never socialized after the weekly visits ended. Now once again they could resume the doctor-patient relationship untainted by personal friendship.

Deanne greeted Len as he walked in the brightly lit office, decorated with an expensive European flair. The dark wood of the furniture was warm and inviting along with the jewel tones of the velvet fabric on the chairs and sofa. The walls were hung with prints of various scenes from Eastern Europe. Len sat in the same seat he had sat in so many other times. He could not escape the irony of his situation. Would Barrett be the right professional for him now? He was wearing a completely different set of shoes this time as a client. Funny, this time his raw emotions caused him to feel more like a true patient instead of the business client he felt he had been in the previous round.

The door opened, and Barrett stood there casually dressed in one of his usual pastel-colored sweater vests and dark-gray trousers, smiling and holding out his hand. Barrett had a medium muscular build. Len noticed that the psychiatrist had lost a good bit of hair since their last visit. But the sparkle in his brown eyes, covered by rimless spectacles, still gave him that unmistakable look of a kind and knowing man.

Closing the door, Barrett turned the handshake into a warm embrace. Len's eyes filled with tears as he felt the warmth of the older doctor's arms. The embrace for an instant reminded him of Leonard Sr.'s warm touch, which he missed so much. Come to think of it, Barrett was probably closer to his father's age than Len had realized—maybe only ten years his junior. Len tried to regain control over his raw emotions one more time.

Barrett sat in his chocolate-brown leather wingback chair while Len took the black leather overstuffed chair across from him. A small dark-wood table bearing only a box of tissues stood between them. Barrett clasped his hands together in his lap and leaned forward.

"Len, I've kept up with the news about the crash and your son Lenny's death. There are simply no words to express my sorrow for what you and your family are going through. What a horrible tragedy the crash has been. Mary and I hope you received the notification for the donation we sent to the charity that was mentioned in Lenny's obituary."

"Yes, we did." Len apologized that the thank-you notes had not made it out of the house yet. "Celia hasn't been able to do very much, and her sisters are handling the notes. And they both work, so you know how it goes."

"I do indeed, and the acknowledgment is not necessary. I just wanted to know if it made it as we've heard nothing from the charity. These things take time. But let's not waste time on formalities. Let's talk about you and the family and how things are going for you."

Barrett was still leaning forward with the intense yet soft gaze that was always such a validation to Len. It was like Len and his problems were the most important issues in the entire world and all that mattered right then. Len felt safe and nurtured when in this professional's presence.

"Well, it's funny. I thought I was doing OK, but I had a pretty bad meltdown a night or so ago. I lose track of time these days. Anyway, I wound up at the church. Father Benjamin found me crying and suggested I see someone professionally. I don't think I'm holding up too well." Len hated to tell him what was going on with Celia.

"Len, if one of my children died, I am certain I would not be handling things any better than you, nor would any parent." Barrett's tone was that of a fellow parent. He did not sound like a psychiatrist at that moment. This parental connection was comforting to Len.

"I guess if I had only myself to think of right now, I could deal with these feelings of being out of control. But that's not the case. I need to keep it together for Bruce and Celia. They need me to be the family leader more than ever right now. And I am not doing too well." Reaching for a tissue, Len was openly crying as he finished his statement.

"Len, look, what you need right now is to give yourself permission to be where you are and feel what you feel. You need a place where you can go and lose it on a regular basis. Before, when we met together routinely, I could see your movement forward when you couldn't. This is a different kind of crisis, but the approach of processing your feelings on a regular and predictable basis is what is called for right now, just as it was when you went through the malpractice suit several years ago."

"Funny, Barrett, but the parallel between the two situations is what caused me to fall apart after the memorial service. I was able to block out the Waterses and their kid's death for the first few weeks, but now that I'm back home in reality, I can't stop thinking about the irony of it all." Len sat back, feeling a little lighter. The elephant he had been silently wrestling up until he'd seen Father Benjamin was out on the table, in the light—now three men instead of one could deal with it.

"Len, there is no way you can come through the loss of your son and have a healthy adjustment to his loss without remembering all of your past. We know healthy mourning brings all past losses into the light, not just the latest one. You can't integrate the loss of Lenny without resolving other issues around the loss of the Waters baby and all issues around previous losses."

"Barrett, you were so helpful to me during the lawsuit. I don't know how I could have made it without your insight, your wisdom, and quite frankly your knowledge of the medical profession and how the whole legal process works. But you've never lost a kid. I see you with your family in church every Sunday. You and Mary have how many kids? Six, last I counted. All due respect, what you know about loss pertains to court cases and defensive posturing and how a doc can survive the system. And maybe what you learned in school in a class on grief. What the hell do you know about losing a kid?" Len's emotions intensified as he finished his statement.

Neither man spoke for what seemed like a very long time. Sitting silently now, Len reflected on how inadequate both he and Celia realized they had been in trying to help other parents who had lost children. Len was starting to believe that guilt about how she had dismissed other parents' grief over the loss of their child was a big part of Celia's drinking. She was staying drunk to avoid feeling her own pain. He wondered when, if ever, she would grieve the loss of Lenny. He was having a hard enough time, and he was sober!

Barrett settled back in his comfortable leather chair, pensive and cautious. This was the moment no psychiatrist liked. It was a decision point. The question always came up and had to be weighed carefully. How much should one share with a patient about one's own life and one's own experience with loss? This was always tricky. If he said too much, the sessions became about him and his pain. If he did not say enough, his true depth of understanding would go unrecognized, untapped, and that would be the greater loss. He decided to go for it.

"Len, we have known each other for many years now. But there are things you don't know about my life that have some relevance here." Barrett took a sip of herbal tea from a black cup bearing a gold-colored Star of David. Something about his tone let Len know that what he was about to share was profound. "You know I am German Catholic?"

"Well, I know we attend the same church, and your last name appears to be German." Len was curious as to where this was leading.

"The *C* in my name is the first letter of my Jewish mother's surname, Cohen." Barrett took his time to share the heaviest part of his message. Len did not interrupt his measured speaking. "My mother was orphaned after World War II. The youngest of seven children, she was the only survivor of a very large Jewish family. She escaped to this country with an American couple before her second birthday. They later adopted her as their own. She grew up without any living relatives. All of my mother's family died in the camps. So family loss is my heritage. I have grown up with its indelible mark on my soul."

Now it was Len's time to become pensive. After a few moments, he spoke.

"Barrett, now I'm the one who's sorry. So sorry for your loss—I mean losses. So you and Mary have six children for a reason. You've been creating a large family to have what so many of us take for granted." Len spoke softly and was now experiencing true compassion for the man he had come to rely on for his own emotional support. "I appreciate your sentiment, but as a physician you know I share my story only so we can get to what will help you. The fact that my mother grew up without her parents, siblings, aunts, uncles, cousins, or any family due to the state of the world at that time has greatly influenced how I live my life—and greatly influenced my decision to make my living the way I do." The older physician met his patient's glance head on and continued.

"I share this with you so you know that I *get* loss and how unresolved grief can harm generations to come. The fact that I am able to help physicians with many issues including living through malpractice suits without succumbing to their addictions, losing their families, and the like is but one of the ways I help people who feel powerless and helpless in the world today. Though you may know only part of my professional life, I can assure you I see my share of others who are struggling with grief."

After a few moments of silence, Len finally spoke. "I'm growing accustomed to feeling shame. And I certainly feel it now." Len looked down at his mismatched socks. Nothing seemed to matter anymore, including how he chose his clothes.

"And knowing what you're feeling and *why* is a big part of getting past feelings that do not serve you any time, but especially at a time like this." Barrett tried to make his point without sounding judgmental or as though he was admonishing his patient.

"So what do I do, and where to do I go with this? With the lawsuit there was always an end in front of me. When the case was settled and I made my decision to stay with the practice of medicine, I dealt with my feelings of guilt by resolving to become a better physician. I took what I had learned with your help and got on with my life. But now, this is different."

"Different how? Of course I can answer that from my perspective, but there is something to be gained by your articulating *the how* that is necessary in your going forward instead of being lost in the spiral of grief and shame so many parents get caught up in."

"Different." Len leaned back and thought for a moment before he continued. "Different in that so much of my identity was built around being a physician, husband, father of two boys, et cetera, et cetera."

"It is the 'et cetera, et cetera' that you need to examine. You are a physician and husband, and we know you fathered two boys. Those are facts. However, one son is alive, and one is no longer on earth. You must learn to grieve the one who is gone while at the same time find energy and time to raise the one who is still with you." Barrett stopped at the look of surprise that appeared on Len's face.

"That's exactly what Father Benjamin said. And I do get that. I just don't know how."

"Father Benjamin and I can help with that. And as time goes by, you'll find others who have a lot to share that will help you. But you must be open to it." Barrett paused before continuing with his message.

"Loss like what you have experienced will make you contract and become smaller, or it will enlarge you spiritually. The choice to grow instead of shrink starts now. It begins the moment you become aware that you have a choice." Barrett's words resonated deeply with Len. It was like he had heard about choice before. He just did not know where or when.

"But I feel I got over the mistakes I made with the Waters baby. How do I get over the loss of Lenny?" The anxiety had come back and embarrassed Len when his question revealed it in the midst of such profound wisdom.

"Len, I'm going to teach you a new vocabulary. You need some new models for healing that will help you talk to yourself in a way that moves you forward. Ideas like getting over the loss of your son or how time heals all wounds and so many other trite terms and phrases will keep you in that spiral I referred to earlier. These ideas keep you expecting something to just happen, and when it doesn't the disappointment keeps you caught up in emotion. The word you're looking for is *transcendence*, a term that better describes our best outcome from traumatic loss."

"What does that mean? In relation to trauma?" Len felt like a gradeschool boy.

"It means we grow beyond the loss. And that takes a commitment to invest the time to do our grief work. When Lenny died in the crash, life as you knew it died too. And yet you are left here on earth, still living the old life—but you can choose to build a new one if you want to. *Transcendence* means you are able to mourn the loss of Lenny while living out the rest of your life in a way that does not punish the people who still need you on earth. Transcendence does not happen overnight, and it does not happen automatically. You first have to surrender and ask for help." Keeping direct eye contact with his patient, Barrett continued. "You have to continue to reach out, just as you did when you went to church and called out to God, talked to Father Benjamin, and called me for this appointment."

"I hear what you're saying. But I think you're giving me too much credit. I seriously wanted to end my life the night I went to church and called out to God. And yet, as you say, there are those who need me who are still here. So I went to the one place where I think I may still be able to be with Lenny someday. Even when my parents died, I never felt so desperate. The idea of there being a heaven never held much meaning for me. But with Lenny's death, it now does. I do believe he is alive somewhere, along with my folks. I just don't know where that is."

"Len, loss like you're describing makes the discussion of heaven relevant like no other time in one's life. You are experiencing a crisis of faith that up until now was only rhetoric." Barrett paused for another sip of tea before he continued. "When a loss of anyone significant takes place, and certainly the loss of a child, humans are faced with the choice to believe in something beyond earth or not. Once we make the decision to believe and follow our faith, we begin to receive the energy and strength we need to carry on. And the one thing that can make life on earth possible in the face of such tragedy is love. I thank God every day that my mother chose love instead of hating the Nazis who killed her family. She chose to love the family who adopted her. If she hadn't, I am certain my five brothers and sisters and I never would have been on earth. You know love and hate cannot exist in your soul simultaneously."

Barrett had summed it up so well in such a short amount of time. Len did not feel better or even relieved, but he did feel understood. He knew Barrett was right—others had been where he was and had made it. Who would have known this psychiatrist personally knew so much about loss? If all of those people from the war went on to create new lives, surely he could. Being in the presence of someone who exuded healthy healing from so much loss gave Len a greater sense of hope.

"Let me get Deanne to set up another appointment. For now do you want to see me a couple of times a week, and then we can go to the standing one time a week, like before, for as long as you need?" Barrett knew Len was fragile. He wondered what was going on at home. Len had not even mentioned his wife or his marriage. Barrett knew too well the fragility of the parental relationship in the first few years following the loss of a child.

"Yes, let's do that. I want to return to work after another week off. I still need to help Celia settle some things before I go back. I'll work with Deanne to get it all set up and the billing. I can't thank you enough. And again, I apologize for my insensitivity around your own family's pain." Len had a lot to process, and this new information had certainly opened his eyes to the reality of what other humans had found a way to live beyond—to transcend.

"No need to apologize. I just knew you needed to know that so many others around you are suffering or have suffered. Having compassion for others and their losses is a major part of how we enlarge our whole frame of reference about our pain in the context of the world's pain. Feeling for others is an important part of healing, as we integrate our losses into our new lives and move forward."

"*Integration* is another new word for me. I never thought about that as part of the grief discussion. You're right; I need a new vocabulary for life experiences I never expected to have."

"Well, I had the opportunity to witness healthy grieving all of my life. Even though my mother was a practicing Catholic like her adoptive parents and siblings, she found a way to honor her Jewish heritage. I grew up knowing many of the prayers, and we celebrated Jewish holidays and practiced much of the ritual. The rabbi was as much a guest in her home as the parish priest. That is an example of the enlargement I spoke about. There are so many ways that our hearts can expand and allow others in. Your involving Father Benjamin and me is a great start.

With that the men shook hands and the session ended—for that day, anyway.

XLI

Confronting the Secret

Len spent the last week of his vacation helping Celia with all that needed to be done as part of completing Lenny's life on earth. Because they were together each day, Bruce was able to stay home and enjoy his parents, his pets, and his toys, plus a trip to the club pool each afternoon. Soon enough kindergarten would start, and he would enter a routine he was looking forward to. Fortunately Celia had registered him for school long before their lives had turned upside down.

While Celia continued to drink heavily, starting as early as breakfast some days with a bloody Mary and moving on to white wine by early afternoon, she had not passed out since that one night after Len's meeting with Howie and his father. Len felt responsible for that. Since the crash it had been the only time that he had left her alone for so long. He was already thinking about what to do once he went back to work. Most nights he was home in time for dinner, but he was talking to Babs and Sheryl about those odd nights when he would need to stay late or return to the hospital due to a delivery.

Learning from his past experience, and now with the grief he and his family faced, Len knew he had to spend more time at home. His plan included sharing much more of his practice and patients with other professionals. Len was determined to have a more rounded life with his family. He wondered if that would be part of his transcendence from the trauma and the loss of his son.

Three days after his first visit to Barrett, he went in for another. He looked forward to the sessions and trusted that visits with the wise doctor would be a major part of his healing. He felt that seeing things from a broader perspective and learning the new vocabulary they discussed earlier was helping prevent him from drowning in emotion. Some days he did better than others in managing his emotions. Sometimes his emotions got the better of him no matter what he tried to tell himself.

Len was having trouble sleeping, and each day he awakened with a sense of dread in his stomach. Once fully awake he would have to accept yet again what the feeling was about. His son had died in a horrible plane crash as a result of a senseless mistake.

Settling back in the black leather chair, Len again experienced the sense of safety and understanding that meetings with Barrett always engendered.

"So tell me what is happening." Barrett leaned forward, with his hands clasped in his lap, as was nearly always his posture when beginning a session.

"I'm getting ready to go back to work after having been off for a little more than a month. Honestly, I know it will be good for me. My staff and colleagues have been so supportive, and surprisingly many of the condolence notes we've received have been from patients and the medical community. I know it will be good for me."

"I'm glad to hear that. I'm sensing you have a concern about doing what's good for you. Are you worried about Celia and Bruce?"

"Yes, I am, frankly. I am very worried about Celia. My sisters-in-law and I have Bruce covered. You may remember that Celia has two sisters—Babs, who is a child psychologist, and Sheryl, who is a high-school counselor. Between them and Babs's twin daughters, who are juniors in high school, and my mother's retired younger sister, Janelle, I have family care for Bruce under control now and after he begins kindergarten in a few days."

"I like that his care right now is largely coming from family. Children need to see as much continuity as possible all of the time, and especially when the death of a sibling or parent interrupts their lives." Barrett validated the plan his patient was laying out before him.

"I do feel very grateful for the support of our family. But Barrett, it's Celia. She is not adjusting well. I mean, I know it's too soon for a lot of things to be normal again, but she's really starting to worry me." Len's genuine concern for his wife was obvious. He held back the facts about the alcohol, yet he knew it needed to be addressed if he was going to get any advice on how to help her.

"Len, I'm going to repeat something we touched on last time. Celia will never be the same, not any more than you will. You both have lost a child. You don't have the same life. Whatever was normal before is never going to be normal again. Losing a child or any close loved one causes us to redefine ourselves, and that takes time. Many people refer to this process as creating a new normal, but I don't endorse those words. There is simply nothing normal about losing one's child, regardless of how it happens. This is about healing. And healing is about surrendering to what has happened and embracing the new life that will flow in if we are open to it, as we discussed last time." Barrett knew he would need to repeat this message many times in the coming weeks.

"But Barrett, Celia is asleep. She is self-medicating with liquor to the point where I'm seriously concerned about the long-term impact on her health and her relationship with Bruce, not to mention our marriage. It's like she's absent in this entire grief process." There. He had gotten in out. The secret that he had been trying so hard to hide.

"I see." Barrett leaned back in his chair, nodding his head as he pondered the newly exposed complication to this family's grief. "Tell me more about what's going on with Celia."

"From the beginning she's made Lenny's death and the crash about her own inadequacies. She is obsessed with her guilt over having been a counselor with so little knowledge of grief. It's true she judged our neighbors whose son died in Iraq. She openly criticized them for what she felt was protracted mourning. And along with her guilt, she is filled with rage toward the airline. She was so rude to the employees who tried to help us when we went to Omaha that I was constantly apologizing for her." Len felt relieved to get his true feelings out.

"And what about her own counseling practice?" Barrett had seen this before. Too many well-meaning counselors learned about grief for the first time after they lost a close family member. Unlike Barrett, who grew up with loss as a part of his life, Celia's experience of counseling about loss was pretty much what she thought bereavement was about and what she read in her studies at university.

"She gave up her practice as the first order of business, right after Lenny's memorial service. And she does not think any amount of grief counseling can help her now. I feel so helpless. She knows I'm seeing you twice a week right now and that these visits are sustaining me."

"You know, this is not unusual. It's almost predictable that when this type of traumatic loss occurs, many people will question their faith in God, their professions, and almost everything they have ever held sacred. It's part of the surrender process that is necessary for building the new life after the loss."

"Barrett, I can see what you're saying, but Celia is drinking so much she's not able to move past her guilt and rage. And I don't know how to break through that cycle that has set in during the past few weeks."

"What about the support group?"

"What support group?"

"I received an e-mail a couple of days ago that one of the local counseling groups is holding a support group for families from Cleveland whose loved ones died in the crash. Did you not receive it?"

"No. Celia has made it clear to everyone that we are not going to meet others who lost family members in the accident."

"Well, I think you might try to get her to attend this group if at all possible. After our session I'll forward the e-mail to you."

"Make sure you use my business e-mail. Celia has been monitoring our personal e-mails at home as part of her aggression toward everyone who's trying to reach out to her."

"I can do that. Len, give her some time. Some people cope like this initially, and then sooner or later, they realize how much they need others. I think you need to try reasoning with Celia, and then if that doesn't work and the support group doesn't work, we'll go to what's next. But for now I want to know more about you and what's going on with you."

Len told Barrett about his sleep problems. He declined sleeping pills or any medications, which he had taken before when being treated by Barrett. He knew going back to work and getting back into his exercise routine with renewed vigor would help him more than drug therapy.

"Tell me about your dreams." Barrett stroked his chin with his fingers, the way he often did when opening up a deeper dialogue.

"I'm not dreaming. If I am, I don't remember when I wake up in the morning."

"You are dreaming; you just don't remember. If you could remember your dreams, it might help us process your deepest emotions right now. I respect your concern for Celia and Bruce, but you must have some time for yourself and your own grief."

"I wish I could dream. I would love to dream of Lenny, but I don't know how to make that happen."

"Tonight try to spend some time in meditation before you go to sleep. Keep a pad and pen beside the bed or in the bathroom, so you can write down anything that comes to you in the night. And don't use your iPad or phone or any digital device. Old-fashioned reading is more relaxing for your brain."

"OK, I'll try it."

Len and Barrett spent the rest of the time talking about what the investigation was showing and the way Len continued to feel about the pilots. As the fifty minutes came to an end, Barrett made a note to discuss the concerns over Celia's drinking in the next session, providing no other challenge became more urgent.

XLII

Struggling to Embrace New Life

Len received the e-mail from Barrett about the support group on his smartphone in his professional inbox. He shared the details with Celia after Bruce went to bed that night.

"Hon, Barrett says many times this sort of group helps people. Even if they're seeing a private grief counselor."

"Research clearly shows that support groups do not help everyone," Celia responded from a clinical perspective—for the first time since the crash.

"I know you're right, but I want to see you do something besides sit in the house each day. I'm starting work on Monday, and I'm going back to the gym. Plus I'm seeing Barrett regularly. I need to know you're going to do something for you." Len touched his wife's hand as he spoke his mind.

Sitting beside her husband on the sofa in the family room, Celia took a sip from her wine glass. "I know I need to do something, but I just don't know what. I feel guilty about doing anything without Lenny. I keep thinking about what we would be doing if he had not died. I would be helping him get his things ready for going off to med school—all the things I did when he went off to college each fall." Celia's tone was genuinely sad.

"Celia, look. You have to accept the fact that Lenny is gone, and there is nothing more we can do for him. Thank God we have a son left to put our energy and attention into."

"I got Bruce ready for kindergarten in the early summer. I bought his uniforms, registered him, and there's nothing to do. His schedule is full.

I like that everyone else is taking over for me with him right now, driving him everywhere and keeping him occupied. I feel so inadequate as a mother. I know I'm not good for him or anyone right now."

"Don't be so hard on yourself. He is fine, and soon enough you'll step back into a routine. But Celia, there is one thing we need to discuss, and now is as good a time as any."

"And what is that?" She poured herself another glass.

Len pointed to the bottle. "It's that. The drinking has to stop."

"I have a couple of glasses of wine with dinner. When did that become a problem? I've always enjoyed wine with dinner, and so did you. I noticed you aren't drinking now. Sooner or later, I thought, you would start having wine again. Actually I don't like drinking alone."

"Well, you'll have to get used to it, because when I feel bad like I do right now, the last thing I want is a depressant in the form of booze."

"I am not drinking hard booze. White wine each day is not like hard liquor."

"It's not what you're drinking but that you are drinking every single day, and it's more than a couple of glasses. You're lying to yourself. I've seen how many bottles are in the trash each day, and it frightens me." There. Len had finally told her his true feelings.

"OK, if you think I'm drinking too much, I'll cut back. I'll have one with dinner each night and let that be enough." Celia was sober enough to feel that her husband was scolding her, and she did not like it.

"That would make me feel better, and I think it might help you regain your desire to get out of the house. And would you give the support group a try? I'll forward you the e-mail, and I'll go with you."

"I guess it wouldn't hurt to go at least once. So yes, I will go with you."

Len went to sleep that night with a pad and pen by the bed. He drifted to sleep remembering early childhood memories of Lenny. But he remembered no dreams the following morning.

XLIII

The Visits

Early the next morning Bruce joined his father at the breakfast counter. Still wearing his ninja pajamas, his height made him appear older than his age. He was already growing taller than the pajamas Celia had purchased earlier in the summer. Len reached over and hugged him, planting a kiss on his cheek.

"Dad, can I tell you something that you promise you won't tell Mom about?"

This type of lead-in to a child's request was always tricky for a parent. However, under the current stressful circumstances, Len nodded.

"I saw Lenny again this morning. He is not dead." Bruce looked directly into his father's eyes as he spoke.

"Again? You mean you dreamed of Lenny again." Len didn't know how to respond to his son's apparent confusion.

"No, it wasn't a dream. When I first wake up each morning, Lenny is sitting on my bed. We talk, and then he says good-bye and goes away. I'm awake, and he looks like he's fine while he's with me."

"What do you talk about?" Len found himself fascinated by his young son's comments.

"He tells me he didn't die in the crash. He tells me he's in heaven and that we'll be together again someday. He tells me he loves me, that everything is fine, and that I should do good in school and make you and Mom proud of me."

Not wanting to be negative about his young son's experience, Len decided to take a different approach. "I'm glad that you see Lenny and that he's showing you that he's fine. Did you try discussing this with Mom?"

"Yes, the first time it happened I told her right away. But she told me I was just dreaming and shouldn't tell anyone about it, not even you. I know it's real, and I wanted to share with you because I thought it would make you happy."

"Well, it does indeed. I like to know that both you and Lenny are OK and that you are connected, even if he can't be with Mom and me in person right now." Bruce's reaction confirmed that Len's response was the right one.

"Dad, can I ask you something else?"

"Of course you can. You can always ask me anything. What is it?"

"Do you believe people come back after they die? I mean to live here again?"

"I never really thought about it. Why do you ask?"

"Remember when you came home from the crash and Aunt Sheryl told you about the crow that came the first day after you left and several days after?"

"Yes, I do." Len had wondered if and when this subject would come up again.

"Well, I read about the crow, and it has to do with people coming back to life. Like when people die, they aren't finished. That people come back. Aunt Sheryl and I read about *carnation* or something, and I liked it. It made me feel good to know that Lenny might come back to stay one day. And then he does each morning, but then he leaves."

This was one morning that Len appreciated Celia's new habit of sleeping later than her routine would have allowed before the crash.

"Bruce, since Lenny died, Mom and Dad are learning a lot of new things. And you are too. I'm talking to someone regularly who's helping me with some of what I'm learning, and I'm trying to adjust to how things are now. Mom may be talking to someone soon too. Would you like to do that? Talk to someone who helps young children talk about things like this after someone they love dies?"

"Dad, I like to talk about Lenny. I miss him, and I'm glad he comes to my room. I hate that airline that killed him." Bruce began to sob.

Len knew his little son had not learned much about the subject of hate before now. Len had a feeling he was repeating some words he had heard from his mother—words that would only harm him as time went on if not handled properly right now.

"Son, you know the crash was an accident. No one meant to hurt Lenny or all of those other people. And it's OK to be angry right now. Just know that you'll get past this time in your life. We all will. Would it be OK if I asked Aunt Babs for the name of someone you can talk with about Lenny and whatever else you want to talk about?"

"Yes, I would like to talk about Lenny and how he might come back someday, more than just early in the morning."

Len took out Bruce's favorite box of cereal and milk from the refrigerator. He served his son breakfast, all the while pondering how different everything was now. Reincarnation was not anything he had ever imagined talking to his children about, and certainly not at such a young age.

Getting Bruce dressed and into the day of play and family fun felt right to Len that morning. After he had delivered him safely to his first activity, he put in a call to Babs's office.

Babs was delighted to get the call from Len. "Of course. I have just the right person to see Bruce. She's great with children and trauma. Let me get back to you. She'll want to see you and Celia first and then meet with Bruce. After that she'll decide how to progress on appointments.

XLIV

Len Gets More Education

Len knew that bringing Celia along to meet the child trauma specialist would not help matters. But he had to tell her about it and what was going on with Bruce. Babs had managed to secure an appointment before he returned to his practice full time.

The evening before he met with the therapist, he broached the subject. "Hon, I know Bruce told you about his dreams of Lenny." He knew this term would cause less pushback on Celia's behalf.

"Yes, he mentioned it." Celia was drinking sparkling water with lime, or so her husband thought. Gratefully Len had noticed the glass of white wine was no longer a constant in her hand.

"Well, I talked to Babs about the dreams and my concern that Bruce might need some support from a child specialist for a few weeks." Len tried to avoid the subject of how Bruce was repeating words he had likely learned from his mother.

"Bruce is fine. You know how resilient children are. I think you're overreacting. I know what to look for as indications that he's not coping well. You should know that too."

"Of course you do. But I also know sometimes parents who are grieving themselves are not always as aware of things as another professional who is evaluating a child's adjustment." Len tried to take a soft approach rather than tell her his true concerns.

"Who is this person?"

"Someone Babs knows and highly recommends." Len was surprised the discussion was going as well as it seemed to be.

"OK. It can't hurt, I suppose, as long as I don't have to go."

Len dropped Bruce off at Babs's house for the twins to watch him while he met with the therapist. Later he would pick up Bruce for his own first session.

Len was immediately impressed with Dr. Caroline when he met her. She was young to have earned a PhD, or at least she sure looked not a day past her midtwenties, likely due to her petite frame. Dr. C, as he would later call her, had short cropped hair and green eyes that sparkled when she spoke. Her office was bright and cheerful and painted with yellows and greens. Children's books, toys, and dolls were dotted about the room, and a giant sandbox took up several feet of space in front of a large window.

"Babs gave me a few details about the trauma that has taken place in your family's life. I am so sorry about your son's death. I've been following news of the accident in the media, and I can't even imagine what you and your family are going through."

"Thank you so much for your kind words. It's been harder than anything I could ever have imagined. I don't think I had any idea how difficult this type of tragedy could be in a family's life."

"Let me say I appreciate the fact that you're bringing your five-year-old son in to see me. It is possible he's coping fine, and you may not need to bring him in for more than a visit or two, but at least I can give you and Mrs. Sawyer my professional opinion about how I think he's coping. And I can give you some pointers on what to look for in case problems arise later. Children really adapt well to trauma if their parents and family give them the attention and support they need."

"Yes, my wife is a therapist, and while adults were her specialty, she had the same thoughts about children and resiliency with regard to trauma."

"I can imagine I would have to take some time off from my practice if one of my children died. When you said adults *were* her specialty, did you mean she's no longer practicing?"

"Actually it's more complicated than that. I do think she just needs time off as we work through the loss of our son. And that brings me to my biggest concern and what caused me to ask Babs for a referral." Len wanted to get off the subject of Celia and onto his major concern.

"Do you mind if I make some notes?" Caroline moved over to her desk and retrieved her iPad.

"Please, go ahead." With that Len explained about the dreams, saving the subjects of the crow, reincarnation, and all that was on his mind about his young son for later.

"I see." Caroline put her iPad down. "What your son is experiencing is quite common with young children. Children of Bruce's age are too young to have absorbed adult views and ideas of death communication and encounters with deceased relatives. Researchers on brain development help us understand that the younger mind, which is more playful, is also more open to spiritual phenomena. And as the brain develops and the verbal side becomes more dominant, children do at some point become more tuned in to what is happening around them than they once were in the nonverbal world, but they may be at a loss."

Caroline went on with what she was saying, despite the quizzical look on Len's face.

"A few years ago, several children about your son's age were playing in a schoolyard when a very large jetliner was descending rapidly toward the earth. It was such a tragedy, as the pilots had no control over the jet, and it crashed in a wooded field a few miles from the school. All onboard died, and it was well over a hundred people. I'm telling you about this as an example of how children have experiences that adults often do not, and it's one of those things that defies explanation." Caroline stopped for a moment, looked off into the distance, and continued, almost like she was remembering a scene in her own head.

"What was remarkable was that a teacher who was with the children later told the parents and other teachers that the children had pointed up at the crashing jet and screamed with joy, 'Look at all of the angels around the plane!' The teacher looked up and saw nothing but the plane falling quickly to the ground."

"I see what you mean by loss. I wish I could see angels and could have a visit from my son." Len was intrigued by what he was learning and feeling envious of Bruce and the openness of the children she was describing.

"What I mean is that the open, trusting, playful nature of a child has many positives, don't you agree?"

"Well, sure, but my son, at five years, is asking questions about reincarnation and the life cycle. Don't you think that's pretty young to be thinking about things like that?" Before he knew it, he had told Caroline about the crow and how Bruce had asked Aunt Sheryl to help him research the subject on the Internet.

"Dr. Sawyer, I know you're a very educated physician, so hope you won't be offended as I speak more about some topics that most adults don't know about. Most child experts believe that around the age of five, children are beginning to have some understanding that death is real. Prior to that age, many children will not believe death is permanent, rather that just as their favorite cartoon character sustains all sorts of injuries and comes back, so will a real human. Children of advanced intelligence, like young Bruce, are likely to understand a good bit more than their parents realize."

"Both my sons were reading at an early age, so you're probably right—there's no telling what Bruce is aware of in many areas." Len looked away as he thought of times Bruce had been alone with Celia and may have heard or witnessed things far more serious than a discussion on reincarnation.

"What matters, Dr. Sawyer, is what you say to him about all of his experiences right now. I can ask some questions about his dreams and what he's thinking about, and I can let you and Mrs. Sawyer know if there's anything you should be concerned about. But the one thing I can advise, if I may?" Caroline paused.

"Yes, please, go on." Len gestured with his hand.

"Validate your son's experiences. Encourage him to talk about what happens when he dreams of Lenny. If he talks of being in his brother's presence, ask him how that feels and what they talk about. My suspicion is you'll find these experiences are positive and help him avoid the depression that loss can often bring into a young child's life, which you may not even be aware of until much later."

"OK. I'll let my wife know what you've said. And just so you know, he does not think he's dreaming of Lenny. He says he is with Lenny and that it feels really good to him."

"I suspected this is the case, and I'm glad to hear that he gets comfort from feeling he's with his brother. I can tell you that I wish more adults were open to experiences like Bruce is having. Our grief process might be improved as well." Caroline felt her young client's father was receiving her message well. "And Dr. Sawyer, when you have an intelligent child who asks questions, answer him as best you can. If he wants to get on the Internet and explore a concept, do it with him. He's young, but he's not too young to understand that some things in life are mysteries and cannot be harmful to explore. Soon enough he'll be caught up in playing with others who will likely be more interested in games, sports, and activities more related to being children. But try to let him know there is nothing wrong with being curious about questions that come to his mind. You want to avoid causing him to feel there's something wrong with him because he's naturally curious. Your son needs to be validated right now. People are never too old or too young to need validation."

"I have one more concern." Len could not leave without discussing the anger issue. "My wife is pretty angry at the airline. I have a different way of viewing professional mistakes due to my own life experience. I hope you can help Bruce with that too. I'm afraid he may be picking up some of her feelings, which I'm concerned will be a problem down the road if not addressed now."

"OK. Sure. I'll look for that. Some of it may be natural, but you're right. Children often mimic a parent's behavior in order to feel closer to them. I'll give you a report on that too."

Len had a good feeling about Dr. Caroline, and he found her last statement interesting. It was entirely possible that Bruce was doing anything he could to get his mother's attention. She was so unavailable, emotionally and otherwise.

"Dr. Sawyer, I just want to remind you that what matters for children of any age when a sibling or parent dies is for them to experience as much continuity and connection as possible."

"Other professionals I'm talking to are saying that same thing. Can you say more about that?"

"Well, whatever was going to happen in his life before his brother died should still happen. Who he played with, spent time with, and enjoyed being with should remain in his life. He lost his brother, and that is enough loss. Try to keep any other changes in his life to a minimum—the ones you can control, I mean."

"Ok, I'm working on that. My challenge has been to manage my emotions well enough to see that I put him first as often as I can. Some days I'm tempted to stay in bed, with the covers over my head." Len smiled as he stood up to leave. Just as he felt about his time spent with Barrett, he felt validated by Dr. Caroline and that much of what he was doing with Bruce instinctively was right on. He now had something else to feel good about.

XLV

The Power of Compassion

Returning to work full time felt right to Len in the fifth week after Lenny's death. What he was not prepared for was the number of people who had themselves experienced trauma and loss in their personal lives who now wanted to share with him. In the first few weeks after he returned to work, he learned more about other doctors, nurses, and all of the medical team members' experiences with grief than he ever would have imagined.

Interestingly, when he had been dealing with the malpractice situation, no one had come forward to share about their personal lives. Len wondered if his peers had any idea how hard that legal case had been on him. And yet when he stopped to think about it, the sympathy was probably reserved for the parents of the infant who died. Now, having lost a son to someone else's mistake, it made perfect sense to him that he had received so little support during his court case.

Something else was dawning on him. In the Waters case, he'd made a mistake that cost parents to lose a son. He was humiliated, and his self-esteem was nearly demolished in the aftermath of the court case, the media coverage, and all that went with it. But Len still went home to his family each night. None of *his* personal connections were lost. He realized now that this had been a business situation for him only.

He found himself wondering about the families of the pilots. Both had been young professionals with children Bruce's age and slightly older. Their spouses were left to raise the children without their mother and father. And what about the parents of the pilots? What about what Walt had said? How much pressure had the pilots been under when they'd tried to land the airplane? What would it be like to lose a child who made a mistake that caused others to die in a tragedy?

Len had plenty to talk to Barrett about at his next appointment. The first few sessions had involved so much of Len's guilt over arguments he'd had with Lenny about going to medical school, and there was so much processing to do each time he went for a session. But now that the first few were complete, Len was ready to explore the feelings he had toward the pilots.

One evening after work, Len walked into Barrett's office with a lighter vibe about him. Barrett noticed it immediately. Over two months had elapsed since Lenny's death, and the grief was not likely easier, but something was different. He waited for Len to tell him of his progress.

"You know, since I went back to work, something has really captured my attention." Len looked away as he spoke, as though he was seeing something in the distance related to his thoughts.

"And what is that?" Barrett was intrigued by the progress this father was making.

"I'm struck by the compassion people are showing me. I mean, sure, when the crash first happened, we got notes, flowers, donations to our favorite charities, and all of that. But when I went back to work, people came out of the woodwork to share with me about their own grief and losses. I had no idea how much pain people were dealing with all around me, every day at work. I mean, I guess it was always there, but I never knew about it."

"Interesting how that works, isn't it?" Barrett rested back in his chair. "Any ideas about why you're just now being included in your colleagues' personal stories?"

"Sure, I guess so. I think it's because knowing about my loss and the grief Celia and I are going through causes others to want to connect with me in a way we couldn't have before."

Barrett nodded.

Len continued, "I was so busy and so unaware. I thought the malpractice suit was traumatic. And don't get me wrong; I realize the loss of that infant was traumatic to his parents and their entire family. But I never knew anything about how they *felt*. All I could think about was myself and what the lawyers advised me to do to lessen the financial impact of my case. And now that I'm the one who's grieving, other people sense my vulnerability and can relate to me on a whole different level."

"Compassion is an amazing phenomenon, especially how it can move healing forward." Barrett was nodding as he spoke.

"I get what you tried to tell me in my first visit after Lenny died. You told me I wouldn't be able to heal from the loss of my son without healing from the losses I experienced with the death of the Waters infant. And now other insight is coming to me about my need to feel for the families of the pilots who died in the crash, parent to parent." Len spoke as though he had put this together before. But he had not. It was in the very moment he spoke the words that the whole thing came together for him.

Barrett knew this was one of those breakthroughs that for some people came years later in therapy and for others never came. He sat silently and allowed his patient to continue, lest he break the clarity Len was receiving from a higher level of consciousness.

"My best friend's father is a retired investigator. He angered me the night I met with him, and he tried to help me understand the many sides of this tragedy. I wasn't ready to accept the innocence of it all. I needed a place to vent my anger. I wanted someone to be the bad guy. And he was telling me something different. He was telling me the monster is the faceless corporation, and the mistakes had to do with things beyond pilot error. But I wanted, or thought I needed, to hate a person, or in this case two."

"And now? What's different?" Barrett leaned into the discussion with his whole body, resting his elbows on his knees, chin in hands.

"And now I just feel compassion in my heart. For myself and my family, all the families whose loved ones died, and for the families of the pilots and the intense trauma they're going through as they hear the words *pilot error* repeated every day in the news and likely will hear about for the rest of their lives."

"What do you want to do about it?" Barrett did not shift his position.

"A lot of things." Len had considered this first action for several weeks now—maybe since right after the crash. "I'm going to write the Waters and tell them how sorry I am. I'm going to pour out my heart and let them know I get it now." He spoke with resolve.

"And what do you expect in return?" Barrett asked—a necessary question.

"Nothing. Not one thing. This is not about an expectation on my part for them to do anything. This is about me coming clean and coming to terms with my own lack of understanding about human nature. I am forgiving myself once and for all, and the pilots too. I want my life to be different now. I don't know what that looks like, but my heart has been broken open. I guess you could say I've surrendered control of my life." Len rested with his last statement, sitting back and feeling free for the first time in a long time—maybe ever.

"I don't want to sound trite," said Barrett. "What you've shared with me today tells me you're no longer a victim of the crash, the mistake in which the Waters infant died, or anything else that now comes into your life. You truly are free, my friend. Nothing can set us free like forgiveness. It is the path out of victimhood. And as you now know, it starts by forgiving ourselves, which must happen before we can truly forgive others."

XLVI

Meeting in the Violet Mist

Life did not change much at home as the cool days of fall turned into the cold, gray days of winter. Bruce was doing well in kindergarten, and the family group—Babs, Sheryl, Aunt Janelle, and Len—were doing things for him that Len had hoped Celia would again resume doing one day. Len had never forgotten the advice Dr. Caroline had given him. The continuity and connection was in full swing, and he owed a lot to Celia's sisters and his aunt and nieces for that.

Overall nothing seemed amiss with young Bruce. After only two sessions with him, Dr. Caroline met with both Celia and Len and gave them a glowing report. He was talking openly about his brother and how he missed him, along with how kindergarten was going. The therapist saw no reason to continue sessions with such a well-adjusted young child who would much rather be tossing a football around or shooting hoops with other children than spending time in her or any other professional's office. The visits from Lenny had stopped, or at least Bruce no longer spoke of them.

Celia was still living life as a shut-in. Television and the Internet were her constant companions. While she had taken to cooking and taking care of their home again, all of which was good for Bruce, Len missed the vibrant, fun, personable woman he had shared his life with prior to the crash. She no longer attended church on Sundays with Len and Bruce. She discouraged visits from Father Benjamin, whom both Len and Bruce enjoyed immensely.

On her own, Celia had engaged one of the plaintiffs' attorneys who had solicited them in the first few weeks after the crash. Her entire life now seemed to be dedicated to seeking revenge for her son's death. In many ways Celia and Len were living separate lives. While they still shared a bedroom, they slept on opposite sides of their king size bed. Len was living in the present, and Celia was consumed with what had happened to her son that night his flight went down in Omaha.

Len had prevented her from knowing that he had not only written the Waters the apology he had told his therapist about, but also had met with them for lunch a few days after he wrote, and they introduced him to their two children—a son and a daughter. They had been moved to read his apology, and yes, they had heard about Lenny. They needed to forgive Len as much as he needed to be forgiven. The three adults talked openly about forgiveness when they met, and while Len would not say they were all friends now, he certainly would not call them enemies.

Len knew Celia was still drinking. White wine had been replaced by vodka. But as far as he knew, Bruce was usually in bed or away for an overnight visit by the time the alcohol intake became obvious. She had gone to the survivor support group a couple of times but did not find it helpful. Len went fairly frequently and found sharing with others to be a meaningful experience. He found comfort in connecting with other people who were attempting to come to terms with the accident and their losses and build new lives in the shadows of their pasts.

Barrett and he were talking about ending his now weekly sessions when Barrett suggested another mode of therapy Len might find helpful. "I know you're still bothered by the lack of dreams of Lenny. I still think in time you'll dream of him. But in the meantime, I would like to see you have a few sessions with a hypnotherapist here in town."

Len found this humorous. "You're joking, right?"

"Actually I'm serious." Barrett knew Len's education about alternative therapies was likely dated, and he didn't know about those that were gaining popularity in so many fields in the present day.

"As we finish our time together this evening, I thought I might share with you a few other ways I know clients of mine have received additional help."

"So you mean this might help me with dreaming about Lenny?" Len was now intrigued.

"Well, actually I do. You, not unlike many of my physician clients, live pretty much in the left side of your brain. And hypnotherapy, which I have never personally had time to practice due to the cognitive focus of my own work, can often relax someone enough to allow for a different type of healing to take place. And since you are still having trouble with sleep, learning to relax on a deep level might help in that way too. I've had many sessions with a hypnotherapist in town whom I find very useful."

"Really?"

"Yes. After my mother died, I began to have recurrent dreams about the camps that were quite distressing. I had known this particular practitioner for years, as she'd worked with me in a psychiatric clinic before she began her private practice. I called her and had three or four sessions. I got at some memories that had been locked away since I was a boy. It had to do with stories my mother told us that apparently were in my subconscious, and I needed to process them. It was amazing how it worked for me. The dreams went away." Barrett could tell Len was receptive.

"I would go only to someone you recommended. I do need to learn to relax better, which in turn might help my sleep. I am open."

Barrett wrote down the number for the hypnotherapist and gave it to Len. The two men embraced and parted ways, at least for the time being.

Len made an appointment with the hypnotherapist for the following day, anxious to try something new. He would miss his weekly visits with Barrett, and this would be a good substitute for a while. Besides, he was curious.

Len entered the office feeling a bit foolish. There he was, a medical doctor having been seen by a well-known psychiatrist for the past several months, and now he was going to see a hypnotist? His concerns were abated when a very attractive middle-aged woman came out into the reception area and introduced herself as Gillian, the hypnotherapist. She was well dressed in normal business attire; she was obviously a professional businesswoman around his own age.

As Len chatted with her, he was surprised and delighted to know that Gillian was a psychiatric nurse who had taken up hypnotherapy when she'd begun to see its effects on patients in the emergency room who were difficult to intubate. She had been in private practice for over five years and had a thriving business. It was only another patient's cancellation that allowed Len to see her so quickly.

Gillian spent some time explaining to Len what her work was all about. The plan would be to spend time with Len for the first session, getting him accustomed to becoming relaxed by the sound of her voice and various induction techniques. Gillian felt sure she could help him with sleep, and he looked forward to learning relaxation techniques in light of the stress he had been under for several months.

Len was surprised by how easily he relaxed with her voice, and he found himself dozing each time she induced him. The fact that she created a CD for him was a bonus. He knew this would be helpful right away in combating his sleep problem. It worked. Celia had, as of a few days before his first visit, begun sleeping in the guest room, so he was free to play the CD beside his bed each night to help him fall asleep without bothering with headphones.

For the second session, Gillian used a technique by which she induced him and then read him positive affirmations about all aspects of his life. Again Len took the recording home and played it before he went to sleep each night. Several of the affirmations pertained to Lenny and, of all things, his life on *the other side.*

Gillian had discussed Lenny becoming spiritual energy when he passed from his physical body.

As they continued discussing the subject of energy, Len found himself asking her about companion animals, like Lenny's dog, Sport. He described Sport's behavior the night of the crash. He felt Sport had been picking up on something, as he could not be quieted. And then for several weeks, they would find him outside Lenny's bedroom door, like he was waiting for Lenny to return. He finally got better when Len and Celia allowed him to sleep at the foot of Bruce's bed.

Gillian introduced him to the term *morphic resonance* and the works of Rupert Sheldrake. She explained that while much of his research into parapsychology had been rejected by traditional scientists, his PhD in biochemistry from Cambridge gave him credibility with many who were able to embrace a world beyond the five senses. Len wrote down his name and made a note to order his book, *Dogs That Know Their Owners Are Coming Home.*

Gillian gave Len some material to read about Einstein and his theory of relativity. They talked more about energy and about what Einstein had taught. Len had always loved Einstein's work but never knew how much comfort could be found in his theory of energy—that one could not create energy, nor could energy be destroyed. Energy simply changed form. Lenny had not been destroyed. Only his body had. His energy existed, along with Leonard Sr. and Len's precious mother and everyone he had ever loved who had died.

Gillian also talked to him about something called the human energy system. It made sense to think of everyone and everything as energy. He liked picturing the colors associated with the human energy system as he practiced the affirmations. He particularly felt a sense of peace when he visualized the center of his forehead surrounded by the color indigo. Gillian told him this was the part of his brain that could receive communication and insight from those he was connected to spiritually.

Within the affirmations were statements to and about his son. As Len repeated the affirmations, he realized he was talking to his son. And strangely enough it felt good. It even felt normal.

"Lenny, I know you are well, as I am well."

"I know you and I are eternally connected."

"I bless and release you to your greatest good."

And so the statements went on and on, releasing Lenny and releasing Len's grief as well.

In the third session, Gillian asked him at first what seemed to be a weird question. "Do you want to see if you can reach Lenny today while you're in hypnosis?" Gillian's matter-of-fact tone lessened his uneasiness.

"You think I can?

"I'm not sure. It might be too soon, but we could try. And then if we don't have success, we could try again a few weeks from now. I think we've had a lot of success with your sleep problem and giving you positive affirmations to replace some of the negative ideation that was bothering you, right?"

"Indeed, and yes, if I can get some sort of two-way communication with my son, I would do anything."

With that Gillian turned on the soft music she played in the background of the inductions. Having listened to the soft patter of her voice scores of times now and considering that he listened to her voice each night as he fell asleep, Len felt drowsiness descending upon his consciousness. Gillian continued by counting backward and leading Len into trance with several suggestions, then she instructed him to see himself standing in a field surrounded by an indigo mist.

Continuing her patter, Gillian regressed Len deeper and deeper with the sound of her voice. Suddenly his sense of smell was overwhelmed by the scent of Old Spice shaving lotion.

"Dad! Oh, Dad!" Len could hardly believe it. Right there in his mind's eye stood Leonard Sawyer Sr. smiling and looking healthy and whole.

Gillian sat for a few minutes. She could see by the rapid eye movements under Len's eyelids that he was in deep hypnosis and obviously having a meaningful experience.

"Can you describe what you're seeing?" Gillian stayed with the same hypnotic voice.

"The scene is alive with the vibrant color of violet! I'm seeing my Dad. It looks like he's in a hospital corridor. And he's pointing to a room. It looks like an operating room. I can see a medical team in their scrubs. I can't see the patient. But I can see it's a delivery." Len went quiet again. "He's showing me something or someone's face."

A few moments later, Len shouted, "It's my son. He's showing me my son! It's Lenny. He's dressed in scrubs, and he's delivering the infant. He's busy and unaware that we're watching him."

Waiting a few moments, Gillian asked for more information.

"Dad is fading away now. The violet color of the operating room is changing back into the indigo."

"What can you see right now?" Gillian pressed slightly.

"Nothing. I'm floating in the indigo mist. I'm hearing something like angels singing. It's not a recognizable song; it's just an amazing harmony. I've never felt like this before."

"Can you tell me what you're feeling?"

"All is well. We are all OK. Lenny is OK. Dad's OK. Mom's OK. The Waters' son is OK. I'm OK. I'm just floating in the indigo mist."

Gillian allowed him a few more moments. When it became clear the meeting had passed, using her same magical hypnotic voice, she began to bring Len back to the present.

"Len, in a moment I'm going to bring you out of trance. We're back in Cleveland, Ohio. November twelve…" She continued with the count-down. "And when I say five, you're going to open your eyes and you will be back here in the room with me, feeling refreshed, clear, and ready to begin your drive home to your family."

Len was awake now, looking wide eyed and surprised. He looked as though he was having trouble understanding all that had just transpired.

"Tell me about your experience," Gillian said, as she always did after an induction.

"I can describe some of it, but what I don't have words for is the feeling that came to me after I saw Dad and Lenny."

"Go ahead and try." Gillian had seen this before. Sometimes, when conditions were just right, people in hypnosis were able to have what some people referred to as cosmic experiences. *Cosmic* meaning they were beyond earthly explanations.

"I felt like I was beyond earth. I was in another dimension, and that dimension had none of the limitations of earth. There was only love, and like my psychiatrist and I discussed in one of my last sessions, Lenny, my dad, the Waters infant, no one is dead. They're just in another dimension."

"So you glimpsed what some refer to as the other side?"

"Maybe. I guess I don't need to have words to describe something beyond earthly experience. I'm OK with the mystery of it all. But I will never forget what I felt just now, and I can't find the words to describe how grateful I am to you for helping me get there—wherever *there* is." Len smiled at Gillian as he gestured toward the ceiling.

Len left that evening with an entire new way of viewing the universe and everything and everyone in it. His new outlook on life gave him confidence like he had never experienced. He had no way of knowing how much time he had left on earth, but he was determined to use every ounce of energy he had to make his life count for something. Len felt that finally he was becoming conscious.

XLVII

The Intervention

Len made several phone calls to Celia's sisters that week, without Celia's knowledge. While she had become more active over the last few weeks, especially with regard to the settlement process with the airline, there were still far too many problems. Recently she had started going back to the gym to appease Len, and today she had agreed to take him up on his suggestion that she go for a spa day. This coincided with a scouting event for Bruce that involved a sleepover with the boys at a nearby camp.

The spa day was part of the plan for prepping for the intervention Len and her sisters were planning. Len felt he had to act before Bruce somehow became victimized by Celia's drunkenness one way or another. Hiding the problem was becoming more difficult.

Lest Celia came home early or otherwise spoiled their plans, the threesome met at Babs's office, which was only a short ride for Len and Sheryl. Babs had made a fresh pot of coffee and was eager to begin the discussion about Celia's alcohol situation, which she knew was now spiraling out of control. Celia had no idea how much her family knew about the hidden bottles, passing out in public, and other signs she was in crisis. Babs had made sure the conference room was free for at least a couple of hours that morning.

Len stirred his coffee and sat down across from his sisters-in-law. "I just want to start by telling you both once again how much it means that you've been there every minute for the three of us. We have a wide circle of friends, as you know, and of course my mother's and father's siblings and folks from your parents' side have been helpful, but only you two know how hard it has been inside my home since the crash. Celia has never hit the bottle this hard. For a few weeks, she seemed to back off, but then I discovered she was substituting vodka for wine, pretending she was drinking sparkling water. She has been intoxicated daily since the Saturday after the crash occurred."

"We know," Babs said "And like you, we had no idea Celia would go this way. In all her adult years, we never saw her abuse alcohol the way she's doing now. We need to do something before she hurts someone else or herself."

"And of course, while we've protected Bruce from knowing what's going on up until now, sooner or later he'll realize what's going on. He is such a smart kid." Sheryl was reflecting on his questioning during the whole sighting of the crow while his parents were away. He got going on a topic and didn't let up until he figured it out.

"I'm out of my element with this." Len was honest in his need for help.

"Well, my specialty is children, as you both know, but I have been talking to some of my colleagues who I think can help. In fact if we can get her to go, I have an appointment set up with a great counselor I think can help her." Babs paused to see what the reception might be.

"I don't know, Babs. Celia is dead set against restarting her own practice, and I don't know if she'll go see someone else. I know she needs help, but I was wondering if we should go ahead and try to get her into rehab and more or less force her or admit her to a program. She is just so obstinate."

"I understand what you're saying. But do you think it will be any easier to get her into rehab as opposed to a counselor's office?" Babs asked.

"Look, this afternoon when she comes in, let's give her the option. She knows she's in trouble, and I think she's aware that sooner or later we're going to confront her over it. Dad and Mom barely allowed alcohol in our home, and this is a problem none of us have experience with. I say let's lay all of the cards on the table and give her the choice." Sheryl ached over the thought of her sister being away from Bruce, but it was going to happen one way or another. The three of them had already agreed to that part.

Bruce was not going to be victimized by his mother, and they needed to be clear about it.

"I think you're right. My friend indicated there are a couple of great places she has sent patients that cater to women with substance abuse problems who also have lost children. I'll get that information and see if we can get Celia in right away. And then we have the fall back of the individual appointment, so she can choose." Babs was already looking in her phone for a contact number for her colleague.

"That would be great," Len said. "If Celia goes away, I can ask Aunt Janelle to help us out in the afternoons. She keeps offering to help more. I can arrange with my colleagues to be home each night, and among us all we can manage." Len was ready for something to change.

"Let me call right now," said Babs. Fortunately she got right through to her colleague's office and was able to ask about the treatment centers. By early afternoon she was assured she would have an answer from one of the locations, if not both. "OK, let's go ahead and figure out how we want to do this, and then as soon as we hear about the availability at the in-patient clinics, we'll be ready to confront her this afternoon when she returns." Babs was anxious to strategize about the flow of the meeting with Celia.

"I plan to be there when she gets home," said Len. "I asked her to call me when she's leaving under the pretense that I might need her to stop and pick up something. She thinks I'm grilling out for dinner. I plan to be there to prevent her from drinking before we have our meeting. Alcohol seems to make her more obstinate. The only thing that seems to bring out her loving side now is when she's around Bruce. The shame is I have to limit that due to the alcohol."

Babs's phone rang as Len finished his statement.

"Great! And you're located where?" Babs was writing notes on her iPad as she listened to the caller. "Very good. We will get back to you later today if my sister decides to go." She hung up the phone and looked at the other two. "Portland, Oregon. The clinic there can take her. So now we have our choice."

Len hurried home to prepare for the meeting. Walking into the kitchen, he caught sight of four family photos that had been taken the summer before the crash, on the beach at Lenny's favorite vacation spot in South Carolina. It had been their last family vacation together. Not too long ago, thoughts about the past would have taken over Len's ability to carry through with what was about to happen. But he was different now. He had a renewed sense of purpose, and he needed to help Celia. She deserved that, and so did Bruce.

He reflected on that day when he saw his father and Lenny while in hypnosis. His family needed to come back together now and live out their lives the best they could. He knew one day the larger family unit would be together again. The others were fine where they were. He knew that now. The family on this side needed to be more connected. It was time.

Len was pleased with the help he had received from Father Benjamin, Barrett, Gillian, friends at work, and even the Waterses. Celia needed to have some help now. And he was determined to see her get it. She needed so badly to have someone who could help her grieve in a way that limited the losses. Losing Lenny was enough, but she could not afford to lose Bruce in the process of grieving—or not grieving, as the case might be.

Len and Barrett had talked a lot about that in their second meeting. Celia's drinking was blocking the grief work she needed to do. As a counselor, intellectually she knew that, but as an addicted person, this knowledge did her no good. The alcohol was blocking her logical mind from helping her, not to mention her spiritual side, which until the crash had been a big part of her life. While Len and Bruce had returned to church the Sunday after Len saw Father Benjamin, Celia did not accompany them. She felt her prayers for her family's safety all those years had been futile. On the Sunday Len and Bruce returned to church, Celia announced she would not be returning—ever.

As planned, Celia's sisters arrived well before four o'clock, which was the time Celia was expected home. At first the fact that she did not arrive on time was not a concern. But when the grandfather clock in the family room struck half past four, the family began to worry.

"Are you sure she left the spa when she was supposed to?" Sheryl asked.

"Yes, I called a few minutes ago, and they told me she left at three, when her massage ended, after she showered and dressed." Len was concerned. Celia knew he was starting the grill by five in order to have dinner around six. She had agreed to call on her way home in case he discovered he needed something for the salad. This was not like her. "I tried her cell again, and it went to voice mail." He was pacing by the time five thirty came.

"Maybe she decided to pick up something on her own and will call a little later, after she's run an errand we don't know about. We're probably worrying for nothing." Sheryl hit the remote's "on" button, and the five o'clock news burst into the room. She quickly hit the "off" button when the cover news story was about the lack of new information on the crash. With their own most recent drama unfolding, news about the crash was not foremost on their minds at that moment.

"This is not like Celia." Len picked up his phone again and tried her cell. Again it went to voice mail.

"Who might she have stopped off to visit? What about her office? Would she have gone there?" Babs was trying to be helpful.

"What office? She hasn't been there since the day of the crash. She hasn't even gone to retrieve her personal things. Her partner took over her files and client base, so that would not be the case." Len could not imagine where she might be. "What if she had an accident on the way home? Maybe I should get in the car and drive the route, just in case."

His thoughts were interrupted by the sound of the ringing phone in the kitchen. "There she is, thank God," Len said as he picked up the phone, expecting to hear his wife's voice.

"This is a call for Dr. Leonard Sawyer," said a woman's voice he did not recognize.

"Yes, this is him. Go ahead." Len got an uneasy feeling in his gut.

"Dr. Sawyer, this is the Westside Hospital emergency room. Your wife has just been admitted following a car accident. Her injuries do not appear to be serious, but the medical team is examining her now. Can you come down and meet with the officers who are awaiting her release? She should be released within the next ninety minutes or so. Oh, and Dr. Sawyer, the reason the police are involved is that she was intoxicated when she backed into another car at a high speed in a parking lot. No one was in the other car at the time. The police called the paramedics. They wanted to make sure she wasn't seriously injured before…before the arrest."

"I'm on my way now." Len hung up the phone and turned to face two women, who were fearful about what might have happened to their sister.

"Celia is in the hospital. Apparently she was intoxicated and hit another car, which fortunately had no one in it. Police called the paramedics. There was concern that she might have some injuries. But the person calling from the hospital said she's OK." The disgust in Len's voice was evident.

"My God, we may have waited too long. Thank God she's not hurt and no one else is injured. It's time to stop her from doing some serious damage." Babs was growing more disappointed with her older sister by the moment.

"Do you want us to go with you, or should we wait? I think one way or another, we must confront her tonight." Sheryl could not imagine the embarrassment Len was feeling. Everyone at Westside knew the Sawyers. The family had been a part of the medical community there for nearly half a century, if you added the tenures of both Len and his father.

"No, stay here. And I need to tell you that we can't do it tonight. Celia is going to jail for three days, per Ohio law. Maybe the shock of what she did and what might have resulted will make her more aware of why we're insisting she make a move toward getting and staying sober." Len felt strongly about their plans, and his voice conveyed his resolve.

• • •

Len entered the ER looking like a local citizen. Even so, several employees spoke to him, as he was easy to recognize, street clothes or not. The nurse in the reception area stopped what she was doing and escorted him immediately to the area where Celia lay in a bed curtained off from others. A policeman stood close by.

"Are you OK?" Len touched Celia's shoulder, as her back was turned to the hallway.

Too ashamed to look at him, Celia spoke quietly. "Yes. I had a lick on the head, but the doc who examined me didn't think I have a concussion or anything. Did you know the police were involved?"

"Yes, the hospital staff member told me. Celia, you may not know this but Ohio requires a minimum of three days in jail for driving under the influence. An officer is standing outside the door. I guess to make sure you don't get away without being arrested." Len could not hide his disappointment with his wife.

Celia rolled over and faced her husband now. "Look, maybe you can talk him out of charging me. It's my first time for anything other than a parking ticket, and I bet if you told him about the crash and Lenny and our story, I could get away with a warning or at least just a citation."

"No, Celia, your drinking has gotten out of hand. I am not going to do anything to enable you to keep going with behavior that could harm you and innocent people. Now, go on and get your clothes on. I'll wait outside with the officer until you're ready." With that Len turned and left.

The police officer smiled at him as he approached. "You must be Dr. Sawyer." The officer held out his hand. "My name is Gerald Bell."

"I'm Len Sawyer, and I am so sorry that my wife apparently got a little out of hand this afternoon," Len said as he took the officer's hand.

"Well, actually it might have been worse. My partner and I watched her walk into the bar around three fifteen. She came out around five o'clock. We were rounding that area of town, as we do every afternoon, and saw her go in seemingly sober, but coming out was a different story. Before we could get to her, she had backed her car into another and hit it so hard, we were worried about a head injury. We still need to formally charge her but wanted to see that she was checked out medically first." The officer was young and obviously very sensitive.

"Yes, I'll wait while you do what you have to do. I hope you understand this is all new behavior for my wife, but I want her to see the ramifications of her alcohol issues. So go ahead and do what you need to do."

"While we were waiting for the paramedics to arrive, she told us about your son and how he died in that crash last summer. Let me tell you how sorry I am. But her blood alcohol level was well above what qualifies for arrest. I am so sorry.

"I appreciate your sympathy, but I want her to face the consequences of her behavior. What happened to our son is tragic, and our grief is fresh. But getting drunk is no way to cope with loss, and I intend to help my wife find other ways to deal with her grief." Len was determined to follow through with his better judgment.

Celia walked out unsteady on her feet. Her blond hair was frazzled, and mascara was smudged beneath her bloodshot, once-clear blue eyes. She reached for her husband's arm and stood while the officer carried out the formal arrest. Officer Bell gave her a second citation for reckless driving due to the speed at which she collided with the other vehicle. He let the couple know the police report would be on file for their insurance company as well as the other driver's insurance company when the time came for the cars to be repaired.

Before helping her into the police car, Officer Bell explained all that would happen next. Celia stood stunned and silent as he explained the details of the arrest. Although the accident had partly sobered her, her rational thinking remained greatly compromised.

XLVIII

Limited Choices

Early the morning Celia was released from the county jail, Len appeared to pick her up and drive her home. He could hardly believe that his wife now had a police record. The couple, once so close and loving, drove to their once happy home in silence. As Len pulled his car into the driveway, Celia caught sight of her sisters' vehicles.

"Did you call the girls about my accident?" Celia had no way of knowing how long they had been waiting for her.

"No. Actually Babs and Sheryl were here the day of the accident, waiting to meet with you." Len was not going to soften as he readied for the task in front of him.

"Were they coming for dinner that evening? I did not remember that." Celia seemed perplexed as she walked toward the kitchen door from the garage.

"Actually, Celia, the three of us were waiting for a meeting with you that afternoon. While this is somewhat delayed, we are going to continue on with family business now." Len opened the door. Both women were seated at the kitchen table, and unlike their normal selves, neither rose to greet their oldest sister.

Suspecting something out of the ordinary, Celia spoke first. "What a surprise to see you both here this morning. I hope you don't mind, but I need a little bit of time to shower and clean up."

"Sit down, Celia." Len pulled out a chair for his wife. Celia sat down and tried to focus. This was not his normal tone—after all, she had been through quite an ordeal.

Babs spoke first. "Celia, first let me say I thank God that you are OK. Len told us about the wreck and the arrest."

Not suspecting the seriousness of where Babs was taking the conversation, Celia responded, "Oh, it was awful. I stopped to get a case of wine because we were running low, and when I came out the sun blinded me, and I hit a car. I was more than a little embarrassed."

"Stop, Celia. Your sisters already know you were driving drunk and that you were arrested for driving under the influence, among other things. Babs and Sheryl have come over this morning because we are no longer willing to be part of your lies about alcohol." Len took command of the conversation.

"Celia, we have watched you for the past several months and have serious concerns about where this is leading. None of us imagined you would ever get into the car and hurt yourself or someone else." Babs spoke next.

"Oh, I have a small bump on the head. And there was no one else involved. The car I hit had no one in it." Celia did not know yet where this was leading.

Sheryl spoke firmly and with resolve. "Celia, that part is irrelevant. Since Lenny died, the person we knew as our sister, Len's wife, and Bruce's mother disappeared. We all support the decisions you've made for yourself about ending your practice, wanting to be a stay-at-home mom to Bruce, and so forth. But we are not going to continue to watch you spiral out of control. We will not watch you use alcohol or any drug for that matter as a way to avoid your grief over Lenny."

"What do you know about grief? You're a school counselor with other people's kids. You don't know what it's like to bear a child and then lose him because of someone else's stupid, stupid mistake!" Celia's words were filled with rage.

"No, I don't know what it's like to be his mother. But Lenny was my godchild, and I loved him too. I know my life won't ever be the same either. But I want to still be a loving part of Bruce's life and do for him all I once did for Lenny. And I want to see him grow up without being scarred by Lenny's death, because he lost his only sibling, any more than necessary. Celia, you are his mother. You have to come out of this and assume that role." The tears in Sheryl's eyes told the story of her own many losses, including her inability to bear a child of her own.

"Celia, look, my practice is filled with children of all ages who are being punished by parents who can't accept the loss of one of their other children." Babs spoke with professional knowledge and nearly two decades of experience as a practicing psychologist. "It's like they lose a brother or sister, and then they lose their parents. The parents are still alive, but they become absorbed in grief over the deceased child. And before you know it, the living children wind up living totally compromised lives because the parents are unable to grieve effectively over the dead child. Grieving is hard enough, but throw in substance abuse on top of it, and the pain of the grief will never be resolved."

Now it was Celia's time to speak. "I am a counselor too. I know the definition of alcoholism. A couple of glasses of wine a day is not like drinking hard alcohol."

"Celia, go tell the officers who put you in jail that you don't have a problem. They will beg to differ with you. And you are not being truthful about the alcohol consumption. You are averaging one or two Bloody Mary's before noon daily, and you're pouring heavy. I've watched you." Len had noticed how quickly the vodka was disappearing, replaced by new bottles. "And you're going through at least a couple of bottles of wine daily, so let's not lie about the amounts."

Celia sat in stunned silence for the second time that day. "Well, I am not going to AA with all the drunks, if that's what you think."

"OK then, if you won't go for local counseling and join AA, then we have arranged another solution." Babs did not hesitate to jump on the opening.

"What, you mean you're shipping me off to a rehab place, away from my baby boy? Len, you don't want me to leave you and Bruce, do you? Isn't being without Lenny bad enough?" Celia looked pleadingly at her husband.

"Celia, yes, being without Lenny is unimaginable. It hurts so much. But we don't have you now anyway. We should be doing things as a family, but you deny us that. You're too drunk most days for Bruce to see you. Eventually he'll know what 'Mom is sleeping in' means, if he doesn't know right now. Since the crash the three of us have done nothing together. You have abandoned our son and me. And now I'm calling you on it."

"Are you saying you'll leave me if I don't go to rehab?" Celia was incredulous and appeared to be catching on to the seriousness of the family discussion fast.

Len had prepared for this moment. "No, but I will arrange for a live-in helper to care for Bruce and run the household for me. Obviously you are no longer capable of doing it." He knew how much Celia hated the thought of a live-in helper or nanny. When she got pregnant with Bruce, the subject came up more than once as a way that she could go back and finish her doctoral degree after his birth. Each time the subject was broached, Celia shot it down. The thought of a stranger living in her home in the middle of her family was about the worst thing she could imagine.

"So here are the options." Babs moved in again. "My colleague, P. J. Bevans, is one of the best in the field of substance abuse, and I hear she's a great grief counselor too. I can get you into a local rehab program, and you can see P. J. on a regular basis, but you will have to commit to going to AA weekly also."

"What other choice do I have?" Celia seemed to be getting the message that she was up against a pretty firm wall, supported by the three adults who were the closest to her in the world.

"Or you can go to a treatment center in Portland, Oregon, that is one of the best in the country. You'll have to be there for three months, but after the first few weeks Len and Bruce can come and see you on weekends."

"What? I lose my son, and now you want to take me away from the one I have left? Does that make sense to you?" Celia was determined to fight.

"OK, then, commit to local counseling and getting into an outpatient program here, including AA, or share our home with a live-in until Bruce can go away to college. The choice is yours." Len hated being a parent to his wife of over twenty years, but she left him no choice.

"How long do I have to think about it?" Celia was wishing for a glass of wine to help her relax. This family session was way too tense for her.

"I am set to start interviewing women from a local agency tomorrow. So you need to tell us tonight what your decision is going to be." Len was firm.

"I need some time. I can police myself. I can commit to a glass of wine with dinner, and maybe one more after that. That's not even half a bottle a day." Celia had to try for some leniency. She did not remember that she had already made this promise and failed to keep it.

"There is no wine or liquor of any sort in the house. While you were in jail, I took care of it. And right now your car is not drivable, and you are not touching my car keys, so I'm not sure where you're going to get anything to drink today. And you can't drink at home anymore. I don't want Bruce to see it. Make up your mind. What will it be?"

"I am not leaving my home." Celia felt like she needed to buy some time to get through this crisis they all seemed to be think they were in. "Babs, I'll go to your friend P. J. Go ahead and have her set up the local rehab. Maybe we can find an AA far enough away that I won't know anyone. I need to go upstairs now. I need a shower and a nap." With those words, Celia left the room and the meeting.

Part 3
Revelations

All the world's a stage,
And all the men and women merely players;
They have their exits and their entrances,
And one man in his time plays many parts...

—As you Like It,
William Shakespeare

XLIX

Reflections

Celia was lying on her back, unable to adjust her position, despite her discomfort. This last stroke had left her paralyzed on her left side. She could use her right hand, but her left hand, like her left leg, was totally useless. Though unable to speak, her memory had not failed her. Unfortunately she could remember more of her life than she cared to. What mattered now was that this life was coming to an end at last.

It had been nearly forty years since the airline had killed her son and taken the joy from her life. Having lived such a successful life up until the crash, she could not understand what she had ever done for God to heap such a punishment on her and her family. Who knew? Maybe it was past-life stuff. Maybe it was her karma to have to live so long physically while having died emotionally and spiritually before the second part of her life had begun.

Somehow her husband, who had preceded her in death by only two short years, had not been taken down by the loss of their firstborn son the way she had. And thank God for that. He was the hero who had raised their younger son and had devoted his life to helping other young men and women in honor of his deceased son. The proceeds from the lawsuit had allowed him to retire earlier than he might have otherwise. This also allowed him to make contributions to countless charities in his son's name. More importantly, he established several scholarships for young students who needed help at various points in their undergraduate education, before they could get into graduate school, where more lucrative economic help was available.

All of this was above and beyond what he had done in conjunction with the Catholic Church in helping boys and girls who were challenged in maintaining the grade-point averages necessary to get into college. In the second part of his life, Len and his companion priest, Father Benjamin, had discovered that most of the students' problems with grades had to do with their home environments, where education and things like homework were not valued, much less supported. Len and Father Benjamin set up an after-school tutoring program. Len spent much of his time tutoring students in math and science after he retired from medicine. Grade-point averages climbed, and the team stopped keeping track of how many local kids became college eligible due to the tutoring program. The first year alone, there were at least twenty students who went from making average grades to well above average and achieved scores on exams that made them eligible for most colleges.

Celia was ashamed of her own life after the crash. Len never abandoned her, but she had trouble understanding why. After the first trip to rehab, she remained sober until Bruce was in junior high. She got away with sipping secretly for a couple of years before Len found her passed out on the floor of their bathroom one morning. He and Bruce had been away for a fishing trip, leaving her alone to enjoy her secret habit.

While he was glad he had come home early and found her, she was not so grateful that he saved her. She did not have the courage to take her own life, and this "accident" would have been an easy way to leave earth without disgracing her family even more with an obvious suicide.

This episode was followed by her second trip to rehab. This time Babs arranged for her to be admitted to an in-patient treatment program in California. She hated to leave Bruce, but she knew Len had been honest with him about his mother's addiction. Even Bruce, then entering adolescence, encouraged her to go.

That time she made it all the way until Bruce went away to college. Looking back now she realized that once he had been admitted to college, she felt she could do as she wanted. Bruce had graduated as valedictorian of his class. He was rewarded with a full-ride academic scholarship to the university of his first choice and was headed toward the same career Lenny and all the Sawyer men had chosen. Of course the airline killed Lenny before he could pursue his medical career.

Len discovered she had fallen off the wagon this time when she was admitted to the emergency room. She passed out at work, and paramedics rushed her to the ER, later to learn she was very ill. Celia was suffering from liver failure. Now she had to stop drinking or leave earth before her second son fulfilled his lifelong dream of practicing medicine.

Fear of death did not stop her from wanting to drink. Celia became physically ill now any time she was even near alcohol. She could not drink even though she wanted to. The nausea and the weakness that followed even one sip made it impossible.

She had never returned to her counseling practice. After the first time she dried out, she needed to find something to occupy her time. Nothing interested her. However, she was relieved to learn that she could get a part-time job at a friend's clothing boutique. She actually found it fun to work with other women who needed help with their wardrobe planning. Her sisters and her other professional friends enjoyed seeing her having fun again and laughingly referred to her new employment as her *jobette.*

They were also relieved that during therapy, she worked through many of her feelings of guilt and shame over her actions toward other bereaved parents before she had become one of them. However, the therapy never allowed her to resolve her anger toward the airline. She never forgave the pilots and became active with an advocacy group. The problem with the group was that their actions were largely fueled by angry people who were not interested in resolving their grief. The group focused on anger and punishment. Their agenda fit Celia well.

All of this stood between Len and Celia. Her sisters, Sheryl and Babs, did not understand why Len did not leave her, but they were grateful that he didn't. Everyone understood the brief affair he had with a young widow he met in the support group three years after the crash—even Celia. Their intimacy, like Lenny, had died with the crash.

But Len never left his family. He lived out his life with meaning and purpose and was recognized by others who honored him with countless awards. His greatest reward was knowing that after Lenny's death, he had committed to living out his life by making earth a better place for others. He felt his life should be a testament to his son. Not an embarrassment, as Celia knew hers had been.

Celia could tell by the way the doctors were speaking that she did not have long now. She was aware when Bruce and Marla came into the room with their three children. She heard the nurse greet her son and his family warmly.

"Dr. and Mrs. Sawyer, I called you because your mother is near the end. I knew you would want to come in as soon as you could." The nurse spoke quietly, with concern in her voice.

"Yes, you're right. I spoke to Dr. Lewis earlier, and he told me the situation is dire." Bruce sounded like his father. He was very direct while at the same time very caring.

Celia was so proud of her second son. He had the height and good looks of his father and his older brother. And he was an outstanding man. She could not take credit for his accomplishments. Her two sisters and her husband had raised him. Oh sure, she was around physically, but an inability to manage her own grief caused her to be absent emotionally from her second son. Thank God their family had pulled together in supporting Bruce after Lenny died. Their success was obvious in the life of this awesome young professional who was a respected physician, family man, and leader in his church community.

The nurse left the room. "Lenny, Soph, and Bo," he addressed his children, "say good-bye to Mama Celia, and then Mom will take you for a treat." Bruce knew he needed some time alone to say his final good-bye. He motioned toward the door with his head. His beautiful dark-haired wife kissed her mother-in-law good-bye and moved toward the doorway.

While his older boy was tall enough to reach her cheek on his own, Bruce held his younger children up so they could kiss Celia good-bye for the last time. A tear rolled down Celia's face as she felt the kiss of the older boy, who had been named after Lenny. More tears appeared as she felt the other kisses. While the stroke had left her unable to speak, the tears reminded Bruce that the lights were still on in the right hemisphere of his mother's brain, at least for a few more moments.

"Mom." Bruce leaned close to his mother's face as he whispered. "Mom, I want you to know what a wonderful mother you were to me and how much I will always love you. You and Dad were the best parents a boy could have, and I will miss you terribly." Bruce's voice broke as he saw another tear appear on his mother's cheek.

"I know I never could have meant as much to you as Lenny did. I know he was special in a way only a firstborn son could be..."

Celia could not believe these last sentences she was hearing. Bruce was a star! He was an incredible son. She needed to tell him this before it was too late.

"Oh God," she prayed. "Let me speak to my son before I leave earth. I beg you, let me speak to him. He has it all wrong. I failed him; he did not fail me!"

Celia had not prayed since Lenny had died. And now she needed God to help her, so she cried out in her mind, though her voice was inaudible. Celia lay unable to speak as Bruce continued taking responsibility on himself for her failure as a mother to him.

*Dear God, please allow me to speak...*Only Celia knew she was thinking these words, as she literally could not speak.

L

Lifting the Veil

"Lenny, oh, my darling! There you are. You're alive!" Celia was ecstatic to see Lenny at her side. Behind him, his father and his maternal grandparents looked on smiling.

Lenny and Len had stood behind Bruce as he'd said his good-byes to Celia. While earthly eyes could not see them, they knew he needed their strength, and as soon as the angels started singing, they recognized it was time for Celia to join them on the other side. While they were there to cross Celia over, they were also there to support Bruce—and would be there whenever he needed them any time while he lived on earth.

Both men's hearts ached when they heard Celia calling out to God for help as she lay dying, unable to express her feelings to her son. They knew Celia had experienced many years on earth where she could have said things to Bruce while they were still together. But she had waited too long, at least for this most recent lifetime on earth. It was not God who had failed her. She had failed herself. Celia had much to learn, and this was the only way to learn what she needed to experience in order to advance her soul's evolution.

Giving his undivided attention to his mother, Lenny wrapped his arms around Celia. His father followed suit as soon as Lenny released her. Within moments her parents joined in on the physical touching, and the family immediately sat down to share their joy of reunion.

Celia's joy continued as she met with old friends and relatives who had departed earth before her. This truly was the heaven she had learned about as a child. She quickly adjusted to this new and wonderful life. Lenny and Len joined her for most meals daily, in spite of their busy medical schedules.

One morning while waiting for the boys to return from the hospital, Celia spent some time reflecting on how quickly her integration to this new life was happening. Being united with Len and Lenny again, along with her parents, was allowing the painful memories of her last life on earth to fade. She was unaware of how much time had passed since her return to the other side. It was true that time, so important on earth, had little meaning here. Lenny had told her that later that same day, she would be moving toward another part of her adjustment in her new life. She was looking forward to discovering more about what he meant. Everything was so pleasant. She understood now why many called the other side heaven.

Celia was allowing the sun to warm her face. No longer concerned about harmful rays, she felt she was coming back to the woman she had been before the crash had thrown her off course. Just as she remembered Lenny's death, she opened her eyes, and there he stood, handsome as ever, right in front of her.

Holding up her cheek for Lenny's kiss, Celia smiled up at him. "Hello, darling. How are you today?"

Lenny was happy to see his mother looking like herself at last. Her last years on earth had taken a toll on her. He hoped next time she would be able to have an easier adjustment when it was necessary. But that would not be anytime soon—there was more to do before that time would come.

"Is Dad still at the hospital?"

"Yes. As we were leaving, the choir started. A young doctor was calling for help. He was handling a case that went beyond his experience level, and there were no senior docs around to help him back on earth. So Dad went to his side. He should be along shortly. Both Mom and the infant will make it, so it should not be long." Lenny spoke with a level of confidence only an experienced physician would have.

Celia was still getting used to the fact that the young college student she had known before he had left earth had been in reality a very seasoned practitioner of medicine many, many lifetimes before she'd borne him as an infant. Everyone assured her this was normal, and it would not be long before this new reality would not seem like a new reality at all.

Celia followed Lenny's index finger as he pointed toward the large white-stone building, which towered over most of the other buildings.

"Are you ready to go to school?" he asked.

"Yes. It's been a while, but last time I went to school, I was a pretty good student."

"I'm sure you'll do fine. No one ever fails the lessons on this side." Lenny did not want to alarm his mother about how the process went, so he left the discussion at that.

"Will we need a taxi? To take us there, I mean?"

"Mom, you'll grow accustomed to the way we travel here. No transportation is needed beyond our thoughts. We can travel anywhere by only directing our thoughts." Lenny pointed to the center of his forehead and smiled as he finished his statement.

Instantaneously Celia found herself standing on the giant veranda of the large white building. Above the giant doors of the building were the words University of Earth.

She wondered why heaven needed an earth school. Why would someone need to go to a school about earth once they made it to heaven? She thought she was finished with earth and had left all that pain behind. She certainly hoped so.

Reaching for his mother's hand, Lenny led the way into the building's large foyer. "Mom, part of moving forward in your evolution is spending some time remembering life on earth." Lenny could tell by the look on his mother's face that the idea of looking back on this most recent lifetime was unsettling.

"I thought the pain from this past life on earth was behind me. It's been so pleasant here. Are you sure I need this?" A look of terror crossed her face as she remembered the final few moments of her life and the pain she had lived through. She'd had no physical pain; it was all emotional. It was almost unbearable. And all the years after the crash… A feeling of dread came into the pit of her stomach.

"Mom, before you can move forward you must review the good and the bad experiences. And only then can you go on to what's next. You had many other lifetimes before this one in which I was your relative, and many of those lifetimes included great experiences, not only painful ones." Lenny was trying to relieve some of the fear he knew Celia was feeling.

Lenny had already reserved one of the viewing rooms. He wanted to get going as soon as they could now that Celia had been briefed about what was coming next. He placed his arm gently on his mother's waist and showed her into the room, where one entire wall was covered by a curtain. Lenny put the "in use" sign in place and closed the door behind them.

"Mom, if you could go back to your most recent childhood and relive one day, the happiest day of your childhood, what day would that be?"

Without hesitation Celia began to describe her eighth birthday with the joy of a child about that age.

With that the curtain opened, and an eight-year-old's birthday party began to take place. A blond girl sat in front of a white birthday cake decorated with eight candles. Two younger blond girls sat on either side of Celia. Their very youthful parents were serving ice cream and organizing the opening of gifts from the other children from the neighborhood, also seated around the table.

The scene was full of joy and laughter. After the group sang "Happy Birthday" and blew out the candles, young Celia opened all of her gifts. There was a knock at the kitchen door, and Celia ran to it. She knew Granddaddy Jack was coming, and he had told her to expect a big surprise.

Granddaddy Jack lifted his small blond granddaughter into his arms and carried her out to a small horse trailer. Holding his hand over her eyes, Granddaddy Jack stood by the trailer while her father led a pony out into the yard.

"Now look!" Granddaddy Jack lifted his hand from her eyes, and she shouted with joy.

"A pony, a pony! Look, Babs; look, Sheryl!"

Lenny and Celia looked on as the day was spent with rides and fun like no other. Celia closed her eyes and reflected on her life after that.

Granddaddy Jack lived on a farm where he kept the pony until a bigger horse was in order, and Celia became a full-fledged equestrian. She rode all the way through college, selling her horse only after she married and became pregnant with Lenny. After that she had settled down to raise her family and eventually started her professional life.

Recalling this wonderful part of her life, which started on her eighth birthday, was an important way to begin her life review. Opening her eyes, she watched many more scenes following this one. Celia was intrigued by the many types of healers she had been over many lifetimes. She now wondered how she had become so determined to drop her profession as a counselor in that last lifetime. She asked Lenny the question.

"That's a great question, but you'll be able to answer that with more time in life review. Every day for a while, you will come to earth school and study your lives from the past, and before you know it, you'll be able to see patterns and themes that repeat over many lifetimes. And more importantly you will be ready to talk about planning your next lifetime on earth."

"Next lifetime. You mean I have to go back? Do I have a choice?" The first part of this discussion sounded good, but not this last part.

"Mom, believe it or not, you will want to go back and finish with earth once and for all in a way that leaves you feeling proud and complete. You will have passed all of the tests that earth school can teach you, and then you won't ever have to go back again. You will have completed that part of your soul's evolution."

"Do I have to relive the trauma in my past lives, like the day you died and the years of mourning?" The good memories were suddenly clouded by memories of her past.

"No, that would be too cruel. And besides, you can see that your greatest fear, that you would never see me again, was not true, so that part would not work. However, you will have an opportunity to meet many of the people you had unhappy experiences with this last time on earth, so you can talk the experiences through for greater insight into the various issues."

"You mean I will meet the people I hated so much at the airline? The pilots, the people who killed you?" Her fear about what he was suggesting was obvious.

"Mom." Lenny hoped she would see the humor in her statement. "Do I look dead to you?"

"Of course not, but I didn't understand what I understand now."

"I know, but you were a woman of faith, and when the crash happened it was time for you to find strength in that."

"Like your father? Lenny, you have no idea how much I wish my life had been more like his after the crash. We had been so much alike up until then. I still don't totally understand."

"And that is why you will go through this process. You have to see it yourself, and you have to talk through the conflicts that existed. The things you didn't complete this last time on earth, you will be able to complete now."

"Then if it all gets resolved over here, why go back?"

"Because to work off human karma, you have to have a human body. Once you are finished and are in control of human emotions, you don't need them anymore—or a body. You are no longer a victim to earth's experiences; you will have passed all of earth's tests. You will have become truly conscious that there is no death, and all is well—just as you are experiencing now."

"It all sounds so easy. But I know it's not."

"No, Mom, but over here you're surrounded by unconditional love, and no matter how painful the experiences on earth that you now must examine, you will feel self-love all the time. That's why you're able to see yourself on a stage from up here. This process allows you to observe yourself without personal suffering. And this will allow you to prepare for your next lifetime on earth."

"I think I understand some of what you're saying, but explain more."

"It's the intention that next time you're in human form and are confronted with what seems like overwhelming trauma and loss of any kind, you will remember you can be an observer of your experience, just like here. And your higher mind, which is dominant in you here on this side, will allow you to survive the experience in a way that you are not victimized by it."

"Like Dad did?"

Lenny hesitated, but he had to tell the truth. "Yes, Mom, like Dad. He was devastated too, and my death was added to his medical mistake that led to the death of little Timmy. His guilt and shame on top of the loss of me could have taken him down. But he made a choice to get in control of his emotions and use that energy to live out his life on earth in a constructive way."

"And why do you think I didn't go that way?"

"You made a different choice." Lenny stated his truth as matter-of-factly as possible. Soon enough Celia would know the answers deep within, and then the truth would be her own.

"Mom, this is enough discussion for today. We can start again tomorrow."

LI

Contracts

Time went by, or so Celia assumed. She quickly adjusted to life without clocks and calendars. She had always been a good student, and her new experiences at the University of Earth proved to be an exciting challenge for her. Right away she was able to see where decisions in the past had led both to good and not-so-good outcomes. She saw examples of where she made decisions in one lifetime that carried over into the next. Usually, when confronted again by a poor choice in the past, she was pleased to see she seldom repeated the same mistake more than once.

The thing that pleased her the most had to do with how many times in her entire evolution she had helped people. She loved watching herself on the big screen when she had been compassionate and caring. One of her favorite lifetimes where she observed this behavior was when she was a midwife. She and Len had been together in that lifetime too. And they had delivered many newborns together. It was amazing in how many lifetimes she, Len, Lenny, Bruce, her sisters, and her parents had played different roles in each other's lives.

The day finally arrived when Celia would sit with the major players who had directed her most recent lifetime. Celia was pleased when she walked in to the university that morning to see that a conference room had been reserved in her name. Walking into the room, she was overjoyed to see all who were sitting at the table. At the head was a man she recognized from several lifetimes including the most recent; he seemed to be presiding over the meeting. Around the table sat Len, Lenny, both of her parents, her grandparents, and several others from her past.

The man at the head of the table turned out to be someone who had agreed to be her guardian again in her upcoming lifetime. His name was Robert, and Celia recognized him from the recent scenes she had been viewing in her past lives.

The subject moved to contracts between Celia and her most recent earthly family. Lenny began the discussion.

"So Mom, as we were talking about early on after you arrived back on this side, you lived most of your life on earth this time in the grace you had earned in previous lifetimes. You deserved all life gave you in terms of your comfort, good health, good looks, and great relationships. You had helped a lot of people in your previous lifetime and many, many more before that."

Celia spoke next. "I did enjoy the finest of things, starting with horses, a hobby that made me the envy of so many others who could barely afford hobbies like tennis and golf. I wondered why I was so lucky. And then I married the best-looking man on campus and gave birth to two beautiful babies. This really did often cause me to wonder why I was so lucky."

Len spoke at that point. "Yes, Celia, you and I and the boys had a contract to do many things on earth with what we had been given."

Celia interrupted. "And then when our big test came, I failed. You passed, but I failed." She looked down briefly, remembering the earthly emotion of shame she once had felt over the failed opportunities.

"Darling Celia." Jack spoke next. "You and Len took on a big commitment when you chose to help advance aviation safety and contribute to many other advancements by losing a son in a preventable crash. Not many parents felt ready to step up to the plate for that. Don't be hard on yourself. And the pilots who volunteered were courageous to take on all they committed to, along with their own families."

"So is that what all of this was about?" Celia was confused.

Jack continued, "For something that affects many, many lives, it's never that simple. There are contracts among everyone on the flight, their parents, and their siblings, wives, husbands, children, and so on. For every tragedy involving multiple souls, like a crash, the ripple of karma is staggering. But what we want to help each other with once we're back on this side is understanding what the contracts were among key players. Our goal is to look at what was learned and determine where we go from here as individual souls."

"So as we were saying," Lenny continued, "You lived off the grace you had earned up until the crash, and then you had to make a choice."

"I was with you up until then." Celia interrupted her son, for whom she had grieved half of her last life on earth. "I was devastated when the crash happened and you died. A part of me died too, and I had no choice. I was left to live out my life on earth with a broken heart. I was not as strong as your father. I wanted to be different, but I could not."

This part of the discussion was always the biggest challenge at this phase in the integration process. The discussion needed to be guided by someone with great wisdom.

Robert spoke up. "Celia, just as you were carried throughout the first half of your life by grace, I and all in the same aura as you supported you completely for quite some time. We know any parent who loses a child needs to be carried initially. And then, to our surprise, when it was time for you to begin to look around and see what all you had to live for—another son, people who needed your leadership and the helping skills you brought to earth after many lifetimes—you chose to self-medicate your current trauma with alcohol. You literally blocked the part of your brain that would allow us to come to you and to help you along. You shut us out with your choice to drink."

"My guilt was so great, and my shame was so intense. Those feelings caused me to choose to numb myself. I never intended to block out higher guidance. That was not a choice I made freely." Celia felt a need to defend her actions.

"Mom, with all your education, you of all people know that substance abuse or any addiction blocks the higher mind. And your faith was always so strong, it was hard to watch you turn away from Spirit at the time you needed God most." Lenny reflected on the many times he had tried to visit his mother the way he had successfully contacted Bruce and his father. But her drunkenness had prevented him from making contact.

"So many times following my departure from earth, and for years after, I tried to reach you. Even when you and Dad were in the hangar that day when our suitcases and belongings were displayed, I tried to reach you. Dad saw me and the others—he saw our souls, as our bodies had already disintegrated. But you were hungover and unable to receive us."

"I remember that. We were in the hangar, and your dad kept trying to get me to see what he could see. I tried, but I could not. You mean you were there?" Celia was incredulous at what she was hearing.

"Yes, I stood behind table number thirty-three, behind my old green suitcase that was nearly destroyed in the fire. I knew Dad picked me up. And I also knew you were unable to at that point. I tried so many times after that, and finally I knew when your death day was coming, so I decided to wait until we could be truly together again." Lenny looked toward Len as he told the story. His father smiled and winked in affirmation of his son's explanation of what he had experienced that day. Shortly after he had arrived on the other side, it was one of the many experiences he had asked his son about. So many times he'd thought his experiences with Lenny were his imagination—and they were, because the part of the brain that can imagine love and connection was indeed the vibration where Lenny and now he and Celia lived.

Len reflected on the day he first knew that while floating in the violet mist. It had been the turning point. While his grief did not end that day, the experience had changed him, and he was awakened spiritually. He never went to sleep on earth again—he committed to remaining conscious for the rest of his life. And when he left earth, just as he saw that day in the hypnotherapist's office, there was Lenny, his father, and all of those he loved, again waiting for him in the violet mist.

Len had also learned that the night he had tried to end his life in his sports car, it was Lenny's voice that commanded his attention and stopped him from ending his life. While the voice was not one he recognized, he had come to terms with the fact that the soul he had called his son was not limited to the young man he had once shared his life with. They were in fact, in heavenly terms, peers.

Len knew he needed to speak up, as it was Celia's evolution that was under discussion. "A lot was learned from that accident. You were intended to be part of that learning. People in support groups and other survivors needed to have more models of people healing and teaching compassion as a result of the personal awareness that loss gives us. But Celia, you chose to turn away with a hardened heart."

"Mom, you had an opportunity to teach love, and you chose to teach hatred. You joined a group of people who continue to hold earth back instead of allowing their pain to soften their hearts and allow greater love to enter earth through the portals of their hearts. Even twenty years later, after great improvements had been made in how airlines and other businesses treated families after tragedies, you and the people in your group continued to talk about the unconscious mistakes made in the past. It was the only way you could get attention—or so you thought, so you kept getting other people upset about problems that had already been addressed and in many cases drastically improved upon."

"What do you mean, teach? I practically became a hermit after your death," Celia answered Lenny.

"Mom, you know that how you live your life is how you teach others to live. Modeling behavior is more important than what you tell others to do. You always told me as a child that people learn more about a person by their actions than by any words they say."

"Celia, look." Robert was speaking again. "You did not know you were making a choice, but you were. We were right there to guide you, but not only did you fail to invite us in, the way you had before the crash, you shut us out with your addiction, the thoughts you harbored, and the people you chose to surround yourself with. Before the crash you prayed several times a day, always inviting us into your mind. You meditated and even led more than one retreat for women who were struggling with addictions. And then the crash happened, and you shut us out. We were no longer invited into your higher mind."

Celia sat quietly for several moments.

Finally Granddaddy Jack spoke up again. "Celia, I know this is a lot to absorb. Most of us have similar demons to confront as we return, again and again, before we are free of the earth school. The most important thing you need to know is that there is no condemnation here for past transgressions. You can take as long as you want to study and get ready for your next big test. And when you are ready, we will come together again as your earth committee and plan your next lifetime. I have every reason to know that next time you will nail that exam. All the pain and suffering of the last lifetime and the learning you are doing now will be in your DNA, and when you need it, we are there."

The committee stayed a while longer and answered questions, even sharing some of their more painful reviews of experiences on earth, which were no less painful than what Celia had just been through. Even on the other side, validation and a sense of connection were never overlooked in advancing earth to a higher level.

LII

Lowering the Veil

The day had finally arrived. A soul who freely chose to return to earth at this time was meeting with the committee and putting final plans and dates on earth's calendar. The guardian and spirit guides had taken great care to brief the soul and answer all questions and concerns.

The astrological chart was being examined so the soul would be drawn into the vortex at just the right moment in earth time. It had to be the exact moment, the exact date, and the right place on earth for the karmic pattern to unfold appropriately. The numerologist had rechecked all of the numbers, and the time for this soul to return to earth for advancement and its evolution was nigh.

Lenny and John sat with Celia and studied the plan with her. All three looked up when Len and Celia's parents, along with Granddaddy Jack, came in for their final good-byes—for now. There was a feeling of joy in the room, similar to the experience of friends meeting and celebrating when another in their group was about to embark on a long, highly anticipated journey.

The mood was heightened when the choir began to sing. Two ancient medicine men, once known on earth as John and Lenny, entered heaven's operating room and took their respective places beside the medical practitioners who had called them to assist by way of their prayers. Lenny took up his position beside the young midwife, and John stood to the left of the young anesthesiologist who had been called in, just in case the newborn experienced breathing problems.

Both John and Lenny knew all would go well with the old soul who was once again returning to earth, having been reborn and died countless times before. But they had once again responded to the angels' choir. They never missed the chance to answer a prayer when their names were called.

The old soul was excited about what lay ahead. After a perfect birth, there would be years of a perfect life; grace that had been stored up from many lifetimes would assure peace, joy, prosperity, and a happy life on earth. And this time, when the karmic lesson came, as challenging as it would be, the old soul knew of the great reservoir that lay within, always guided by the great energy on the other side. There would be no failure this time.

LIII

Earth Again

A blond, blue-eyed infant tumbled down the birth canal of a raven-haired young woman once called Marla. The old soul being reborn had once been called Celia. The young handsome first-time father had been called by the name of Bruce in his last lifetime on earth.

"It's a girl!" the midwife called out with glee. She knew it was no surprise to anyone, but bringing a new baby into the world was so exciting, she always felt it important to announce the gender.

Her exclamation was suddenly drowned out by the perfect birth cry as the old soul completed the journey to earth, for one more lifetime.

John and Lenny were watching the excited young parents as the umbilical cord was cut, when suddenly another choir began. This chorus told a different story. The experienced healers walked quickly to the birthing room next door to assist in a more complicated delivery.

Lenny placed his hands over the hands of the female doctor who was trying to assist the baby struggling to be born, while John assisted the anesthesiologist who was helping the young mother breathe as her blood pressure rose dangerously.

Working hard to assist the old soul, the mother, and the medical team, Lenny and John knew it would all be OK. They had reviewed the chart before the birth moment came for this infant, too. Unlike the old soul in the first room they had been in that morning, this soul had chosen to experience medical problems early in life as part of his and his parents' karmic lessons this time on earth.

Two births that morning had started the invisible doctors with yet another busy day on the other side. And both men knew there would be more births to come that morning. Once the second birth was complete, Lenny and John looked back in on their first birth of the day. The only hymn the angels sang in those moments surrounding Celia's rebirth was om, om, om—peace, peace, peace.

Printed in Great Britain
by Amazon